St. George J. Mivart

The Origin of Human Reason

being an examination of recent hypotheses concerning it

St. George J. Mivart

The Origin of Human Reason
being an examination of recent hypotheses concerning it

ISBN/EAN: 9783337368036

Printed in Europe, USA, Canada, Australia, Japan

Cover: Foto ©Andreas Hilbeck / pixelio.de

More available books at **www.hansebooks.com**

THE ORIGIN OF

HUMAN REASON

BEING AN EXAMINATION OF

RECENT HYPOTHESES CONCERNING IT

BY

ST. GEORGE MIVART

PH.D., M.D., F.R.S.

LONDON

KEGAN PAUL, TRENCH & CO., 1, PATERNOSTER SQUARE

1889

CONTENTS.

THE ORIGIN OF

HUMAN REASON.

———•◦•———

CHAPTER I.

INTRODUCTORY.

THE question of evolution by the agency of natural
selection has now been debated for one whole generation. The result of the battle, so far, has been to
concentrate almost the entire interest of the struggle
upon the question whether or not the mind of man can
have been evolved from the psychical faculties of the
lower animals. We have not hesitated to declare, again
and again,* that such an evolution is necessarily impossible ; but our critics and opponents, from Professor
Huxley † downwards, have evaded, rather than com-

---

* See " The Genesis of Species " (Macmillan, 1870) ; " Lessons
from Nature " (John Murray, 1876) ; " On the Development of the
Individual and the Species," *Proceedings of the Zoological Society*,
June 17, 1884 ; " A Limit to Evolution," *Nineteenth Century*,
August, 1884 ; and " Nature and Thought " (Burns and Oates,
1885 : 2nd edit.).

† See his article entitled " Mr. Darwin's Critics," in the *Contemporary Review*, 1871, and reprinted in 1873 in Professor
Huxley's " Critiques and Addresses " (Macmillan and Co.), p. 251.

B

bated, the arguments whereby we supported our position.

We hail, then, with much pleasure and very sincere satisfaction, the publication by Mr. Romanes of his recent work on human mental evolution.* In him we have at last a Darwinian who, with great patience and thoroughness, applies himself to meet directly and point-blank the most formidable arguments of the anti-Darwinian school, as well as to put forward persuasively the most recent hypotheses on his side. Mr. Romanes is exceptionally well qualified—amongst the disciples of Mr. Darwin—to assume the task he has assumed. For a long time past he has made this question his own, and has devoted his energies to the task of showing that there is (as Mr. Darwin declared) no difference of kind, but only one of degree, between the highest human intellect and the psychical faculties of the lowest animals. Mr. Romanes has become the representative of Mr. Darwin on this special and most important field of inquiry, and he has accumulated, in defence of the position he has taken up, an enormous mass of facts and anecdotes, which he regards as offering decisive evidence in his favour. His new book on this subject is written with great clearness and ability, and though it is, of course, possible that other advocates might have avoided this or that erroneous inference and mistaken assertion (as we deem them) of Mr. Romanes, we are convinced that no one could, on the whole, have

* "Mental Evolution in Man : Origin of Human Faculty," by G. J. Romanes, M.A., LL.D., F.R.S. (Kegan Paul, Trench and Co., 1888).

made out a better case for his side than he has done ;
no other naturalist could, we are persuaded, have done
more, or done better, to sustain Mr. Darwin's great thesis.
We say " Mr. Darwin's great thesis," because in main-
taining it the modern Darwinian school are faithful
followers of their master.   For the late Mr. Darwin declared that to admit the existence of a distinction of kind
between the origin of man and that of other animals
" would make the theory of 'Natural Selection' valueless," and that, under such circumstances, he " would
give absolutely nothing for the theory of Natural
Selection," adding, " I think you will be driven to reject
all or admit all."   That Mr. Romanes is a faithful
exponent of his master's views is certain, for Charles
Darwin has told us again and again that he saw no
distinction of " kind," but only one of " degree," between
our highest intellectual faculties and the feelings of a
brute.   He has also proclaimed the doctrine which
denies to us the possession of any intellectual and
moral faculties that could not have been evolved by the
chance action of natural forces, from the powers possessed by brutes, to be a doctrine which " rests upon
ground that will never be shaken." *

The question to which Mr. Romanes applies himself
—the question as to the existence of any essential
distinction between the lowest human intellect and the

* This shows how little justified Mr. Alfred R. Wallace was
in bestowing on his recent work, the name of " Darwinism "—a
work which, however fully it may maintain the doctrine of the
origin of species of plants and animals by " Natural Selection,"
culminates in a distinct denial of that which we thus see Mr.
Darwin regarded as an essential part of his whole contention.

highest psychical powers of any brute—is, as he says, "a most interesting and important" one, and is, in Professor Huxley's words, an "argument fraught with the deepest consequences."

The doctrine which Mr. Romanes, Professor Huxley, Professor Haeckel, Mr. Herbert Spencer, and others agree in asserting—the doctrine of the essential bestiality of man—is declared by one of the ablest and most honest and outspoken teachers of that school, Professor Ray Lankester—to be the very flower and culmination of modern philosophy.*

Very worthy, then, in our opinion, is Mr. Romanes's work of the most careful and candid consideration—a work on which he has lavished so much time and labour.

He has been very unreasonably blamed for attaching the importance he has to the question of "difference of kind," and for affirming † that such a difference involves a difference of origin ; and it has been asserted

---

* His words are, "Darwin, by his discovery of the mechanical principle of organic evolution, namely, the survival of the fittest in the struggle for existence, completed the doctrine of evolution, and gave it that unity and authority which was necessary in order that it should reform the whole range of philosophy. The detailed consequences of that new departure in philosophy have yet to be worked out. Its most important initial conception is the derivation of man by natural processes from ape-like ancestors, and the consequent derivation of his mental and moral qualities by the operation of the struggle for existence and natural selection from the mental and moral qualities of animals. Not the least important of the studies thus initiated is that of the evolution of philosophy itself. Zoology thus finally arrives, through Darwin, at its crowning development ; it teaches, and may be even said to comprise, the history of man, sociology, and psychology" ("Encyc. Brit.," vol. xxiv. p. 820).

† As he does on p. 3, in a note.

that creatures really different in kind may have been continuously produced, in succession, simply by evolution. To say this, however, is to confound a real, philosophical difference of "kind" (which, of course, is what Mr. Romanes has in view) with a mere popular use of the word. It is as if a man were to say he liked three "kinds" of toast for breakfast—"dry," "buttered," and "French." But a real difference of kind, a difference of *essential nature*, cannot be evolved. It cannot possibly admit of "more" or "less." It simply "is" or it "is not." Mr. Romanes has rightly apprehended the task before him, and has vigorously applied himself to it. He does not "palter with us in a double sense," but honestly and honourably strives to meet, point-blank, the strongest arguments of his adversaries.

Before beginning our examination of Mr. Romanes's work, we think it well to state distinctly what our own position exactly is.

We deem this necessary, because, as will shortly appear, our views have been so singularly misapprehended by Mr. Romanes. We therefore cannot but feel sure that other persons less gifted, or less interested in the subject than he is, may, not improbably, have misunderstood us also. It therefore seems to be incumbent on us to take what pains we can to obviate such misconceptions, by giving as plain and full a statement of our convictions as it is in our power to do.

A careful study of the facts of life (human, animal, and vegetal) has impressed us with the following convictions :—

(1) Although our intellectual and volitional nature

is essentially distinct from that of any mere animal, there is none the less abundant evidence that certain physical conditions are necessary for its external manifestation. In the absence of those conditions it may, as in sleep, remain latent. That. often, when not externally apparent, it may for all that really persist in a latent condition, is plainly shown us by the fact that it can and does become subsequently manifest—as on waking—when the needful conditions have been supplied, as, *e.g.*, through sufficient rest.

(2) Each human being is a true unity which possesses, simultaneously, the powers of two natures—one animal and the other rational—both sets of powers * co-operating in the whole mental life of each individual. We cannot, therefore, separate, for examination, our intellect from our sensuous activity, while our intellectual nature modifies the exercise of even our mere sensitivity. Nevertheless we can sufficiently distinguish the qualities of either set of faculties to be aware of the great difference which exists between them.

(3) We know, both by common sense and careful observation, that brutes do not make manifest externally an unequivocally intellectual nature. But though we know that such manifestations do not occur, we cannot know all that animals are or may be. We cannot, therefore, venture positively to affirm that, in the absence of

---

* In our work "On Truth" (Kegan Paul, Trench and Co., 1889) we have described at length—pp. 178-223—both our higher and our lower mental powers. We shall be compelled again and again to refer our readers to this work, which was sent to press before that of Mr. Romanes appeared. Had it not been so sent the present volume would have been superfluous.

intellect, they do not possess one or more powers or faculties which we do not, and which, therefore, we cannot imagine or fully understand. Did they possess, however, an intellectual nature, we are very confident that they would very soon make us distinctly and unmistakably aware of the fact by external signs.

(4) But animals do not make signs ; for a sign is a token or device addressed to eye or ear, depicting, by an external manifestation, some newly arising combination of ideas. Such a manifestation must be made with the intention of conveying to the understanding of another, a knowledge of the combination of ideas possessed by the mind of the sign-maker. Otherwise it is not and cannot be a "sign."

(5) The accounts we sometimes meet with of a quite exceptional display by animals of psychical powers which seem to be truly intellectual, must, then (occasional mendacity apart), be due to one of three causes :—

(*a*) Errors of observation or mistaken inferences—and the actions of animals are very easily misapprehended.

(*b*) The possession by such animals of some power or faculty which we have not, and therefore cannot imagine.

(*c*) The possession by animals of an intellectual nature like our own (making them truly moral and responsible beings), which nature they are hindered from making manifest externally, owing to the absence of some requisite physical conditions. This view, instead of degrading man to the level commonly assigned to brutes, raises them to the level of mankind. It is nevertheless a view which appears to us to be absurdly unwarranted and one not only without evidence but against it.

(6) As to infants too young to show intelligence, and as to savages so degraded (if any such there be) as not to appear unequivocally intellectual, we judge of their essential nature by the outcome of education in the first case, and by the analogy of their fellow-men in the second case. This outcome and this analogy lead us to credit such infants and such savages with the possession of a latent intellectual nature which physical conditions (their undeveloped frame or their unfavourable environment) do not allow them to make externally manifest. We judge the very opposite (also from outcome and analogy) in the case of brutes.

(7) Thus we deem that no human state of existence, however abnormal, can be really "brutal," and that the psychical activity of no brute, however startling, can be really "intellectual." We should expect, moreover, that an adult human being, who could give no evidence of rationality, would (being in an *abnormal* condition) be capable of even less than a mere animal—the non-intellectual condition of which is *normal*. Similarly, the possession of intellect, as well as passions and a power of will, would lead us to expect to find occasionally amongst mankind, more perverted and more profoundly irrational actions than in the case of brutes, which, we believe, have no voluntary power of applying their intellectual and physical activities in consciously perverted modes.

(8) We consider that it is congruous and according to

analogy that our intellectual nature should require the exercise of merely animal faculties as a condition precedent to manifestations of intellect. We so consider because, in the first place, we find that the world of plants, in order that they should live, require to possess, as they do possess, the physical and chemical powers of inorganic nature; secondly, because we find that animals need and possess, not only the physical and chemical powers of inorganic nature, but also the vital activities of plants, as well as their own specially animal powers. We might then expect to find, as we do find, that we men possess at one and the same time the powers of the inorganic, vegetal, and animal worlds, as well as the special faculties of human nature.

Having thus made profession of the biological and psychological faith that is in us, we may proceed to address ourselves to our task — an examination of recent hypotheses, and especially a careful consideration of Mr. Romanes's arguments. He relies mainly on the phenomena said to be presented by infants and savages to justify his assertion that such a gradual series of transitions in psychical power exists between man and brute, as suffices to make plain the fact that the difference between them is not one of "kind"—not a fundamental, essential difference—but merely one of "degree."

He starts by urging that there are four *à priori* reasons in favour of his contention. Putting aside for the moment the question as regards man, he tells us* that "the process of organic and of mental evolution has been continuous throughout the whole region of life."

* p. 4.

" On grounds of analogy, therefore," he adds, " we should deem it antecedently improbable that the process of evolution, elsewhere so uniform and ubiquitous, should have been interrupted at its terminal phase."

But this continuity we altogether deny as regards the domain of irrational nature, and whatever force his argument has, tells (if we are right) directly against his contention, instead of in favour of it. That there is an absolute break between the living world and the world devoid of life, is what scientific men are now agreed about—thanks to the persevering labours of M. Pasteur. Those who affirm that though life does not arise from inorganic matter now, nevertheless it did so " a long time ago," affirm what is at the least contrary to all the evidence we possess, and they can bring forward nothing more in favour of it than the undoubted fact that it is a supposition which is necessary for the validity of their own speculative views.* There is, then, one plain evidence that there has been an interruption of continuity, if not within the range of organic life, yet at its commencement and origin. But we go further than this, and affirm, without a moment's hesitation, that there has, and must necessarily have been, discontinuity within the region of organic life also. We refer to the discontinuity between organisms which are capable of sensation and those which do not possess the power of feeling.† That all the

* Thus, *e.g.*, Dr. A. Weismann says, " I admit that spontaneous generation, in spite of all vain efforts to demonstrate it, remains for me a logical necessity." See his " Essays upon Heredity, etc." : Oxford, 1889.

† Mr. A. R. Wallace, in his recent work, " Darwinism," p. 475, does not hesitate also to affirm this ; declaring it to be altogether

higher animals "feel" will not be disputed. They give all the external signs of sensitivity, and they possess that special organic structure—a nervous system—which we know supplies all our organs of sensation. In the absence of any bodily mutilation, then, we have no reason to suspect that their nervous system and organs of sense do not act in a manner analogous to our own. On the other hand, to affirm that the familiar vegetables of our kitchen-gardens are all endowed with sensitivity, is not only to make a gratuitous affirmation, but one opposed to evidence, since no vegetable organisms possess a nervous system ; and it is a universally admitted biological law, that structure and function go together. If, then, there are any organisms whatever which *do not* feel, while certain other organisms *do* feel, then (as a door must be shut or open) there is, and must be, a break and distinction between the one set and the other.

Some persons may object: "The transition is so gradual, it is impossible to draw an exact line between sentient and insentient organisms." Even if this assertion be true, such an objection would be of no avail, because an apparently continuous and uninterrupted course of action is often not really such, but only seems to be so on account of our organization—our very limited power of vision. Let us suppose an action to take place at precisely such a rate as to permit of our seeing

preposterous to assume that at a certain stage of complexity of atomic constitution, and as a necessary result of that alone, sensitivity should arise. "Here," he tells us, "all idea of mere complication of structure producing the result is out of the question."

its steps separated from each other by just appreciable intervals; then we have but to suppose the period needed for our nervous activity to be slightly increased, and it would necessarily follow we could no longer perceive the intervals, and the supposed action would seem to be continuous—as does that of the hour-hand of a clock. Let us next assume that a really interrupted action is so slow that we cannot detect any separate intervals and acts in its course; we have but to suppose the rapidity of our nervous activity increased, and we should be able to clearly perceive them. So much for continuity as to conditions of succession. As to the continuity of conditions of simultaneous existence, it is notorious that the microscope is continually showing us the existence of intervals and interruptions in what, to our unaided senses, appears continuous. It is also notorious that the universal presence of intervals and a perpetual absence of continuity, is set forth as the real condition of material existence by those thinkers who are most earnest in denying the existence of an interval between human and brute intelligence—namely, by all those who uphold the mechanical theory of the universe. For they believe that everything we know, even every gas, is made up of a cluster of more or less widely separated molecules and atoms.

But that absolute interruptions and really instantaneous actions do take place on all sides of us in nature, is indisputable. Such is the case in every act of impregnation, wherein there is, and must be, an instant before and an instant after the contact of the ultimate sexual elements. We have again, at a later reproductive stage, the final separation of the embryo from the body of the parent. Universal and persistent continuity in nature does not exist. There are distinct interruptions, some of which our senses can perceive, while others are only evident to our intellect through reasoning and mature reflection.

But reason assures us, as we have already pointed out, that if any real distinctions of "kind" exist at all, there must be distinct steps and absolute breaks. For the very essence of a nature or kind, is that it does not admit of "greater" or "less"—of augmentation or diminution. It absolutely "is" or it absolutely "is not." There is no possibility of any intermediate condition. To assert that there may be a really intermediate condition between death and life, or between absolute non-sensitivity and sensuous existence, or between feeling and thought, is covertly to beg the question and categorically to deny the absolute possibility of any distinctions of kind whatever. Just as the atomist writers, before referred to, assert the existence of real material breaks and differences of kind in what appears to our senses to be one existing material whole, so we assert the existence of real dynamic breaks and differences of kind in what appears to our senses to be one evolving dynamic whole. If any one chooses to assert that stones are living things, accidentally prevented by circumstances from showing forth their latent life, and that all plants are sensitive beings, accidentally hindered from making their sensitivity manifest, we cannot, of course, refute him; but we also cannot but regard him as superstitious and credulous. We need not trouble ourselves to controvert him, because "*quod gratis asseritur gratis negatur,*" and he has, and can have, nothing but an *à priori* prejudice to bring forward in support of his assertion.

Because we cannot actually see or feel the origin of an intellectual nature or any other nature, no argument thence arises against such origins, for we have no experience and can know nothing, save by rational inference, of any origin whatever. It may well be that there have been a countless multitude of breaks and distinct origins—one even for every species—hidden beneath a process of evolution that appears to be continuous to our sense perceptions. Reversing, therefore, Mr. Romanes's declaration, we say, "On grounds of analogy we should deem it to be antecedently probable that the process of evolution at its terminal phase (the advent of the rational animal—man) had been interrupted because it is continually interrupted now, and has notably been interrupted at the introduction of life, and again at that of sensitivity."

Mr. Romanes's second *à priori* analogical argument reposes on the fact that every human individual goes through "a process of gradual development and evolution, extending from infancy to manhood ; and that in this process, which begins at a zero level of mental life and may culminate in genius, there is nowhere and never observable a sudden leap of progress, such as the passage from one order of psychical being to another might reasonably be expected to show. Therefore," he adds, "it is a matter of observable fact that, whether or not human intelligence differs from animal in kind, it certainly does admit of gradual development from a zero level."

But, as we have said, this is covertly to affirm the very thing to be proved—that intellect can be gradually developed from a zero level. We altogether deny that it can, though a nature of a certain kind, existing *ab initio*, may only make its real nature plainly manifest as impediments disappear and needful conditions for its showing itself, become provided. No "order of psychical being" is perceptible by us in itself, but only through its effects; and we know quite well (through persons who, from accident or disease, are temporarily or permanently deprived of speech or even reason) that an "order of psychical being" may be certainly in existence, and nevertheless unable, from accompanying physical conditions, to make that existence manifest; while we also know (through the further education of children already plainly intellectual) that one and the same "order of psychical being" may become better able to manifest its latent power through changes in its environment, *e.g.*, through education. Therefore the indisputable fact that no "sudden leap" in individual human evolution takes place, is an argument that the same intellectual nature has existed from birth, and that it is only changes in environmental agencies and bodily growths—i.e. *physical conditions*—which have enabled powers latent from the first, to more and more plainly make themselves manifest. The fact that the psychical difference between the immature and the mature human being is marked by no obvious and conspicuous interval, while the difference between the psychical manifestations

of man and brute is marked by an obvious and conspicuous interval, constitutes an *à priori* argument in
favour of the existence of a difference of kind in the
second case, and not in the first.

The third *à priori* argument of our author * is the
following one : it is an " undeniable psychological fact "
that the human mind, in its individual development,
" ascends through a scale of mental faculties which are
parallel with those that are permanently presented by
the psychological species of the animal kingdom." Here
Mr. Romanes relies upon his own views as expressed by
his initial diagram. According to that diagram, an
infant of a week old has the memory of a starfish ; at
twelve weeks it is comparable in intelligence with a
frog, but in a fortnight more has mounted to the
mental level of a lobster ; at five months it can "communicate its ideas" as freely as a bee, and in three
months more understands words and pictures as well as
a bird. All this we regard as quite fanciful and base-
less, and really unsustained by any of the arguments
adduced either in his previous works or in the present one.
We shall, by-and-by, meet with † facts brought forward
by Mr. Romanes himself (with respect to his own and
other children) which abundantly prove that infants of
a few months old, give unmistakable evidence that they
possess a really intellectual nature and true abstract
ideas.

Man is an animal,‡ and, therefore, he might be

* p. 5.   † See below, chaps. iv. and v.

We cannot in this chapter afford space to consider at length
Mr. Romanes's assertions about animals ; but we may most briefly
advert to the entirely unsatisfactory nature of some of them.

expected to undergo (as he does undergo) an anatomical and sensuous development similar to what we find in those animals, the adult condition of which he most nearly resembles. But even here there is a startling difference. In no known apes are the young nearly so slow in their bodily development as children are, and in no mere animals do the psychical powers shoot forward so wonderfully in advance of bodily evolution as they do in man. These facts we rely upon with confidence as affording another strong *à priori* probability the exact reverse of that for which Mr. Romanes believes he has found evidence.

The fourth and last *à priori* argument of our author is drawn from the fact that "the intelligence of the [human] race has been subject to a steady process of gradual development" in the arts and appliances of life. Therefore, he urges, since mental evolution has continued in man since he first appeared, we must deem it probable that it continued before he appeared, and so produced *him.* But here again the facts seem to us to

Birds are compared for intelligence with infants eight months old ; but how great is the divergence between different birds as to their psychical powers! Hymenoptera (wasps, bees, ants, aphides, ichneumons, etc.) are compared with infants of five months ; but how great, again, is the difference between an entirely sluggish cochineal insect and an ant! Instead of these circumstances tending to prove that there is no difference of kind between man and brute, it might rather indicate that different kinds of animals have a radically different fundamental nature, and that however their bodily form may have been—to our sense perceptions—continuously evolved from that of antecedent species, the formation of their really essential nature has been due to some discontinuous action parallel with, however inferior in intensity or degree to, that which has formed the essential nature of man himself.

C

establish an *à priori* probability of an exactly opposite kind.

Though it is not true that all races of men, or that most of them, are and still less have ever been, thus continuously progressive ; and though it is true that a certain enlargement of brain, and probably an increase in practical intelligence, have taken place in animals, yet the difference as to psychical advance between men and animals is vast. In no species of mere animal have we an approximation towards the evidence of advance— since that species existed as a species—which is comparable with the advance which some races of men have made.

Herein we find a difference which we cannot measure, and the probability which thence naturally arises is that there must be a difference of kind, and not of degree, between creatures whose capacities are so extraordinarily diverse.

Taking, then, these several *à priori* considerations together, they must, in our opinion, be fairly held to make out a very strong *prima facie* case in favour of the view that there has been a positive interruption of the developmental process in the course of psychological history, and that the mind of man can never have been evolved from the sensitive faculties of any brute. For these considerations show, not only that on analogical grounds such an interruption must be held to be in itself probable, but also that there are facts with respect to the human mind which are quite incompatible with the supposition of its having been slowly evolved ; seeing that no race in human history is known to have undergone the process in question, and that no individual mind does undergo it now.

In order to overturn so great a presumption as is thus created on *à priori* grounds, the biologist may fairly be called upon to supply some very powerful considerations of an *à posteriori* kind, tending to show that the general consent of civilized mankind * is wrong in denying to brute beasts those truly intellectual, volitional, and moral faculties which it is commonly supposed that they do not in fact possess.

In proceeding with his argument, Mr. Romanes remarks on the emotional resemblance between animals and man. This we have always not only admitted, but affirmed, as being a necessary consequence of the corporeal nature common to man and beast. Nevertheless, though the sensations and lower emotions of both are probably similar, it is not so with the higher emotions,† which depend upon distinct intellectual and moral perceptions. Thus we are convinced that Mr. Romanes errs in attributing to animals ‡ the emotion of the "ludicrous," since that emotion essentially depends on an intellectual perception ; though emotional excitement and facial contortions more or less like those of man, may be induced in some animals, especially in apes, by tickling. Such "laughter," however, is radically § different from a feeling of the ludicrous

---

* Some of the lower races of mankind think little of the distinction between themselves and the brute creation (see " On Truth," p. 497). The appreciation of man's exceptional dignity has grown with civilization.

† See " On Truth," p. 221.   ‡ p. 7.

§ See the *Forum* for July, 1887, p. 492.

—always accompanied by some perception of incongruity.

Similarly with regard to the instincts which are concerned in nutrition, self-preservation, reproduction, and the rearing of progeny, Mr. Romanes says,* "No one has ventured to dispute that all these instincts are identical with those which we observe in the lower animals." But, so far from wishing to dispute this identity, we have again and again affirmed it to be a necessary result of similarity of bodily organization. Reason, however, is one thing and instinct another,† a matter we shall have to deal with later on.

Soon, however, we come to a startling misstatement as to the cognitive powers.‡ Mr. Romanes says, § "Enormous as the difference undoubtedly is between these faculties in the two cases, the difference *is conceded* ‖ not to be one of kind *ab initio.*" But with our utmost power of insistance we deny this, and affirm that man's nature is intellectual, and absolutely differs in kind from that of the highest brute, from the first moment of his existence.

Another noteworthy assertion occurs on the same page. Mr. Romanes says, "It belongs to the very essence of evolution, considered as a process, that

---

* pp. 7, 8.

† See "On Truth," pp. 175, 184, 358-365, 427, 515-518.

‡ We say "cognitive powers" to avoid any possibility of injustice to Mr. Romanes. He, indeed, speaks of "the faculties of the intellect," but in a note (p. 8) declares that he does not use that term in a "question begging sense," but only to avoid "coining a new term." Without doing this, he might have availed himself of our term, "sense perception," or "sensuous cognition."

§ p. 9.　　　　　　　　　‖ The italics are ours.

when one order of existence passes on to higher grades of excellence, it does so upon the foundations already laid by the previous course of its progress." This is equivalent to saying that it is of the essence of evolution that there is no such thing as a distinction of kind at all, so that to assert evolution is, for him, to assume as certain the very point which he has to prove.

The true statement of the case should, we think, be very different, and we would express it as follows: When a higher order of existence succeeds to others of lower grades, it does so upon the foundation already laid by preceding existences of lower orders. Thus the vegetative nature of a plant manifests itself upon the foundation already laid by the preceding inorganic world, in the powers and properties of which it participates. The sensitive nature of an animal manifests itself upon the foundation already laid by the preceding inorganic and vegetative worlds, in the powers and properties of both of which it participates. Similarly the rational nature of man manifests itself upon the foundation already laid by the preceding inorganic, vegetative, and animal worlds, in the powers and properties of all three of which man, in turn, participates.

Moreover, although each distinction of kind is absolute, and must be due to a distinct origin, nevertheless the higher forms of each superior kind present us, in a way for which " natural selection " will not account, with a sort of adumbration of the superior kind which has to follow it, and the advent of which it thus, as it were, predicts. Thus in crystals and such forms as dolomite and spathic iron, we have an adumbration of organic forms ; in the insectivorous plants (*Drosera* and *Dionœa*, and various others *) we have an adumbration of animal life ; in the relatively complex higher Protozoa we have structures (radically different in kind) which are an adumbration of the organs of the Metazoa ; in the Marsupials we meet with adumbrations of various orders of placental mammals.   Again, amongst the latter, the lowly organized lemurs so prepare the way for the apes that they were classed in one order with them, and not even separated into a sub-order by themselves, till we ourselves so separated them.† However distinct, then, man may be, analogy would lead us to expect to find amongst animals, some which so far approach, and simulate in a lower order, human characteristics, as to constitute a foreshadowing, or adumbration, of man himself.

After quoting,‡ with seeming approval, a passage from a presidential address delivered by us (to the British Association, at Sheffield, in 1879), but objecting to a criticism on Professor Huxley therein contained,§

---

* See "On Truth," p. 335.
† See " Proceedings of the Zoological Society for 1864," p. 635.
‡ p. 10.
§ Speaking of the sensations of animals, Professor Huxley had said (" Critiques and Addresses," p. 282), "What is the value of the evidence which leads one to believe that one's fellow-man feels ? The only evidence in this argument from analogy is the similarity of his structure and of his actions to one's own, and if that is good enough to prove that one's fellow-man feels, surely it is good enough to prove that an ape feels," etc. We (who assert as much as Professor Huxley can do) that animals truly feel, had criticized this statement, saying, "Surely it is not by similarity of structure or actions, but by *language* that men are placed in communication with one another." This criticism of ours Mr. Romanes

he goes on to observe that animals are capable of no small degree of *ratiocination*, "if we use the term Reason in its true, as distinguished from its traditional sense." Here by the word "traditional" Mr. Romanes refers only to views which are not traditional, but modern, and which would limit the use of the term

pronounces "feeble," and adds, "It seems sufficient to ask, in the first place, whether language is not action; and, in the next, whether, as expressive of *suffering*, articulate speech is regarded by us as more 'eloquent' than inarticulate cries and gestures?" Cries and gestures may, and ordinarily do, denote suffering; but they may occur without it—as during operations under an anæsthetic. However eloquent they may be, they may be ambiguous in a way which conscious verbal declarations cannot be. Moreover, the question did not refer to "suffering" only, but to feelings generally; and it is simply nonsense to say that the feelings we make known by speech, we make known by actions, because all articulations *are* actions. Breathing and deglutition are made up of action as much as speech, but they are respectively actions of diverse and definite kinds, and it is absurd to confound them with emotional and intellectual gestures, and articulate and inarticulate sounds, under the one indefinite name, "actions." We know quite certainly that men and animals feel, but we are enabled to attain, by conversation, to a knowledge about the feelings of our fellow-men which we can never attain to concerning those of animals or even of infants. It is common enough to hear expressions of regret that a child is too young to be able to describe its feelings, and so guide the judgment and action of a medical man. But Professor Huxley is an ardent admirer of Descartes; we may then cite, as an *argumentum ad hominem*, the following contradiction of the Professor's assertion by Descartes himself: "Il n'y a aucune de nos actions extérieures qui puisse assurer ceux qui les examinent que notre corps n'est pas seulement une machine qui a remué, de soi même, mais qu'il y a aussi en lui une âme qui a des pensées, excepté les paroles, ou autres signes faits à propos de sujets, qui se présentent, sans se rapporter à aucune passion" ("Œuvres de Descartes," par Victor Cousin, vol. ix. p. 724; cited by Professor Max Müller in the *Nineteenth Century* for March, 1889, p. 408, note 5).

"reason" to processes of "inference." According to views which are *really* traditional, the word "reason" should denote and include all intellectual perception, whether it be direct and intuitive, or indirect and inferential. Under neither head are to be included, as we shall endeavour hereinafter to point out, the sensuous perceptions and merely practical inferences of animals. Mr. Romanes fails altogether to distinguish between those mere associations of feelings and emotions in animals which may produce an unconscious expectant feeling of sensations to come,* occasioned by some feelings already excited (the practical inference † of animals), and true inference. He confounds ‡ them both together under the denomination, "*reason properly so called.*"

Mr. Romanes makes a very grave mistake when he tells us, on the same page, that human immortality can only have become known to us by "revelation." We do not, of course, affirm that man's immortality is directly to be perceived as being a necessary truth like the principle of contradiction or the law of causation ; but we confidently affirm that a scientific analysis of our being, with a consequent perception of the nature of the human soul, make its indestructibility (without a miracle) a reasonable inference.§ When, further, we reflect on God's existence and nature, together with our own ethical perceptions and our observation of the facts of history, this inference becomes raised to the level of certainty, quite apart from revelation. The value of

---

* See "On Truth," p. 195.   † Ibid., p. 345.
‡ p. 12.   § See "On Truth," pp. 388, 487.

Mr. Romanes's judgment is, however, seriously imperilled by a perfectly amazing assertion he makes in a note on this subject. He there tells us,* "The dictum of Aristotle and Buffon, that animals differ from man in having no power of mental apprehension, may be disregarded ; for it appears to be sufficiently disposed of by the following remark of Dureau de la Malle : ' Si les animaux n'étaient pas susceptibles d'apprendre les moyens de se conserver, les espèces se seraient anéanties.' "

So, then, animals have first to learn how to live, and then go on living afterwards ! The sucking action of the new-born infant, the grain pecking of the freshly-hatched chick, and the nutritious properties of the leaves whereon any insect's eggs may be laid, must all be learnt before the creature's impulses are turned to practical account !

This statement could never have been written but for the flagrant ambiguity of the term " to learn " made use of in it. That such a sentence should ever have been written by De la Malle is wonderful, but that it should be quoted nowadays by Mr. Romanes, and supposed by him to overpower the assertions of Aristotle and Buffon, is astounding. It is difficult to imagine how such an intelligent and painstaking author as Mr. Romanes could fall into such a bathos. We shall see, however, shortly that he is led by a correspondent's cockatoo to step over the edge of an abyss of absurdity even more profound.†

But though the zeal with which our author endeavours to establish his thesis thus causes him every now

* p. 12.   † See below, chapter iii.

and then to commit regrettable indiscretions, we frequently come upon statements as admirably expressed as they are true. Thus in contrasting * the views of those he regards as his leading opponents, he makes the following excellent remarks concerning the relation existing between religion and morality, and an intellectual nature : " It is certain that neither of these faculties could have occurred in that species [the human], had it not also been gifted with a greatly superior order of intelligence. For even the most elementary forms of religion and morality, depend upon ideas of a much more abstract, or intellectual, nature than are to be met with in any brute. Obviously, therefore, the first distinction that falls to be considered is the intellectual distinction."

Rightly, therefore, does Mr. Romanes begin his detailed discussion of the subject with a consideration of mental processes, and his second chapter is accordingly devoted to an exposition of his views concerning " ideas."

Before following our author upon his psychological excursion, it may be well to set down certain general considerations bearing upon the question of the existence and origin in man of a nature essentially distinct from that of any other animal whatever.

Now, such a distinct, absolute origin is of course unimaginable ; but, then, every absolute origin is unimaginable, and yet both sensitivity and life must have had a beginning. It is a first requisite in our scientific inquiries to distinguish between the imagination and

* p. 18.

the reason. Nothing can be *imagined* by us which has not been directly or indirectly experienced by our sensitive faculty; but many things may be *conceived* of which have never been thus experienced,[*] and our inability to "imagine" anything should be no bar to our accepting it as true if reason shows that it necessarily or most probably is such.

Mr. Wallace, in his recent work,[†] has well pointed out the impossibility of the mathematical, musical, and artistic faculties having been developed by the action of "Natural Selection," and (as before said) has also insisted upon the necessity of a "new cause or power" having "come into action" at the origin of life and sensitivity, as well as at the origin, of man himself.

But if such a new mode of action—an action different in kind—is to be admitted as having occurred once, *e.g.*, at the origin of life, why should not new kinds of action and new causes occur several or very many times—or even occur constantly and repeatedly?

If once the *possibility* of such a thing is demonstrated by but a single case of its actual occurrence, new origins and actions not only cease to be improbable, but their probability is thereby established.

Mr. Wallace [‡] also agrees with us [§] in affirming the active agency of immaterial principles in bringing about the phenomena of nature, organic and inorganic. But if the necessary intervention of an intelligent, immaterial agency be accepted to account for the origin of any part

---

[*] As to this, see "On Truth," pp. 111–113, 411.
[†] "Darwinism," pp. 461–476.   [‡] Ibid., p. 476.
[§] See "On Truth," pp. 507–510.

or power of the material world, why not also for the origin of man ? It is impossible for us to picture such action and agency, because the requisite anterior experience is lacking to us, and we cannot imagine what we have never had any experience of. Whatever mental picture we frame for ourselves of such action and agency must, our reason assures us, be unreal and false ; but that is no ground for our not accepting the real existence of an action and agency which we cannot picture. It has been objected, by Professor Tyndall, against such conceptions, that they cannot be "mentally visualized ;" but so far is this condition from being a proof of delusion, that we may rather say, whatever in such matters can be "mentally visualized" is necessarily untrue, and it is often the more untrue the better it can be so "visualized."

If such a prejudice, such a gross and manifest delusion of the mere imagination, thus possesses the mind of a distinguished physicist, a general commander in science, it is no wonder that it besets the rank and file of the scientific regiments. When we say that reason indicates the existence of an immaterial principle as forming that in every material existence which is active and dynamical (so that in each organism it is rather that principle than any combination of matter, which may be said to constitute such organism),* we are met by the protest, "Such teaching is not science." But the protest is an unreasonable one, and directly contradictory of the truth. For what is science ? It is and must be the highest and most certain knowledge

* See "On Truth," p. 432.

attainable by us. Now, our most careful and complete investigations in all departments of nature are science—physical sciences of different kinds—but they are not and cannot be the highest science, or science *par excellence*, for they do not embody the "most certain knowledge." Observations and experiments are of the greatest value ; nevertheless, in the last resort, when we have done observing and experimenting, we depend for the result entirely on our knowledge of absolute and necessary truths. Were it not for our implicit knowledge of such truths, we could not know that we had ascertained the facts we had ascertained ; neither could we know their necessary bearings and the most certain deductions from them.

Science has to do with self-evident, necessary truths —first principles which underlie and maintain every kind of physical science. When, then, truths seen by the intellect to contain their own evidence, or which result from reasoning logically carried on, are declared to be uncertain, or even false, because they do not agree with what is (by a confusion of terms) called "the scientific imagination," as great an absurdity is committed as if it were said that it must be false that any vessel has gone directly against the wind, because a sailing vessel is unable so to do.

It is, of course, true that mechanical conceptions have been and are of great utility. It is, therefore, not only permissible, but laudable, to make use of them as working hypotheses. But it is a very different thing to represent them as absolute truths. Yet much of what is often spoken of as "science" is really un-

deserving of that name—it is an attempt to inculcate
the truth of such hypotheses, and to "picture" and
"visualize," in terms of sense perceptions, matters which
reason tells us are altogether beyond the power of sense-
perception.*   Thus it is deemed especially "scientific"
to regard all the phenomena of nature as being essentially nothing but matter and motion.   Whereas, in trying
so to regard them we are but "following the line of least
resistance," and yielding to the temptation of dwelling
upon those imaginations which experience has made
easiest for us. †   It is this which causes the mind to take so
readily to the idea of motion, and to feel "at home" therein.

Hence the favour with which mechanical theories of
the universe are accepted, and vibrating molecules and
atoms regarded with special favour.   A firm faith in
"small balls in motion" is deemed a faith which unless
a man keep whole and undefiled he shall without doubt
perish everlastingly from the roll of scientific worthies.
It is, indeed, a short cut to seeming knowledge when
a man can allow his imagination to "visualize" variously
moving balls of various sizes, and then with mental satisfaction exclaim, "That is feeling!"   "That is thought!"
Yet to say that the fidelity and affection of the dog, the
maternal care of the nesting bird, or the actions of the
insect which prepares food it cannot eat for a progeny
it will never behold—to say that such things (to say
nothing of intellectual conceptions) are but minute
motions to be explained by mechanics, is to mock us
with unmeaning or delusive phrases.

* See "On Truth," pp. 89, 101, 127, 128.
† Ibid., pp. 193, 410, 411, 443.

We are in this nineteenth century only beginning to get free from that dark cloud of materialism which shrouded the latter half of the eighteenth. But the cloud is passing, and we may already, here and there, catch a glimpse of its silver lining. When it has finally vanished, thinking men will once more appreciate what science really means, and look back with even more wonder than contempt at not a few of the so-called "scientific speculations," of our day—as Aristotle despised the materialism his system combated and ultimately for ages subdued.

The name of Aristotle suggests an answer to yet another prejudice which the candid seeker after truth has now to struggle against, and about which a few preliminary words need saying. We refer to theological prejudice. The popular science of the day is truly "denominational." The *odium antitheologicum* has become established and endowed, and, as men are ordinarily under the temptation to consider others like themselves, the opponents of a mechanical theory of the universe are accused of working, not in the interest of philosophic truth, but of a creed. We ourselves have had such accusations hurled against us, with others who have been declared to be scientific workers for whom things "ought to be made unpleasant."

With a view, therefore, to guarding against such a system of "poisoning the wells," we think it incumbent upon us to make a brief statement concerning this matter.

No one has more decidedly and uncompromisingly asserted the difference of nature between man and beast than has Aristotle. Yet no one can pretend that he was actuated by theological prejudice in arriving at the conclusions he did arrive at. It is quite otherwise with the most prominent advocates of the bestiality of man That doctrine has again and again been declared to be, for them, a necessary doctrine. They speak truly ; for to establish the separate and essentially distinct nature and origin of man, is practically to refute the mechanical theory of the universe. With the proclamation of man's essential rationality, the folly of the maintainers of that theory is simultaneously proclaimed.

Thus the assertion of man's bestiality is the very *articulus stantis vel cadentis eccelsiæ* for the whole school which numbers amongst its followers, Darwin, Haeckel, Vogt, Huxley, Herbert Spencer, Tyndall, and Prof. Lankester. But it is very different as regards their opponents. We, at least, are by no means bound, in the interest of any Church or system, to maintain that an essential difference of nature and origin *does* exist between man and brute. We are free, the most Ultramontane Catholic is absolutely and entirely free, to hold that the saint and the philosopher, the faithful hound and the tormenting parasite, all possess a fundamentally common nature, and that an analogous immortal destiny awaits them all. This we do *not* believe ; but our disbelief is grounded upon science and philosophy alone, and theological convictions have no part or share therein.

Again, as to early man, the most fervent Catholic, who deems that man has an essentially distinct nature, is none the less absolutely and entirely free to hold that creatures in all minute degrees and shades of physical distinction between an anthropoid ape and man, might have existed for untold ages, such creatures approximating more and more by the increasing complexity of their actions, and perhaps by their articulate cries, to man who was yet "to be." He is, further, perfectly free to hold that when at last the time came for the advent of the human animal, that animal, possessing an essentially rational nature, might nevertheless have long existed before the circumstances of his environment rendered it possible for him to display in act his potential rationality as set before us in Adam. His progeny, again, the men of long prehistoric times, may be deemed* to have dwelt in lands entirely uncultivated, with no weapons but sticks and unchipped stones, as unable to hunt as to till, and destitute of every kind of art. He also not only may, but should, further hold that speech was the spontaneous product of a being of the kind— that he evolved a language insignificant as to the number of its terms, it may be at the lowest grade possible for a creature who could think at all.

What more "freedom of thought" in this direction can science possibly require?

But although, in the interests of truth and fairness, we have thus drawn out what such a believer may consistently hold, we desire distinctly to state that we ourselves do not hold it. We attribute to early man

---

* That the reader may see this is no exaggeration, he is referred to a paper (first published in *Le Muséon*) by the Rev. Monseigneur de Harlez (Professor of Sanscrit at the University of Louvain), entitled, "La Civilisation de l'humanité Primitive" (Charles Peeters, Louvain, 1886).

D

higher powers and more developed faculties ; but most assuredly we attribute such powers to him, not on the strength of, or as a concession to, any theological dogma, but simply because, in our poor judgment, the balance of argument seems to incline that way.

We do not, of course, for a moment wish dogmatically to affirm that early man was so conditioned ; but we believe him to have been so—while we remain quite ready to reject that belief and accept the opposite view as soon as ever we meet with evidence which seems to us sufficient to justify our so doing.

Having made this preliminary statement and explanation of our own views and position, we will proceed, without further preface, to address ourselves to the examination of Mr. Romanes's psychological views.

CHAPTER II.

MENTAL STATES AND PROCESSES.

THE whole attempt of Mr. Romanes to show that the intellect of man is but a development from the psychical power of brutes, reposes upon his mode of representing the various orders and degrees of cognition and intelligence, and this again rests upon his analysis and classification of mental states and processes. By dividing and subdividing these according to a certain system, by ignoring various more important distinctions which exist between some of them, and by exaggerating the significance of some minor differences, he is enabled to draw out what, to the unwary, may look like a transitional series of psychical states. On this account it is absolutely necessary that we should examine with great care the whole of the three chapters (his second, third and fourth chapters) which he devotes mainly to psychological analysis. In this section, however, he anticipates, to a certain extent, what has to follow in his section on language,* while in the latter he carries out further and more completely elucidates, his own psychological views. In our present chapter, therefore, we also cannot quite neglect the subject of language, nor, when we

* His chaps. v., vi., vii., viii., and ix.

come to treat of the latter, can we be altogether dispensed from reverting occasionally to questions about mental states and processes.

Although he does not treat of "self-consciousness" till he comes to his tenth chapter, yet in a summary which he gives of his first four chapters he speaks * of it as the faculty "whereby the mind is able, as it were, to stand apart from itself, to render *one of its states objective to others,*† and thus to contemplate its own ideas as such." Now, we should very much like to know what are "the other states" which thus examine "the one," and what is "the one" which has thus the power of passing the "ideas" in review ? Surely, at the beginning of a treatise on psychological analysis and classification, it is imperatively necessary to try and make the reader understand the fundamental facts and principles upon which his classification reposes, and how and why it is that what is represented as being such a passive abstraction as a mere "state," should be credited with action and searching power of a "faculty."

Mr. Romanes expressly repudiates such questions on the ground that they are "quite alien to the scope" of his work. We, on our part, think we have good ground to complain of such repudiation, seeing that Mr. Romanes expressly adopts a very distinct philosophical system. He could not give to the psychical states he describes even the appearance of a transitional character from "sense" to "intellect," but that he starts by assuming the system of Locke. To affirm that system, however, is to affirm that every group of faint, or revived,

---

* p. 397.   † The italics are ours.

sensations is an "idea"; and since every brute* has such groups of feelings, the point in dispute is thereby at once assumed.

Mr. Romanes affirms, and professes to agree with his opponents in affirming, that the presence of "self-consciousness" is the line of demarcation between man and brute. We might fairly expect, then, that he should have some clear apprehension of that which he thus puts forward as so important. Yet he candidly avows † that it is a problem "which does not admit of solution." Now, the one task which Mr. Romanes has undertaken, the one object of his whole book, is to show that the difference between a self-conscious being and one without self-consciousness is a difference not of kind, but of degree. Yet, instead of placing before us, as we think he should, his convictions as to consciousness, he postpones his consideration of that faculty till he comes to his tenth chapter,‡ and then declines to grapple with it, retreating, as we shall see, into a profession of Idealism. Yet Idealism is fatal to his position, which is essentially that of a materialist. We did not, of course, expect to find in Mr. Romanes's book a treatise on philosophy; but we did expect to find a statement of principles, and one not inconsistent with the position he had taken up. Chemistry and mathematics are different sciences; but nevertheless, if in a chemical treatise statements are

---

* Mr. Romanes states (p. 395) that "nowadays no one questions" that such phenomena are "common to animals and to men." We should like to know what philosopher ever questioned it, save some follower of Descartes? By all the Scholastics it would not only have been unquestioned, but positively affirmed.

† p. 194.   ‡ See below, our chapter iv.

made which involve mathematical error, the assertion
that mathematics are "alien to the scope" of a work on
chemistry will neither save the credit of the chemist
nor that of his statements. We will for the present
abstain from any further criticism on this matter, after
thus briefly calling attention to what appears to us to be
a very noteworthy and significant evidence of some
fundamental confusion of mind.

That section of the work which is mainly devoted to
an examination of mental states is divided into a
chapter (the second chapter) on "Ideas," one on
"The Logic of Recepts," and one on "The Logic of
Concepts."

In his second chapter,* Mr. Romanes applies himself
to the task of describing various kinds of mental processes, and presenting them † in a tabular form. All
these he calls "ideas," and by the very mode in which
he uses this term he at once really lays the foundation
of what we deem his subsequent errors—a foundation
he amplifies by his unintentionally misleading treatment
of the mental processes he so names.

He begins by quoting and accepting, as before said,
certain declarations of Locke respecting the psychical
processes of men and animals, thus at once assuming the
very position which we, his selected opponents, deem to
be the most profoundly mistaken one. For we regard
Locke and Descartes as twin sophists, upon whose confused and misleading notions, as upon a foundation,
subsequent writers have again and again tried in vain
to rear a durable and consistent system of philosophy.

* p. 20.   † p. 39.

But we make our appeal to the reason and common sense of our readers alone, and deliberately put aside all authorities of whatsoever kind.* We decline not only

* Mr. Romanes rather strangely asserts (p. 22) that " Realism was gradually vanquished by Nominalism." The fact is that during the period of their struggles, Nominalism twice raised its head and was twice defeated, and at the time when, with the Renaissance, all scholastic disputes went out of fashion, moderate Realism had conquered all along the line. All the followers of Thomas Aquinas, and all the followers of his critic Scotus, were opposed to Nominalism, and they prevailed. In fact, Nominalism never got the upper hand, never had any standing, in the schools. Of course, with the neglect of Philosophy which accompanied the rise of Cartesianism, Nominalism (with almost every other exploded error) once more raised its head. This was not wonderful, seeing that its founder, Descartes, never understood, never even studied, the Aristotelian system, which, having gone out of fashion, was soon simply thrust aside and neglected by the Cartesians and by their contemporaries and followers here and on the continent, from Hobbes, Locke, Hume, etc., to Hegel, Spencer, and Cousin. Nominalism was argued down, and argued off the field. It never argued its way back, but simply reappeared, as a noxious weed may reappear in a field left uncultivated, or cultivated according to mistaken methods. Some of the arguments used against Nominalism were as follows : (1) Had not the intellect universal ideas, common nouns would be meaningless, whereas consciousness tells us we have a meaning in using them beyond denoting an individual or a collection of individuals, and more than a mere material sound ; for a common noun in an unknown foreign language has no meaning for us. (2) There is no sign which does not signify something ; *prius est esse quam significari ;* and unless we had in the mind something distinct from the individual, the collection, and the material sound, no such sign would ever have existed. We have no signs for the absolutely unknown—*e.g.,* for classes of animals in the planet Mars—and mental perception must precede the use of signs, which would also be useless unless their connection with what they signify was understood. (3) The most ultra-Nominalists must admit that they possess the faculty of perceiving the general nature of certain entities—namely, of certain *words.* Were the human mind incapable of perceiving the universal, this would be impossible. But

to follow Locke, but to follow any one, whoever he may be.

Mr. Romanes tells us that he passes "on to consider the only distinction which can be properly drawn between human and brute psychology. . . . The distinction has been clearly enunciated, from Aristotle

if we can perceive the general nature of certain words and classes of words, why not of other entities also? (4) We can perceive similitudes between certain objects, therefore we can perceive the universal, for every similitude perceived, reveals our power of perception of the same quality, or essential lineament, in distinct individuals, *i.e.* an universal. (5) The Nominalists admitted that we have *collective* ideas ; but collective ideas presuppose the perception of the universal, without which no "number" and no "aggregate of individuals " could be recognized as such. (6) Again, it was said, Nominalism destroys all certainty, for if nothing objective corresponded to our terms, we could know nothing but subjective modifications, and this would destroy the validity of the law of contradiction. If the term and idea " being" represents nothing objective, the whole system of truth disappears. (7) It was also objected that Nominalism was fatal to all science, which necessarily treats of order and laws arising from certain common properties, or similar essential characteristics, perceived to exist in individuals. Science, even physical, is primarily concerned with what is abstract and universal, and has always to fall back upon it in the ultimate analysis ; but if the universal has no objective reality, science becomes a mere *lusus mentis*—a contemplation of a mental panorama of worthless, because truthless, figments. (8) Nominalists were also taxed with confusing the objects of cognition with the means of cognition ; objects being known *directly* through (by means of) our mental affections, and not *mediately*, as results of mental affections which are themselves primarily cognized—a position from which, of course, Idealism follows, such as that from Berkeley and Hume, through Kant and Fichte, to our last living representatives thereof. By such arguments the Schoolmen completely extinguished the Nominalists, who tried by endless quibbles to avoid being forced into that Idealistic Scepticism which reduces science to a knowledge of distinct, individual modifications in a state of chaotic disorder, since it affirms no real objective relations of interdependence, or of any other kind.

downwards, but I may best render it in the words of Locke :—'It may be doubted, whether beasts compound and enlarge their ideas that way to any degree ; this, I think, I may be positive in, that the power of abstracting is not at all in them.'"

Mr. Romanes, by this quotation, introduces to the mind of his reader the suggestion that beasts have "ideas," and that "our ideas" are things similar to the "ideas" of brutes, only compounded and enlarged.* And this suggestion is quietly introduced, as if it was a simple, uncontested matter, instead of being a doctrine which his opponents regard as a fatal and radical error.

We define an idea as "a similitude of any object or action, generated in and by the intellect," and distinguish it fundamentally from a sense-perception, which we define as "the phantasm of an object or action generated in and by the imagination."

The passage quoted contains, further, the following statement as to brutes : "If they have any ideas at all, and are not bare machines (as some would have them), we cannot deny them to have some reason. It seems evident to me, that they do some of them in certain instances reason, as that they have sense ; but it is only in particular ideas, just as they received them from their senses. They are the best of them tied up within those

---

* We do not, of course, object to the term "idea" being used in so broad a sense as to include both intellectual and sense perceptions, if a distinction is carefully drawn between the term as used in a *wide* and in a *strict* sense. Such a distinction, carefully maintained, would obviate the confusion to which we object. But that confusion is part of the very system of Mr. Romanes, and hence his mode of using the term.

narrow bounds, and have not (as I think) the faculty to enlarge them by any kind of abstraction." Here again we have a passage which, if allowed to pass unchallenged, would provide all the materials most essential to construct such a temple of error as Mr. Romanes has, in our opinion, reared. We affirm that no brute gives evidence that it possesses any "idea," any power of "abstraction," or any faculty of "reasoning;" as also that our "ideas" are not formed by the compounding or enlargement of anything which we have in common with the brutes. None the less, we not only most freely allow, but we positively affirm, that brutes possess complex groups of associated sensations and emotions;* that, in their way, they can apprehend not only individual creatures, but kinds of creatures, and, by their feelings and resulting actions, can draw what may be called "practical inferences." That by this we mean something very different from what Mr. Romanes means, is shown by our utterly different positions as regards the relations of the human intellect.

Our own meaning we will do our best, as we proceed, to make perfectly clear. Mr. Romanes begins by observing,† "Psychologists are agreed that what they

* This is, indeed, all that Mr. Herbert Spencer would allow to man. His "Psychology," upon which his whole philosophy reposes (as he himself declares), is one continued endeavour to resolve our higher faculties into our lower by ignoring intellect altogether. Mr. Romanes is, we believe, a devout and faithful disciple of Mr. Herbert Spencer, and it is, of course, easy enough to derive man's highest faculties from his lower, if by the former be understood (as Mr. H. Spencer understands) nothing but certain groups of his lower faculties.

† p. 22.

call particular ideas, or ideas of particular objects, are
of the nature of mental images, or memories of such
objects—as when the sound of a friend's voice brings
before my mind the idea of that particular man.
Psychologists are further agreed that what they term
general ideas arise out of an assemblage of particular
ideas, as when from my repeated observation of numerous individual men I form the idea of Man." In this
passage there is an ambiguity against which it is
necessary to be on our guard if we would avoid confusion of thought. It is, of course, quite true that
general ideas, or "universals," only arise in our mind
after we have experienced corresponding groups of
sense-impressions. The ideas "camel," "triangle," etc.,
cannot arise in us before we have had visual or auditory
impressions related to one or the other. We must first
have seen, felt, or heard descriptions of such things.
Therefore, in a certain loose and inaccurate way of
speaking, such ideas may be said to arise "out of" such
sense-impressions. But this by no means implies that
they *consist of them*, and "*are*" but assemblages of
such impressions further aggregated or otherwise modified. Nevertheless, to use the expression "arise *out of
them*," does lend itself to and favour this latter meaning,
which we shall see directly is the meaning of Mr.
Romanes himself. He continues as follows: " Hence,
particular ideas answer to percepts, while general ideas
answer to concepts: An individual perception (or its
repetition) gives rise to its mnemonic equivalent as a
particular idea ; while a group of similar, though not
altogether similar perceptions, gives rise to its mne-

monic equivalent as a conception, which, therefore, is but another name for a general idea, thus *generated* by an assemblage of particular ideas." * Here again the word "generated" is an equivocal expression. What follows, however, is clear and unequivocal. He says, "Just as Mr. Galton's method of superimposing on the same sensitive plate a number of individual images gives rise to a blended photograph, wherein each of the individual constituents is partially and proportionally represented ; so in the sensitive tablet of the memory, numerous images of previous perceptions are fused together into a single conception, which then stands as a composite picture, or class-representation, of these its constituent images."

These superimposed images we have elsewhere carefully referred to,† and have distinguished such affections

---

* p. 23.

† See "On Truth," pp. 103, 191, 206. In addition to the power we have through each sense-organ to apprehend its own special object (*e.g.* colour through the eye, tone through the ear, etc.), our consentience (and therefore that of animals also), is affected in an analogous and to a certain degree similar manner, by the same object felt through different sense-organs (*e.g.* a triangle as seen or felt, or a fox as seen or smelt), owing to previous associations of sensations, and which object thus comes to be apprehended by this internal feeling. Similarly the several synchronous impressions which have been received from different objects all of the same kind, give rise to a corresponding, more or less vague or blurred, internal impression (analogous to a Galton photograph). Such a photograph, however, whatever may be the number of individuals from which it is constructed, remains, after all, a strictly individual thing—a single particular impression. It is the same with the image of the imagination, which is only called "sensuous universal" by analogy, and which, of course, is not truly general or "universal" at all. It is only a particular image, which, from the mode of its production and the purposes it serves, has an analogy with true universals.

as "sensuous universals" from true "universals," and pointed out how utterly distinct they are in nature from "ideas." That the idea of any object—*e.g.*, a horse—is not a mere amalgam of modified imaginations, or a generalized mental image, is plain from the fact that the imaginations which have helped to call it forth may persist in the mind side by side with it, which they evidently could never do if the idea was made up of such imaginations. Neither can our idea of a horse be an imagination generated by antecedent impressions and imaginations, for the notions implicitly contained within it show it to be something of an altogether different kind. The notions we refer to are those of "existence," "similarity," "distinction," "unity," "truth," "materiality," "life," and "animal existence of a certain kind." Such things are beyond the domain of the senses, and cannot be contained in any mere images or sense-impressions. For a proof that these notions are really contained in the idea, the reader is referred to our previous work, wherein the fundamental differences between "ideas" and "groups of feelings" are more fully drawn out—in a way which cannot here be repeated at length for lack of space. We claim to have shown that ideas differ from such feelings by their simplicity;* by the same idea being capable of elicitation by different senses,† while different ideas may accompany a single set of sensations. Ideas are abstract,‡ reflective,§ and self-perceptive, while they cannot be too intense. Ideas may remain the same,

---

* See "On Truth," p. 106. † Ibid., pp. 107, 116.
‡ Ibid, pp. 207, 212. § Ibid., pp. 207, 216.

while the sensations which accompany them change.* They are apprehensions of abstract qualities grouped round a unity,† and can perceive the "whatness" of things.‡ Ideas are not tied down to sense and imagination,§ but can exceed sensuous experience, ‖ while they can perceive existence, which sense cannot.¶ There is one idea, "being," at the root of all,** while there is no corresponding one fundamental sensation. Ideas are relatively multitudinous †† compared with sensations. Sensations become associated according to the proximity in place or time of their occurrence, but ideas may be associated according to their logical relations.‡‡ The intellect, unlike feeling, can recognize the truth, goodness, beauty, or objective necessity of its acts,§§ as well as its own supremacy,‖‖ while it can recognize itself as the energy of a unity ¶¶ which is essentially inorganic.***

It has been said that ideas are only groups of feelings to which names have been assigned, and that the only unity and distinctness about them is the unity and distinctness of the name. "A name," it is objected, "is of course very different from a group of feelings, but there is nothing which is one and distinct, beyond such feelings, save only the word or name." This objection we have already met,††† and have shown that mental conceptions are both logically and historically

---

* See "On Truth," p. 106.   † Ibid., p. 207.
‡ Ibid., p. 211.   § Ibid., pp. 89–101.
‖ Ibid., pp. 109, 110, 217.   ¶ Ibid., p. 208.
** Ibid., p. 209.   †† Ibid., p. 210.   ‡‡ Ibid., p. 217.
§§ Ibid., p. 217.   ‖‖ Ibid., p. 113.   ¶¶ Ibid., p. 387.
*** Ibid., pp. 317, 388.   ††† Ibid., pp. 224–234.

prior to the terms which denote them. Rational conceptions can exist without words, but rational words cannot exist without conceptions or abstract ideas, and new terms are continually invented to denote ideas which have been freshly conceived. We may suddenly come to apprehend not only an idea, but a whole argument, far too rapidly for oral expression, and it may cost us very perceptible efforts and an appreciable period of time to put it even into mental words. These relations between thought and speech will come before us again and again in our examination of Mr. Romanes's work, so that it does not seem needful to say more at present on the subject.

Having thus referred to the leading distinctions between ideas and feelings,* and having cautioned our readers against the implications of Mr. Romanes as to the "generation" of ideas, we will next proceed to notice some of his remarks about "abstraction."† He says, truly enough, that our power of forming "general ideas," or "universals," depends upon this faculty as a *sine quâ non.* But the nature of this faculty he, in our judgment, misapprehends and misrepresents, while in connection therewith he introduces some very misleading implications. He tells us,‡ "I desire only to remark two things in connection with it. The first is

---

* In our work "On Truth," p. 203, we have, we may again remind the reader, specially called attention to the great importance of the distinction between our higher and our lower mental faculties. It is a distinction which has been strangely ignored, while it is probably the most important one in the whole range of psychology.

† See "On Truth," pp. 12, 211, 213, 214, 345, 409.   ‡ p. 25.

that throughout this history [that of the development or growth of abstraction] the development is a *development:* the faculty of abstraction is everywhere the same *in kind.* And the next thing is that this development is everywhere dependent on the faculty of *language.*"

Now, in our present work we have to encounter a singular difficulty. We have, by means of written language, to make it clear to those who read and who mostly think in words, what thought is and can become *without* words. Fortunately, Mr. Romanes agrees with us in perceiving that, in man, abstraction and the formation of distinct, unequivocal ideas, can take place without words.* As we shall have occasion, later on, to consider his examples, we will defer citing any ourselves till the occasion referred to arises.

But Mr. Romanes introduces ambiguity and confusion at once, saying,† "All the higher animals have general ideas of 'Good-for-eating' and 'Not-good-for-eating' . . . for . . . the animal . . . subjects the morsel to a careful examination before consigning it to the mouth. This proves, if anything can, that such an animal has a general or abstract idea of sweet, bitter, hot, and, in general Good-for-eating and Not-good-for-

---

* He quotes M. Taine's account of a little girl eighteen months old, who was amused by her mother hiding in play behind a piece of furniture and saying "Coucou." Again, when her food was too hot, when she went too near the fire or candle, and when the sun was warm, she was told "Ça brûle." One day, on seeing the sun disappear behind a hill, she exclaimed, "'A b'ûle coucou," which showed, of course, that without speech she had formed concepts, which might be expressed by the terms, "Bodies giving forth heat," and "The action of hiding behind an object."

† p. 27.

eating—the motives of the examination clearly being to ascertain which of these two general ideas of kind is appropriate to the particular object examined."

Now, the inner nature and faculties of an organism can only be judged of by the outcome of its powers, whatever these may be. If these "higher animals" really had ideas of the kind, and consciously performed voluntary acts of examination in order to see "which of two general ideas" might be applicable in any given case, then of a surety we should soon be made unmistakably aware of it by other, less equivocal, manifestations of their possession of intellectual faculties like our own. But it is evident that a profound difference between the psychical powers of men and brutes does, in fact, exist, and therefore the interpretation of their actions which Mr. Romanes gives, cannot be the right one. Interpretations of that kind might carry us very far. We might say that plants have abstract ideas of " Suitable-for-nutrition" and "Not-suitable-for-nutrition," and of the still more abstract ideas, " Big-enough-to-be-worth-a-prolonged-effort " and " Not-big-enough-to-be-worth-a-prolonged-effort." For the plant called Venus's looking-glass (*Dionæa*) will snap together the blades of its singular leaf to catch an insect, but not to catch a non-digestible object. More than this, if the blades of its leaf have closed on an insect of insignificant size (not worth its catching) they will unclose and let it go again ; while otherwise they will hold it till it is killed and digested. Even the sundew (*Drosera*) exhibits what might be called a similar process of estimation due to "general ideas," since the actions of its glandular hairs are similarly discriminating. We, however, do not attribute even sensation to these plants on the strength of their economical, practically purposive, actions. Neither do we attribute to the higher animals the possession of the ideas "Good-for-eating," or "Not-good-for-eating" on the strength of those unconscious, instinctive actions of theirs which have a superficial resemblance to our acts of intellectual, voluntary discrimination. Not only the "higher animals," but very lowly animals also, possess multitudes of complex associations of feelings and motions. Amongst them are associations of definite pleasant odours as preceding definite and corresponding savours, as well as associations between various affections of sight and touch and similar pleasant savours. What, then, is more to be expected than that when a group of previously unexperienced sensations are brought before an animal (the new object submitted to the animal's senses) such commonly habitual actions as smelling it, feeling it, and looking round it, should automatically take place? Thus, instead of saying, "When we see animals determining between similar alternatives by" actions externally like our own, "we cannot reasonably doubt that the psychological processes are similar," we should express ourselves as follows: "Knowing by the widest inductions that we and brute animals are fundamentally different in nature, we should expect *à priori* that actions externally similar were due to causes internally diverse." Mr. Romanes says, "If I see a fox prowling about a farm-yard, I infer that he has been led by hunger to go where he has a general idea that there are a good many eatable things to be fallen in with—just as I myself am led by a similar impulse to visit a restaurant." We should say, "The fox has been led by hunger to visit a place presenting appearances and giving forth odours which have become associated in its sensitive faculty with pleasant consequences on previous occasions." We not only concede, but affirm that even very lowly animals have sensuous cognitions and sense perceptions of the kinds of creatures on which they prey, or which may be their enemies. But such affections need not be (and the general outcome of their psychical faculties forbids. them to be) more than those "sensuous universals" before referred to, which are fundamentally and utterly different in nature from the very lowest kind of ideas.

We have elsewhere * taken all the pains we could to draw out distinctly and fully, to the best of our ability, the distinction between those lower psychical faculties which we evidently share with brutes, and those intellectual powers in which we are convinced they have no share. We have shown how, merely by means of associated feelings, such sense-perceptions, sensuous general cognitions, and sensuous inferences may take place even in us, quite apart from true perceptions, general ideas, and inferences.

With this reference we must pass on to what we have lately said Mr. Romanes next treats of—namely, the process of "abstraction."

The power of abstraction, he tells us,† depends on

* See " On Truth," chaps. xiv., xv., pp. 178–223.
† p. 30.

reflection, and this again " on Language, or on the power of affixing names to abstract and general ideas."

To this we reply, (1) that abstraction does not depend on reflection, but takes place in us spontaneously without it, and (2) that abstraction does not depend on language, but also takes place without it.

As to our first reply, we would point out that animals have a sensitive faculty which, when stimulated by the presence of external objects, can associate together in groups and groups of groups, the sensations such external objects excite, and can combine them with revived past feelings of similar kinds, thus forming "sensuous perceptions." *   On the occurrence of similar but slightly varied experiences, this faculty can give rise to those compound impressions which we have termed "sensuous universals," † and which Mr. Romanes (as we shall see) calls " Recepts, or generic ideas."

All these affections we men (inasmuch as we are animals, though rational ones) also possess ; but we have a further faculty which brutes, we are convinced, have not. Upon the occurrence in us of such sensuous perceptions as have just been referred to, we have the faculty of generating — spontaneously and directly, without reflection—true, intellectual, abstract, general ideas. These ideas also may be elicited, continue to exist, and be communicated, without words. For, as we shall see abundantly, later on, they may exist in deaf-mutes, and can be conveyed from mind to mind by manual signs. Each man, however, consists of both an immaterial energy (one form of which is intellect) and an animal

* See " On Truth," p. 188.   † See above, pp. 44, 45.

body—the two being most intimately united so as to form a true unity—as reflection upon our own experience will suffice to show us.* He cannot, therefore, exercise his intellectual power without some mode of accompanying bodily activity. This may be a nervous activity, producing the utterance or imagination of words or other sounds, or the making of some gesture, or the imagination of such, or of some other visible or tactile sign. Such signs are necessary to serve as a material basis for every intellectual act—every conception, however abstract it may be.† We shall, later on, give various examples of distinct intellectual abstractions and true general conceptions, existing fully developed in the entire absence not only of the power of speech, but of sight and hearing also. How widely divergent from the truth, how profoundly mistaken, must, then, be the views of the Nominalists! Such views, as expressed by M. Taine, are quoted by Mr. Romanes ‡ in the most uncompromising manner, as follows : "Names *are* our abstract ideas, and the formation of our abstract ideas is nothing. more than the formation of names." Now, a name can only be a certain sound, or, if written, a certain sight, and therefore is and must be a definite individual entity. But the concept it serves is different indeed. The latter can neither be seen, heard, smelt, tasted, or felt, nor can it consist of any combination of our. sensations. It can only be thought, and it can be thought and recognized to be absolutely one and of the some kind, by the aid

* See " On Truth," pp. 386–392.
† Ibid., pp. 88, 224.   ‡ p. 32.

of very different "feelings." A triangle can be apprehended by means of sight, by feeling, or by hearing its
description ; and the general conception, "triangle," can
be also understood to be one and the same by means of
sight and feeling, or by means of feeling and hearing,
or by hearing and sight. The more abstract idea,
"extension," may exist apart from sensations of sight,
for it exists for the blind. It can exist apart from
sensations of touch or of muscular effort, for it may be
revealed by sight alone.*

Mr. Romanes says † that if the term "abstraction"
be confined to what is marked by a name, "then undoubtedly animals differ from men in not presenting
the faculty of abstraction ; for this is no more than to
say that animals have not the faculty of speech. But
if the term be not thus limited . . . then, no less
undoubtedly, animals resemble men in presenting the
faculty of abstraction. . . . In accordance with the latter
view, great as may be the importance of affixing a name
to a compound of simple ideas for the purpose of giving
that compound greater clearness and stability, the essence
of abstraction consists in the act of compounding, or in
the blending together of particular ideas into a general
idea of the class to which the individual things belong."

But "abstraction" is not in any way a "blending"
or "compounding," but is an ideal separation, or separate
intellectual apprehension, of qualities and conditions
which actually exist in concrete realities.‡

Mr. Romanes does not seem to regard it as possible

* "On Truth," p. 106.   † pp. 32, 33.
‡ See "On Truth," pp. 211–216.

to deny that "abstraction consists in the compounding of simple ideas," with which inane notion he, *mirabile dictu*, credits * both of the two psychological schools he is dealing with. The classification of psychical states he draws out for us is, therefore, as might be expected, confused, misleading, and with cross-divisions, as we will endeavour briefly to point out.

He submits his classification as follows :—

"The word 'idea' I will use . . . as a generic term to signify indifferently any product of the imagination, from the mere memory of a sensuous impression up to the result of the most abstruse generalization." This is, indeed, for him a convenient confusion in one lump, of things essentially distinct. Were it once conceded that no difference of kind exists between the sensuous memory of an impression and a really intellectual generalization, it would be altogether idle to inquire whether any difference of kind exists between the psychical natures of man and brute. A concession of the sort would render it impossible for any one whose reasoning powers were not exceptionally defective, to maintain the existence of such a distinction of kind.

He next tells us, " By 'Simple Idea,' 'Particular Idea,' or 'Concrete Idea,' I understand the mere memory of a particular sensuous perception." But what sort of "memory" is here meant? There is true memory, in which we are conscious our recollection refers to the past, and there is the exercise of that retentive faculty which recalls past images without intellectual advertence to them. The latter is only improperly called

* p. 34.

memory, and is to be distinguished as "reminiscence" or "sensuous memory." * It is evident, however, from the connection in which it is used, that Mr. Romanes only refers to sensuous memory; but the sentence is exceedingly ambiguous.

"By 'Compound Idea,' 'Complex Idea,' or 'Mixed Idea,'" he tells us, "I understand the combination of simple, particular, or concrete ideas into that kind of composite idea which is possible without the aid of language." Now, both sensuous and intellectual cognitions are possible without the aid of language; but again the context shows us that Mr. Romanes here really intends to denote only what he, a little further on,† calls "Recepts," which are what we have distinguished as "sensuous cognitions," and which may and obviously do exist both in animals and in ourselves.

Lastly, he informs us, "By 'General Idea,' 'Abstract Idea,' 'Concept,' or 'Notion,' I understand that kind of composite idea which is rendered possible only by the aid of language, or by the process of naming abstractions as abstractions." Against this we must once more, in passing, briefly protest, and affirm that general ideas or concepts are not composite, but simple, and that they do not depend for their existence on language.

---

* The subject of memory is most important to any one who would investigate the psychology of man and animals. We must refer the reader to our work "On Truth," the second chapter of which is devoted to the faculty of memory generally, while sensuous and intellectual memory are described at pp. 186 and 220 respectively. That curious power of mere "organic reminiscence," which has most improperly been spoken of as memory, is treated of at p. 169.

† p. 36.

Discoursing on his own classification, Mr. Romanes tells us * that his first division (simple, particular, or concrete ideas) " has to do only with what are called percepts." This term we cannot allow to pass uncommented on. The term "percept" should be used to denote a thing "perceived," and intellectually perceived ; since intellectual perception is alone really perception in the proper sense of that word. It may be loosely used to denote a mere sensuous discrimination ; but it should then be distinguished by some qualifying, limiting term. Thus, as we have said, this passage is an exceedingly ambiguous one. Mr. Romanes's term includes two classes which differ *toto cœlo*—namely, (1) sensuous perceptions, and (2) intellectual perceptions of individual concrete objects or actions, or of affections of the individual who perceives.

His intermediate class of " recepts " he very strangely considers a *terra incognita* which he has discovered and named for the first time, forgetting that we have spoken of them as " sensuous universals," and not knowing that they were distinguished six hundred years ago, and have been so again and again since, under the title of *Universalia Sensûs.*" †   Indeed, he distinctly

---

* p. 35.

† By St. Thomas Aquinas, and other Scholastics. We may refer Mr. Romanes to Quæstio LXXVIII. articulus iv., entitled, " Utrum interiores sensus convenienter distinguantur," of Aquinas's " Summa Theologica," for a treatment of this so-called " terra incognita." Further, we may refer him to Quæstio 34 of the "Questiones Philosophicæ" of Father Maurus, S.J. (who died 1687), and to a recent work, Kleutgen's " Philosophie Scolastique " (Gaume Frères, Paris, 1868), vol. i. pp. 62–65. The problems of cerebration investigated by Prof. Ferrier, and the speculative theories of Prof.

affirms * that "this large and important territory of ideation is, so to speak, unnamed ground. . . . So completely
has the existence of this intermediate land been ignored,
that we have no word at all which is applicable to it."
On this account he coins his word "recept." We have
no objection to the term in itself, although as he uses it,
error is connected with it. He says † that "in order to
form a concept, the mind must intentionally bring together its percepts (or the memories of them), for the
purpose of binding them up as a bundle of similars, and
labelling the bundle with a name. But in order to form
a recept, the mind need perform no such intentional
actions." The distinction is surely here drawn in the
wrong place. The mind must be active in either case,
but need act intentionally in neither—and, certainly, in
forming general ideas, or true universals, it never collects
and builds up its sensuous cognitions into bundles.

On the occurrence of the requisite reiterated sensations, a sensuous cognition, or "recept" (an entity of the
same essential nature as sensations) is formed.

On the occurrence of the requisite sensuous cognitions, an intellectual general idea, or concept (an entity
of an essentially different nature from sensations) springs
forth spontaneously in the mind, without the need of
our exerting any intentional activity.

In introducing his list ‡ of ideas at the end of his
second chapter, he tells us that for the sake of avoiding
confusion he makes use of the term *generic* instead of

Weismann refer to no matters the principles of which were not,
in principle, discussed by the Scholastics of the Middle Ages.

* p. 35.   † pp. 36-37.   ‡ p. 39.

the term *general* in naming his intermediate class, and he sums up as follows :—

IDEAS
$\begin{cases} \text{General, Abstract, or Notional} = \text{Concepts.} \\ \text{Complex, Compound, or Mixed} = \text{Recepts, or Generic} \\ \quad \text{Ideas.} \\ \text{Simple, Particular, or Concrete} = \text{Memories of Percepts.} \end{cases}$

In order to make clear the precise divergence of view which exists between Mr. Romanes * and ourselves, we subjoin a tabular statement of corresponding subdivisions which may respectively be made in the two groups of activities which we regard as fundamentally distinct in kind—namely, intellectual perceptions and sensuous cognitive affections. To one group of the latter we have applied the new term " sencept," for which we feel much apology is due. We have used it as conveniently matching with Mr. Romanes's term "recept," and as serving to distinguish one simple set of affections from those which we ourselves term "sensuous universals," but which we have no objection to denote by the term which Mr. Romanes has himself coined :—

IDEAS
$\begin{cases} \text{General, or true Universals} = \text{Concepts.} \\ \text{Particular or individual} = \text{Percepts.} \end{cases}$

SENSUOUS COGNITIVE AFFECTIONS
$\begin{cases} \text{Groups of actual experiences} \\ \quad \text{combined with sensuous} \\ \quad \text{reminiscences} \\ \text{Groups of simply juxtaposed} \\ \quad \text{actual experiences} \end{cases}$
$\begin{aligned} &= \text{Sensuous Universals, or Recepts.} \\ &= \text{Sense-perceptions, or Sencepts.} \end{aligned}$

In his third chapter Mr. Romanes reviews what he

* In his chapter ix., pp. 184, 185 (on Speech), he further distinguishes between (1) lower and (2) higher recepts, as well as between (3) lower and (4) higher concepts—distinctions which further aid his attempt to bridge over the gulf which yawns between sense and intellect.

calls the " Logic of Recepts." Before proceeding to its examination, we would ask our readers to bear carefully in mind eight special points, some of which have been already adverted to either in our introductory chapter or in the present one, but which we deem it necessary to here especially insist upon :—

(1) It is abundantly evident, and it is freely admitted by Mr. Romanes himself, that animals, even the highest, do not exercise the intellectual powers which we exercise ; though it is plain that they possess abundantly the sensitive faculties of feeling, imagination, and emotion.

(2) Besides our powers of feeling, thinking, and willing, we possess both a faculty of instinct * and a power of forming habits.† These powers account for the existence, even in ourselves, of a number of actions which our possession of intellect will not account for,‡ and it is an unquestionable fact that instinct is more largely developed in animals,§ notably in insects, than it is in ourselves.

(3) These faculties of instinct and habit, do not form part of our conscious life. We are, of course, conscious of the actions we perform, and we can recognize them as having been instinctive or habitual. But we have no conscious experience of those faculties, while we have conscious experience of our powers of reasoning, think-

---

* As to this faculty in ourselves, see " On Truth," pp. 175, 184.

† Habit is the determination in one direction of a previously vague tendency to action. Its existence presupposes this active tendency. See " On Truth," pp. 174, 358, 362.

‡ Such as the sucking of the infant and various activities attending adolescence.

§ See " On Truth," p. 358, for various cases in point.

ing, imaging, or feeling, at the time we exercise them. We are only conscious of the *effects* of our faculties of instinct and habit. It results from this that we cannot imagine a faculty of instinct or a faculty of habit, for we can never imagine anything of which we have not had experience. Therefore, although our reason tells us that these faculties not only exist but have acted in us, they nevertheless seem to possess a specially mysterious character. Thus it is that we come to feel a temptation not to believe that there are any such special faculties at all. But groups of feelings and thoughts, on the other hand, can be most easily imagined because they are constantly experienced, and this alone would suffice to prevent our feeling any temptation to doubt the existence of our sensitive and cognitive faculties, which would seem to be even more absurd (though it is not really so) than is a doubt as to our own continued, substantial existence.

(4) We may, then, well expect to find that animals possess powers which we cannot imagine, and in the existence of which, therefore, we may find it difficult to believe. Such are some of the truly marvellous instinctive faculties of insects and other lowly organisms, and the seemingly intelligent powers of some plants.* But these various faculties are no more really wonderful than are our powers of sensation (which are quite as inexplicable), and are vastly less wonderful than are our amazing powers of cognition—especially our knowledge of necessary and universal truths.

(5) We should carefully distinguish between direct

* See "On Truth," pp. 334, 335.

and reflex cognition. Even in ourselves, who possess true intellect, we may often, by reflection, detect the past, latent presence of feelings which were not perceived. We do not mean by this that we have apprehended something without adverting to our apprehension. That is a thing we constantly do. It is very rarely that we perceive, or advert to the fact that we are thinking whatever we may happen to be thinking. What we mean is that we can perceive that we had a sense-perception of an object without knowing the object— a sense-perception without consciousness,* as when walking along in a town we suddenly recollect we have seen a name over a shop-window sometime before.

· Such an impression cannot be a "percept," which is a state the existence of which implies consciousness.† Instead, then, of "percept" and "perception," I, for this, shall venture to employ the terms "sencept" and "senception." Surely in animals which give us no evidence of reflective power, or, as we shall see, of the presence of "consciousness" as distinguished from "consentience," we should expect to be able to account for the most seemingly intelligent actions of animals by "sencepts" and "recepts" (and we ought to do so if we could), without supposing the existence in them of "percepts" and "concepts," which, if they existed, would certainly produce very startling effects which we do not see. By "consentience"‡ we mean the faculty of receiving divers

---

* See "On Truth," pp. 89, 187.

† To call any "thing not perceived" a percept—that is, a "thing perceived"—is a glaring contradiction in terms.

‡ See "On Truth," pp. 183, 219, 354. As to such an "internal sense," see also above, p. 44, note †.

orders of sensations in one common sensorium. It is by it that the sleep-walker receives and accurately responds to the varied impressions which surrounding objects make on his organs, and its existence suffices to account for the simultaneous effect of sounds, sights, and smells upon an animal seeking its prey or trying to escape from pursuit.

(6) We should also take pains to understand and appreciate the distinction which exists between true "inference," which is an essentially intellectual apprehension of a truth as implicitly contained in other truths, and that mere sensuous reinstatement of past impressions which may simulate it. The latter affection, which we have distinguished as "sensuous or organic inference," * manifests itself as follows : Let any group of sensations have become intimately associated with certain other sensations, then, upon the recurrence of that group, an imagination of the sensations previously associated therewith spontaneously arises in the mind, and we have an expectant feeling of their proximate actual recurrence. Thus, the sensation of a vivid flash of lightning has come, by association, to lead to an expectant feeling of the thunder-clap to follow. Such mere association of feelings, some of which when freshly experienced lead to an expectant feeling of the others, and to a feeling of satisfaction when the sense of expectation is fulfilled, may certainly exist in animals as well as in ourselves, and its presence will fully account for all those actions which are so often taken as indications of the existence in them of a truly reasoning faculty.

* See "On Truth," pp. 194, 201.

(7) We have already indicated what we deem to be the true nature of the process of abstraction ; but before entering upon a consideration of the statements made by Mr. Romanes in his second chapter, it may be well, at the risk of tediousness, to repeat that so far from its being a separation and segregation of feelings, it is radically different from every sensuous process. It is the spontaneous starting forth in the mind of an intellectual cognition, or idea (upon the reception of certain sensuous experiences), like Minerva from the head of Jove. One of the earliest of our abstractions is also one of the most ultimate—namely, the idea of "being." This never was and never could have been a feeling, though the idea must have accompanied every feeling recognized by us as such. Thus abstraction is so fundamentally different from the power of forming sensuous universals, that it may be said to be a process directly contrary to it ; since the latter agglutinates sense-impressions which the former discards as it emerges and escapes from amongst them.

(8) Lastly, we should be very careful to distinguish between feeling, knowing, judging, inferring, and classifying *formally*—*i.e.* when we perform this act with a distinct intention to perform them—and feeling, knowing, judging, inferring, and classifying *materially*—*i.e.* when we do so in a more or less automatic manner, without intention or advertence. This distinction takes note of the difference between direct and reflex cognition.†

* See "On Truth," pp. 205, 208, 234.

† As to this, see "On Truth," pp. 8, 23, and also p. 189 as to the three senses of the word "know."

Thus there may be—

(*a*) Unconscious, merely sensuous cognition, accompanied by "consentience"—as in the actions of certain sleep-walkers and idiots.

(*b*) Intellectual cognition of the lowest order : where general consciousness is present, but where there is no distinct consciousness, not only as to the nature of an act performed, but even as to the fact of its performance ; so that the act is far indeed from being one done with a deliberate intention of doing it. Thus, when out shooting, and in a normal state of consciousness, on firing and missing our aim, we may make some sudden gesture by which a bystander can see what has happened, though we had no intention of so indicating it, and had no distinct consciousness of the fact of our bodily movement. Such a movement is no true "sign," for the gesticulator has no intention of conveying his ideas to another by depicting any fact. If, then, a spectator exclaims, "That gesture is a sign he has missed his aim," such a spectator uses the term "sign" improperly, by a loose analogy. Similarly we may, without any intention or distinct consciousness, make a movement from which a bystander can tell in which direction an animal we have been watching may have gone.

(*c*) Intellectual cognition, accompanied not only with a general consciousness, but with a consciousness of an act performed, yet without special advertence to it as being a fact or to any intention we may have had on performing it. Thus we may suddenly raise our arm and point in a specially selected direction, with the

F

intention of showing which way any creature has gone. Evidently a consciousness must attend a gesture thus made to indicate direction which was absent in an aimless, altogether unintentional movement produced by vexation at having made a bad shot, however practically indicative the latter may have been. Therefore such a movement is a true "sign," being a movement made depicting a fact with the intention of conveying to other minds the ideas of the sign-maker.

(*d*) We may do the same thing not only with consciousness and intention, but with express advertence to the fact of our intention in the act deliberately performed.

We may know without adverting to our knowledge, and we may feel without knowing that we feel. Now, since such is the case with us, it must be, to say the least, probable that animals also may feel without knowing it.

With these premisses, we may proceed to the examination of Mr. Romanes's third chapter, entitled, "Logic of Recepts." Therein he tells us,* "The question which we have to consider is whether there is a difference of kind, or only a difference of degree, between a recept and a concept. This is really the question with which the whole of the present volume is concerned."

We call attention to this passage as an excuse for, and a justification of, what we fear some of our readers may deem too great minuteness and reiteration in this analysis of mental states. Great care is, however, necessary not to yield to the temptation of hurrying

* p. 45.

over and treating incompletely a matter which is of the very essence of Mr. Romanes's whole contention.

As to his mode of procedure, he observes,* "First of all I will show, by means of illustrations, the highest levels of ideation that are attained within the domain of recepts ; and, in order to do this, I will adduce my evidence from animals alone, seeing that here there can be no suspicion—as there might be in the case of infants—that the logic of recepts is assisted by any nascent growth of concepts."

Before, however, applying himself to this task, he discusses his own expression, "logic of recepts."

He tells us,† in the first place, that "all mental processes of an adaptive kind are, in their last resort, processes of classification; they consist in discriminating between differences and resemblances."

Now, in this sentence much confusion of thought is indicated. In the first place, the word "discriminating" is used ambiguously, as—neglecting the distinction we have above indicated ‡ as No. (8)—it is applied to both "formal" and "material" discrimination ; and yet these acts are of a radically different kind. A mere sieve *materially* "discriminates" between coal-dust and cinders of a certain size ! It is also false to say that "all mental processes of an adaptive kind" "*consist*" in either a material or a formal discrimination ; although, of course, like all other mental acts, they are accompanied by something of a discriminating nature. To know that any object (y) possesses any quality (x), implies that x is discriminated from the group of

* p. 46.   † p. 46.   ‡ See above, p. 64.

things, "not *x* ;" but this may be a mere unimportant accident of such mental process. Yet even a mental process as adaptive as is the determination to bolt, and the bolting of, a bedroom door, cannot be properly said to *consist* of a discrimination ; although, of course, it is "accompanied " by a formal mental distinction between "doors bolted" and "doors unbolted," and by the material distinction of adding one to the group of "doors actually bolted." Mr. Romanes goes on to say, " An act of simple perception is an act of noticing resemblances and differences between the objects of such perception." But such an act by no means consists in taking notice of qualities, but in *perceiving an object* by means of the impressions it makes on the senses, which impressions (and the qualities they imply) have their effect without being adverted to. They hide themselves in making the object itself known.* The impressions and the resemblances and differences with which they correspond, cannot themselves be noticed without a distinct reflex act.

Still more objectionable is Mr. Romanes's next sentence : " Similarly, an act of conception is the taking together—or the intentional *putting* together—of ideas which are recognized as analogous." To this we reply, A thousand times, No ! A mental act of "conception " does not take place in a way similar to that in which an act of sensuous perception takes place ; which latter, as we have seen, Mr. Romanes includes under his term " percepts." Neither is conception a " taking together," and still less is it an " intentional putting

* See " On Truth," pp. 91, 96, 101.

together" of ideas in any sense—and *à fortiori* not in the sense in which Mr. Romanes uses that much abused word.* There need be no "recognition" of any analogy existing between objects in order that a concept should be formed. Men can form a concept of the sun who do not know, or suspect, that any other sun exists. Even in the commonest cases, as in the concept "apple," we by no means need to advert to or "recognize" an analogy existing between different kinds of apples or different specimens of one kind of apple, though, of course, we can turn back our minds and, by reflection, "recognize" such analogy. All that is necessary is that there be such a *direct* apprehension of an object, as an object of a kind and possessing qualities or existing in one of various states ; but there need be no advertence either to the qualities or states, which are, nevertheless, implicitly apprehended in every direct perception and conception.

But, putting aside the sensuous meanings which Mr. Romanes attaches to the term "idea," and taking it in the sense of a truly intellectual act of perception, even then a "conception" *is* not "a taking together" of such ideas, though it may be elicited *through* our apprehension of different ideas. Thus our conception of the idea, "a marsupial mammal," may be elicited by our acquisition of ideas concerning the structural and physiological characters, and the environing conditions of the existing and extinct animals belonging to the zoological order, Marsupialia. Yet the idea itself is one single idea.

* Namely, in the sense of "any product of imagination, from the mere memory of a sensuous impression up to the results of the most abstruse generalization " (p. 34).

The matter in which we deem Mr. Romanes most mistaken is his notion that an "intentional" putting together of ideas is a necessary preliminary to our forming any mental conception. The infant who sees one or several dogs, does not fulfil any mental intention when it forms its corresponding concept. Neither do the first observers of an object new to them, intentionally put together ideas and group them into a plexus ; but their mental experiences give rise to a spontaneously formed new intellectual product or concept—which may be very imperfect and inadequate, but which *is* a concept notwithstanding.

Mr. Romanes continues : * " Hence abstraction has to do with the abstracting of analogous qualities." The expression, " has to do with," is an exceedingly vague one, and Mr. Romanes's meaning in using it is consequently obscure. We will not, therefore, further criticize it, contenting ourselves with once more observing that abstraction is much more than "the abstracting of analogous qualities," as most notably of all in the formation of that highest abstraction, the idea of " being."

" Reason," our author tells us, " is ratiocination, or the comparison of ratios." In saying this he further shows himself to be a disciple of Mr. Herbert Spencer, and errs with him. " Reason " is not equivalent to "ratiocination." It is a wider term, which includes inference, or ratiocination, but is by no means confined to it ; for it also includes "intellectual intuition." †

It is by our reason, but certainly not by any process

* p. 46.   † As to this, see further, " On Truth," p. 220.

of *inference*, we see that nothing can both be and not be at the same time, or that we know we have any feeling which we may have at the time. That ratiocination cannot be the whole of our reason, or even the most important part of it, is evident. For all proof, or reasoning, must ultimately rest upon truths which carry with them their own evidence, and do not, therefore, need proof. Consequently, the most important, because ultimate, department of our reason must be that which apprehends such self-evident, necessary truths. But inference, or ratiocination itself, is not a comparison of ratios. It is the process of making latent and implicit truth into explicitly recognized truth, in an orderly manner, according to the laws of thought—that is, according to logic.* Denying, therefore, *in toto* Mr. Romanes's assertion of the similarity of nature between sensuous and intellectual perception, and between recepts and concepts, we none the less freely let pass, without objection, his term "logic of recepts," not only allowing, but strenuously affirming, that the sensitive, imaginative, and associative power of living organisms has its own innate orderly laws, according to which all their feelings, imaginations, and sense-perceptions take place. For the very same reason, however, we cannot agree with Mr. Romanes in objecting† to the terms "Logic of Feelings" and "Logic of Signs." For the fact that Feelings belong to the sensitive and emotional side of life, is no reason why they should not occur, and group themselves according to their own laws. "Signs," it is true, are the expression of psychical con-

* See "On Truth," chap. v., On Reasoning.   † p. 47.

ditions, and not such conditions themselves, but they none the less correspond with the orderly arrangement of ideas on the one hand, and of emotional states on the other ; being, as Mr. Romanes says, "A reflection of the order or grouping, among the ideas [and feelings] which they are used to express."

Our author continues : " Even within the region of percepts we meet with a process of spontaneous grouping of like with like, which, in turn, leads downwards to the purely unconscious or mechanical grouping of stimuli in the lower nerve-centres.   So that on its objective face the method has everywhere been the same : whether in the case of reflex action, of sensation, perception, reception, conception, or reflection, on the side of the nervous system, the method of evolution has been uniform ; it has everywhere consisted in a progressive development of the power of discriminating between stimuli, joined with the complementary power of adaptive response."

How, it may be asked, can Mr. Romanes tell what are the various minute changes in the nervous system which respectively accompany the conscious processes of sensation, perception, conception, and reflection ?   It is difficult to understand how he can venture to speak dogmatically on so obscure a subject.   The term " discrimination " is commonly applied to denote rather a mental than a mechanical process.   That some corporeal modification accompanies, in us, every intellectual act, we do not for a moment question, and it may be that there is a close analogy between the physical processes in each case.   But the passage cited implies much more than this, and is misleading on account of its reference to psychical as well as physical processes. It tends to give rise to a persuasion that psychical acts, which our own minds show us to be different in nature, are themselves fundamentally similar, because there may be a similarity in the physical processes which accompany both.

Mr. Romanes makes * the great distinction between recepts and concepts to consist in the former being "*received*," while, he tells us, the latter "require to be *conceived.*" But in forming recepts as well as concepts, we need to be active agents as well as passive recipients. In both cases the psychical entity energizes and evolves something new, according to the nature of the entity which acts. A merely sensitive psychical entity, or Soul, † can (it is admitted on all hands) evolve *recepts* as a consequence of receiving due sensuous stimuli. A rational Soul can (it is admitted on all hands) also evolve *concepts* as a consequence of receiving due intellectual stimuli. It evolves in either case active, psychical states, which existed potentially before stimulation, but, of course, not actually. So much must be universally admitted. We, of course, further contend that a merely sensitive psychical entity, such as the soul, or principle of individuation,‡ of an amœba, an ant, or an ape, cannot by any stimulation be made to evolve an intellectual product.

Mr. Romanes proceeds to ask,§ "To what level of

---

* p. 49.

† As to this term, see "On Truth," pp. 390–392, 422, 424, 427, 430, 434.

‡ As to this term, see Ibid., pp. 422, 433–435.   § p. 50.

'ideation' can recepts attain without the aid of concepts ? . . . How far can mind travel without the aid
of language ?" He then applies himself to answer
this question by relating various anecdotes of animals.

In considering the value of such relations, we should
ever remember to what very curious lengths instinct
may go in insects, and how numerous and complex are
the responsive actions which may take place even in
ourselves in the absence of consciousness.* We should
recollect how we every now and then have experienced
a sort of "*malaise*," which has been relieved by finding
something which was missing from its place, although
we were not conscious of the cause of the *malaise* (the
absence of the object) till the shock experienced on our
having automatically found it, has called our attention
to the matter. We ourselves have frequently experienced this when one of the many objects we habitually
carry in our pockets has been unconsciously transferred
from one to another. We can, as every one knows, do
many things automatically and without consciousness,
which we often perform with full consciousness. This
fact makes it probable that similar actions may take
place in animals, and another fact is also very significant:
this is the notorious circumstance that persons deprived
of one of their senses often have their remaining senses
made more acute. It is also commonly affirmed that
some savages, who have little intellectual activity, have
much keener powers of seeing, hearing, and, perhaps,
even smelling, than we have. How much greater, more
acute, more complex, and more far-reaching, then, may

* See " On Truth," pp. 183–200.

not be the sensitive powers of creatures whose whole
being is entirely given up to sensitivity, without its being
interfered with by any intellectual activity ! It should
surely cause us little wonder if we found them doing
many things altogether beyond our power under such
conditions to effect. That thirsty dogs should run into
hollows,* that an elephant should blow on the ground
beyond an object it wished to drive towards him, that a
bear should similarly draw near a piece of floating bread
by pawing the water, or that dogs, "accustomed to
tidal rivers or to swimming in the sea," should feel and
automatically allow for currents, need occasion no surprise whatever. Such actions are surely just such as we
might confidently anticipate would take place under the
given circumstances.

Mr. Darwin is quoted † as having written about a
bitch of his, which, on hearing the words, " Hi, hi, where
is it ? " rushed and looked about, even up into trees.
He is also quoted as having asked, "Now, do not these
actions clearly show that she had in her mind a general
idea that some animal is to be discovered and hunted ? "
To this we reply, No doubt the hearing of such words
uttered, as we are told, " in an eager voice," excited the
dog's emotions, and raised phantasmata (images) in its
consentience—awoke reminiscences of before-experi-
enced groups of smells, sounds, colours, and motions, and
relations of various kinds between them—but this is
very different from a "general idea." In other words,
imaginary recepts were aroused in the dog, but not
percepts, and, therefore, no such thing as a mental

* p. 51. † p. 52.

conception. Mr. Romanes quotes from Mr. Belt an anecdote concerning ants in South America which learnt to tunnel under the rails of a tramway. But such facts need surprise no one who remembers some of the more wonderful actions of ordinary insects nearer home. No doubt these burrowing ants were well-accustomed to make tunnels, and had instinctively made them again and again on the occurrence of other obstacles to surface progression. To say, as Mr. Romanes says, "Clearly, the insects must have appreciated the nature" of the obstacles, "and correctly reasoned out the only way by which they could be avoided," is not a little absurd. If they could really appreciate a "nature," and truly "reason out" a way to avoid injuries, we should quickly have such plainly and distressingly inconvenient evidence of their rationality, that there would be no need to go so far as to South America to find an instance of it.

With respect to the fear which wolves have of traps and their detection of man by the sense of smell, the following remark is cited* from Leroy: "In this case the wolf can only have an abstract idea of danger—the precise nature of the trap laid for him being unknown." That the wolf has a fear of man, no one can doubt, and it is highly probable that his sense of smell would lead him to abstain from taking a bait. This would be enough to account for the fact cited, without crediting the animal with "an abstract idea of danger," to credit it with which is to credit it with an intellect such as man has. Mr. Romanes also tells us that Leroy "well

* p. 53.

observes, 'Animals, like ourselves, are *forced* to make abstractions. A dog which has lost its master, runs towards a group of men, by virtue of a general abstract idea, which represents to him the qualities possessed in common with these men by his master." But the dog runs towards the men because the sense-impressions it has received from them raise pleasurable feelings of anticipation and of the completion of a sensuous harmony unconsciously craved.* There is no more need for an act of abstraction in this case than there is in the case of a stag which "doubles" on its own footsteps, and sometimes practises before retiring to rest "the artifices which he would have employed to throw out the dogs, if he were pursued by them."· Such actions are clearly "instinctive proceedings." Mr. Romanes adds,† "It is remarkable enough that an animal should seek to confuse its trail by such devices, even when it knows that the hounds are actually in pursuit ; but it is still more so when the devices are resorted to in order to confuse *imaginary* hounds which may *possibly* be on the scent." The fact would be curious indeed if, as the words quoted seem intended to imply, the stag consciously employed such devices as a consequence of thinking that hounds might be on its scent, and formed an intention to deceive them accordingly. There is not, however, the slightest need to adopt so absurd a notion. The action is sufficiently accounted for by instinct. It is done instinctively, as a dog instinctively turns round and

* For further detail as to instances of precisely the same kind, see " On Truth," p. 350.

† p. 55.

round on a drawing-room hearthrug before lying down, just as if it were in its ancestral home in the greenwood, the herbs of which needed thus treading down and pressing round, to make a comfortable bed.

Very funny is the tale cited * from Miss Bramston about a certain archiepiscopal collie-dog, which had acquired a habit of hunting imaginary pigs every evening directly after family prayers. Mr. Romanes makes much of this, but really nothing could well be more simple or natural than the association of feelings and imaginations thereby implied. Indeed, the case may well be cited as a type of others, the explanation of which may seem, from a less complete knowledge of the circumstances, to present some difficulty. In this instance we are told that the collie had been formerly accustomed "to be sent to chase real pigs out of a field ; " and, of course, the sound of the word "pigs," and the pleasurable action of running about after them, became associated in its imagination. We are then told, " It became a custom for Miss Benson to open the door for the collie after dinner in the evening, and say, ' Pigs ! ' " when he very naturally ran out, and ran about according to his previously-acquired habit. Soon this exercise became in its turn a matter of habit, and the phenomena attending the termination of dinner and of family prayers very naturally gave rise in the collie to an expectant feeling † of the door being opened for the accustomed pleasurable excitement. If the door was not opened, the habit being now well-established, the expectant feeling, always growing more and more vivid,

* p. 56.   † See " On Truth," p. 195.

could hardly fail to elicit barks, tail-waggings, and movements towards the exceptionally unopened door, and the
constantly accumulating excitement would surely lead
it at last to run out and bark without waiting for the
uttering of the word " Pigs "; nor is it in the least surprising to learn that the phenomena attending family
prayers at Miss Bramston's house should arouse in the
animal the same expectant feelings and therewith associated actions, which had become so ingrained during its
residence at the Archbishop's.

Mr. Romanes gives us yet again the oft-told tale
of the crows which "seem able to count." It is thus
related,* after Leroy, by our author: When about
to shoot the nests, in order "to deceive this suspicious
bird, the plan was hit upon of sending two men into the
watch-house, one of whom passed on while the other
remained ; but the crow counted and kept her distance.
The next day three went, and again she perceived that
only two returned. In fine it was found necessary to
send five or six men to the watch-house in order to put
her out of her calculation."

But what wonder is there that a crow, seeing a man
go beneath her nest with a gun, should keep clear till
she had seen him go away ; even if, for a time, he had
hidden himself behind a bush ? Why, then, should it
be wondered at that the bird's mere sense-perception
felt a difference between the visual picture presented by
a group of three men and another presented by only
two ? The wonder rather is that the creature should
not be more discriminative, as we always wonder that a

* p. 57.

bitch or a she-cat does not seem to miss a single pup or kitten which may have been taken away from the others in her litter.

Mr. Romanes naturally makes a great deal of the chimpanzee "Sally" at the Zoological Gardens, which, he tells us,[*] has been taught "to count correctly as far as five." The result of our own investigation with regard to this ape was as follows :—

It is most true that the animal is finely gifted, and that it does separately pick up from the ground, place in its mouth, and then present "in one bunch, two, three, four, or five straws, as may be demanded of it, or only one. It has distinctly associated the several sounds of these numbers with corresponding groups of picked-up straws. The ape will also, on command, pass a straw through a large or small hole in the fastening of its cage, or through a particular interspace of its wire netting. It will also put objects into its keeper's pocket, play various odd tricks with boy visitors, howl horribly when told to sing, and hold on its head pieces of apple, remaining perfectly quiescent till a particular expression is used. This last trick, however, is one of the commonest of those performed by pet dogs, and the putting of objects into the keeper's pocket is nothing remarkable. The passing of a straw through a special aperture on command would be more so, but for the fact that the basis of the whole superstructure of such tricks was laid by the animal itself (as the keeper told us), which had spontaneously taken to the trick of picking up a straw and passing it through a small hole near the keyhole of

[*] p. 58.

the door of its cage.* Having thus itself acquired a habit of picking up straws and passing them through a hole, there could be little difficulty in getting it to pass the straw through other holes, and not much in getting it to pick up more straws than one. That it should associate certain motions with the sound of certain words, is no more than dogs, pigs, and various other animals lower in the scale will accomplish.

There remains, then, as the single distinguishing peculiarity of this case, the association in the ape's imagination and consentience, of the words, one, two, three, four, or five, with the picking up, holding, and handing over a corresponding number of straws. This fact of association is, so far as we know, exceptional, and it is therefore very interesting. But it does not prove that the animal has any idea of these five numbers —not, of course, as numbers †—but as so many separate things. The matter would be the same if the animal could discriminate up to ten or more. We know abundantly already that various animals may be made to associate very complex bodily movements with sounds,

---

* Possibly as a result of having seen a key put in and out of the keyhole.

† The idea of "number" implies comparison, with a simultaneous recognition of both distinctness and similarity; although, of course, it is not necessary that the fact of our having such apprehensions should be adverted to. No two things could be known to be two without an apprehension that while they are numerically distinct they can in some way be thought of as belonging to one class of entities. We could not say "pink" and "a high rate of interest" were two, unless it were two "thoughts." By so speaking of them we should unite them under one conception which is common to them both as two "ideas." As to this, see further, "On Truth," p. 241.

G

and to associate a repetition of the same movements more or less frequently with different sounds is an act of essentially the same kind as the former. That the thing seems at all marvellous is due to a trick of our own imagination. The words of command in this case are words which express for us the highly abstract idea of number; and our imagination having become connected therewith, we are apt to picture to ourselves a like connection in the cognitive faculty of the ape. But its presence there is by no means necessary to explain the action, while if such a highly abstract idea was present there, the animal would not allow us to long remain doubtful as to the fact. We particularly questioned its keeper whether the ape ever pointed to any object or used any gesture with the evident purpose of calling his attention to some fact or passing occurrence. Although he was evidently well disposed to extol the powers of his charge as far as truth would permit, he distinctly told us it did not do so. If any one came in with a gun the creature would show extreme terror, but "Sally" never pointed to it or by gesture called the keeper's own attention to the dreaded object. We could neither see nor hear of anything rendering it possible to attribute to this very interesting brute a psychical nature of a higher kind than that possessed by any other brutes. It appeared to us plainly to have only the same kind of powers with them, although they might be more developed in degree. But this, surely, is just what we should expect. The rational nature of man has been conferred only on an animal of a special kind, with a body resembling very closely that of an ape.

We might, then, confidently expect to find in that animal such higher powers of mere sensitivity as should almost fit it to be the receptacle of a higher nature, which higher nature could not evidently act in conformity with its requirements in the body of some very differently constituted beast, such as a horse, an ant-eater, or a whale. The powers and activities possessed by apes and monkeys are just those we should expect to find in animals closely resembling ourselves in body, but devoid of mind. They exhibit phenomena which are those of the life of a mere brute nature, but yet are the phenomena of a brute nature the sensitive powers of which are somewhat exceptionally developed, as of a brute nature which had been formed in preparation for and as an adumbration of what was to follow.

Mr. Romanes objects*—as from the position he takes up he is forced to object—to our declaration (in which we have the advantage of having the great physiologist, Müller, as well as Hegel, on our side) that the formation of abstract conceptions under the notion of cause and effect, is impossible to animals. He declares† that, in his opinion, "needless obscurity is imported into this matter, by not considering in what our own idea of causality consists. . . . All men and most animals have a *generic* idea of causality, in the sense of expecting uniform experience under uniform conditions." Here the word "*expecting*" is used ambiguously, and is therefore misleading. To "expect" in the sense of to perceive what may or should follow, is what we utterly deny any brute can do. To "expect,"

* p. 58 † p. 59.

meaning thereby an unconscious sense of craving for something needed to complete a harmony amongst sensations and emotions, is what we have not only allowed the brutes, but have distinctly attributed to them.* Mr. Romanes goes on : "A cat sees a man knock at the knocker of a door, and observes that the door is afterwards opened : remembering this, when she herself wants to get in at the door, she jumps at the knocker, and waits for the door to be opened. Now, can it be denied that in this act of inference, or imitation, or whatever name we choose to call it, the cat perceives such an association between the knocking and the opening as to feel that the former as antecedent was in some way required to determine the latter as a consequent ? " We have already objected to and denied, upon definite and distinct grounds, the existence of perceptions in animals ; but for the purpose of Mr. Romanes the word " feels " might be substituted for the word " perceives," so we will let this passage pass without further protest. However, the whole circumstance referred to can be accounted for simply by the association of feelings—including emotions and desires. Nevertheless we are inclined to believe that the narration is a little exaggerated, and that some further sensuous experience on the part of the cat would be needed than the mere seeing "a man knock at a door" and its being thereupon "opened." But Mr. Romanes continues: "What is this but such a perception of causal relation as is shown by a child who blows upon a watch to open the case—thinking this to

* See " On Truth," p. 350.

be the cause of the opening from the uniform deception practised by its parent—or of the savage who plants nails and gunpowder to make them grow?" We say it is something very different indeed, as is shown by the other circumstances respectively attending the action of the cat on the one hand and those of the child and the savage * on the other. Some plants move about their tendrils to find a suitable point of support, and a blind man may move about his hands to find suitable support ; but the two actions, though *materially* similar, are very different *formally*. It is a recognized logical fallacy to conclude because two things are alike in some accidental circumstance, they are alike altogether or essentially. Mr. Romanes further relates to us † some of his own experience of a dog afraid of thunder, in connection with apples shot down on the floor of an apple-room. "My dog," he says, "became terror-stricken at the sound ; but as soon as I brought him to the apple-room and showed him the true *cause* of the noise, he became again buoyant and cheerful as usual."

This is a curious example of reading into an animal what the observer expected to find. There is not the slightest reason to suppose that the dog in this instance even receptually ‡ apprehended causation, or felt any relationship between the noise which had previously frightened him and his feelings in the apple-room when taken there. What could there be to frighten him in

---

* We confess to some incredulity as to the asserted planting of nails and gunpowder by savages.

† p. 60.

‡ As to the mere feeling of causation, as distinguished from its perception, see "On Truth," pp. 48, 195, 220.

the presence of his master, who had called him and was kindly noticing him?

Still more curious is the tale told about an American monkey which had found out the way to unscrew the handle of that object which is often so much too easily unscrewed, namely, a hearth-brush. He delighted in screwing it on and off, and soon began to unscrew all the unscrewable articles within his reach, so as to become a nuisance to the household. This, we are told,* showed that the monkey had "discovered the mechanical *principle* of the screw"—an "intelligent recognition of a principle discovered by the most unwearying perseverance in the way of experiment" (!). To do what it did, needed as little the "intelligent recognition of a principle" as any white mouse which had learnt to turn rotating objects, or, as a canary, which had learnt to pull up a small vessel of water suspended by a thread, need apprehend "principles" of mechanics and hydrostatics. We are told that the monkey, "however often he was disappointed at the beginning [of the screwing process], never was induced to try turning the handle the other way; he always screwed from right to left." This would seem to show (on Mr. Romanes's method of interpretation) that the monkey had much greater intelligence than is possessed by many human beings, who often *do* try screwing the wrong way, when their efforts to screw the right way have not succeeded. The misleading language into which Mr. Romanes allows himself to be betrayed by his credulous enthusiasm about his monkey is far more remarkable

* p. 61.

than anything else in the anecdote. We are told that after having discovered this " mechanical principle," his little beast " proceeded forthwith to generalize." Concerning the objects thus mischievously unscrewed, screwed, and unscrewed again and again, we are gravely assured, as to the separated parts, that the monkey "was by no means careful always to replace them "—as if he was ever careful to do so, and as if those which were replaced were replaced by a sort of quasi-ethical, deliberate intention! Next follows * an interesting account of the raising by a minute spider of a house-fly twenty times its weight, through a very ingenious process, but one in no way really more wonderful than many other curious contrivances of which spiders instinctively avail themselves.

Mr. Romanes afterwards remarks how the gradually increasing receptual power of animals prepares the way for the formation of concepts, a remark with which we agree in our own sense. Knowing, and ever asserting the necessary dependence of the exercise of intellect in us rational animals upon a foundation of associated feelings of all kinds, we also affirm that in animal evolution, mechanism is gradually more and more perfected in anticipation of that intelligence which was to be introduced into the material world with the advent of man. Our author adds,† what is indeed most true, he has not yet proved " that the ideation which we have in common with brutes [our sense-perception] is not supplemented by ideation of some other order, or kind. Presently," he continues, "I shall consider the arguments

* p. 62. † p. 64.

which are adduced to prove that it has been, and then it will become apparent that the supplement, if any, must have been added in the smelting-pot of Language —a fact, be it observed, which is conceded by all modern writers who deny the genetic continuity of mind in animal and human intelligence." The last assertion is one which is indeed remarkable. It shows that Mr. Romanes has not apprehended what is the fundamental position, on this subject, of the school to which he is opposed. The "intellectual," as opposed to the "sensational" school, energetically affirm that the supplement added was not "language," but "a distinctly rational nature," whereof thought, language, and moral responsibility are alike results.

In concluding this chapter, its author makes an assertion which we have sincere pleasure in agreeing with and supporting. It is the assertion that children do not commence their intellectual life by special and particular perceptions from which they generalize, but that they generalize at once. Nevertheless, his mis-apprehension of the distinction between recepts and concepts, and his notion that a distinct intention is needed in order to form the latter, naturally make themselves manifest. As to recepts and concepts, Mr. Romanes truly says, "Classification there doubtless is in both cases ; but the one order is due to the closeness of resemblances in an act of perception [*i.e.* senception], while in the other order it is an expression of their remoteness from merely perceptual [*i.e.* sensuous] asso-ciations."

The concluding sentence of this chapter is, however,

very misleading, and really once more begs the whole question which its author has to prove. He says,* " The object of this chapter has been to show, first, that the unintentional grouping which is distinctive of re-cepts may be carried to a wonderful pitch of perfection without any aid from the intentional grouping which is distinctive of concepts ; and, second, that from the very beginning conscious ideation [which here means our consentience] has been concerned with *grouping.* Not only, or not even chiefly, has it had to do with the registration in memory of particular percepts ; but much more has it had to do with the spontaneous sorting of such percepts, with the spontaneous arrange-ment of them in ideal (or imagery) systems, and, conse-quently, with the *spontaneous reflection in consciousness* of many among the less complex *relations*—or the less abstruse principles—which have been uniformly encoun-tered by the mind in its converse with an orderly world."

Certainly the world is orderly. Certainly its co-existences and sequences make manifest, objective relations and principles which pervade and govern it. Certainly, also, these objective conditions modify the sentiency of irrational organisms, and certainly, as we have elsewhere pointed out,† such objective conditions correspond, as "objective concepts," with internal per-ceptions or "subjective concepts in us." But this in no way even tends (as it is represented as tending) to bridge over the gulf which exists between sentiency and intellect. We might *à priori* expect to find a certain

* p. 69.   † See " On Truth," pp. 136, 137, 386, 445.

parallelism of results in the effects of one set of objective external conditions acting upon two distinct
kinds of internal subjective powers—one sentient, the
other rational.   The wonders of vegetable life, of sentiency, and of intellect, are all parallel and similarly
inexplicable.   In plants we have chemical combinations
organized and vivified ; in animals we have vegetative,
organic life raised to sentiency and receptive power ;
and in man we have animal, sentient life raised to
perception and conceptual power.

His fourth chapter Mr. Romanes devotes to a consideration of the " Logic of Concepts."   He begins it by
affirming (what no reasonable person can deny) the great
importance of " sign-making " and " symbols " for the
growth and advance of intellectual life.   But he gives
us no definition or explanation as to what he means by
a sign, while he makes observations, by the way, which
must not be allowed to pass without criticism.   Thus
he says : * " By the help of these symbols we climb into
higher and higher regions of abstraction : by thinking in
verbal signs we think, as it were, with the semblance of
ideas : we dispense altogether with the necessity of
actual images, whether of percepts or of recepts : we
quit the sphere of sense, and rise to that of thought."
But so long as life, as we know it, lasts, we can never
dispense with the use of mental images (phantasmata)†
of some kind—whether it be of sights or of sounds or of
some form of our own activity.   Such images, however,
are not the " semblance of ideas," but survivals and
reminiscences of sensuous experiences.

* p. 71.   † As to this, see " On Truth," pp. 87, 88.

Mr. Romanes illustrates his contention by a reference to mathematics, which demonstrates for us with especial clearness the great value of symbols. We are told,* " Man begins by counting things, grouping them visibly [*i.e.* by the Logic of Recepts]. He then learns to count simply the numbers, in the absence of things, using his fingers and toes for symbols. He then substitutes abstract signs, and Arithmetic begins." But no man could begin really counting the simplest things unless he already possessed the idea of number ; and, as Mr. Romanes truly says, "before the idea of number can rise at all," a distinct power of intellectual conception must be present.† The very essence of "counting" is *numerical* distinction. To suppose that a man could voluntarily begin to count, without any idea of such distinction, is absurd. But men, like animals, may "group objects visibly" without counting. To separate objects in groups —were they in groups which accidentally had definite numerical relations—without any regard to their number, could never be *counting.* To suppose that a man by " not counting " could learn to count, or that he could acquire the idea of "number" by performing actions wherein he took no note of real numerical relations, is to add absurdity to absurdity. He could not possibly take note of any numerical relations without having the idea of numerical relation, that is, without possessing very abstract ideas and having already an intellectual nature. We dwell on this point because it is a good

* p. 72.
† For what is implied in the idea of " number," see "On Truth," p. 241.

instance of that "intellectual thimble-rigging" which all men of the sensist school, from Hume downwards, must perform in order to make the innocent on-looker think he has found the pea of "intellect" under the thimble of "sense." We dwell on it the more be-cause the sincerity and honesty which are conspicuous amongst the other merits of Mr. Romanes, show how he himself has been deceived and is all unconscious of the ways of some of his masters. It is none the less true that he is completely justified in affirming,* with Sir W. Hamilton, that signs of some kind are needed "to give stability to our intellectual progress," that "words are fortresses of thought," and that "thought and language act and react upon one another.† Not, however, that we can for a moment admit that any change in mere verbal expressions, which are not the *result* of a modification of thought, can improve the latter. It is thought alone which can really improve language, though verbal modifications acting with it and produced by it may greatly aid it and hasten intel-lectual progress.

Mr. Romanes begins the real substance of his fourth chapter as follows:‡ "From what I have already said, it may be gathered that the simplest concepts are merely the names of recepts." This we altogether deny. In the very simplest concepts, the ideas, "existence," "kind" or "nature," "reality," "possibility" and "impossi-

---

* p. 73.

† Here we may ask at once, by anticipation, "If thought is thus admitted to be able to improve language, why should it be thought unable to originate it?"

‡ p. 73.

bility," and "truth," etc., are latent and implied.* But such is not the case with recepts, every one of which, moreover, not only contains, but consists of, phantasmata —imaginary phenomena which accompany, but are far indeed from constituting, every concept.

Mr. Romanes offers us, as examples of recepts (sense-perceptions), the impressions severally produced by water, ice, or dry land, on the psychical faculties of diving birds and men. Man, he tells us,† "like the water-fowl, has two distinct recepts, one of which answers to solid ground, and the other to an unresisting fluid. But, unlike the water-fowl, he is able to bestow upon each of these recepts a name, and thus to raise them both to the level of concepts." But it is his very power of conception which enables him to give them a name. No concepts, therefore, can possibly be "merely the name of recepts;" they are results of, and embody that marvellous power which enables man to bestow a name.

Man, he tells us, "must be able to set his recept before his own mind as an object of his own thought : before he can bestow upon these generic ideas the names of 'solid' and 'fluid,' he must have *cognized* them *as* ideas." Here there is some confusion of thought. We do not bestow names upon our sensuous cognitions or recepts, unless we are occupied about psychology—unless we are considering mental processes. But we bestow names upon what we perceive to be objects of certain kinds, or upon qualities which we perceive concretely existing, as, *e.g.*, in this land or that water. We do not perceive the various groups of sensuous affections we

* See "On Truth," pp. 103–105.　　　　† p. 74.

experience, as so many ideas—which, indeed, they never were and never will be.   What we perceive are so many objective realities, and by turning back the mind to consider our mental experience, we can recognize that the presence of those objective realities has been revealed to our minds by means of the various unnoticed sensations and sense-perceptions, excited in us by them. These sensuous affections, as before said, hide themselves in making such objects and ideas known.   But it is evident that they do not *constitute* such things, for, as we have pointed out, they persist and remain side by side with the ideas to which they minister.

Mr. Romanes further says : " Prior to this act of cognition, these ideas [of man] differed in no respect from the recepts of a water-fowl."   Now, we do not desire to deny this—the question is for us quite immaterial.   Nevertheless we do not think that such *complete* similarity can with reason be so dogmatically affirmed.   It is by no means clear to us that the recepts formed by different animals from the very same objects must always "differ in no respect."   The innate natures of different animals—*e.g.* birds and fishes—may so differ that the action of the same object on both may produce in those two classes of animals results more or less decidedly different.   Mr. Romanes adds,* " In virtue of this act of cognition, whereby he assigns a name to an idea known as such, he [man] has created for himself a priceless possession: he has formed a concept."   But our author has previously affirmed, with great truth, that before a man can bestow names, he must have ideally cognized what he so names.

* p. 75.

Moreover, a man does not assign a name "to an idea known as such" (unless, as before said, he is occupied about psychology), but he assigns a name to an object of which he has already formed some sort of conception. How could a man name a thing of which he had no sort of conception whatever?

Mr. Romanes remarks * that "names are not concerned with particular ideas, strictly so called : concepts, even of the lowest order, have to do with generic ideas." Now, concepts "have to do with" general ideas ; but, nevertheless, there are such things as individual concepts. We may have an idea of some individual man or animal, the absolute individuality (or "hæcceity")† of which forms so essential a part of our conception of it, that the conception would be essentially different without it.

But Mr. Romanes well expresses one relation in which intellectual perception stands to its sensuous antecedents. "The Logos," he says,‡ "does not come upon the scene of its creative power to find only that which is without form and void : rather does it find a fair structure of no mean order of system, shaped by prior influences, and, so far as thus shaped, a veritable cosmos."

The reader has, however, in reading Mr. Romanes's work, to be almost constantly on his guard against misleading expressions which are very frequently introduced —we are convinced, in simple unconsciousness. Thus we read, "All concepts in their last resort depend on recepts, just as in their turn recepts depend on percepts."

* p. 76.   † A very convenient scholastic term.   ‡ p. 77.

This statement is founded on a fact which it deforms. It is quite true that we can have no sense-perception without preceding or accompanying sensations, and no idea without some accompanying imaginations; but the expression, "in their last resort," implies that ideas are fundamentally only recepts. One thing *is* not another because it cannot exist without it. All active steam-engines depend on water, but they *are not* water. Similarly the teaching contained in Mr. Romanes's book depends on printer's ink and printer's devils, yet it is altogether different from either.

It is but natural, then, in him to tell us that "the most highly abstract terms are derived from terms less abstract, until, by two or three such steps at the most, we are in all cases led directly back to their origin in a 'lower concept'—*i.e.* in the name of a recept." This statement is based partly upon the fact that the most abstract terms have had, originally, concrete significations. Indeed, as we shall later on have occasion to point out, we cannot, even if we would, make use of terms which have no concrete meanings. This, however, is no reason why such terms should not also serve to give expression, by analogy, to meanings which are altogether beyond the range of sense-perception.* They are certainly able to do so now, and we think it will by-and-by be made evident that they must always have done so. The idea "equality" is "abstract" enough; yet deaf-mutes have expressed it by placing their forefingers side by side. Why, then, should the

* That conception and intellect are not bounded by our sensitive powers, see "On Truth," pp. 109–111.

relatively concrete and sensuous expression, "fingers-parallel," be unable also to denote the abstract idea "equality"?

Mr. Romanes admits * that a concept may cease to bear any easily perceptible likeness to what he calls "its parentage," "owing to the elaboration it subsequently undergoes in the region of Symbolism." †

After reiterating statements of his view (already criticised by us) as to the relations of concepts to recepts, and as to what he deems the necessity of an intentional mental act in order to form a concept, he makes ‡ the somewhat startling assertion : "So far as my analysis has hitherto gone, I do not anticipate criticism or dissent from any psychologist, to whatever school he may belong"! What is above all remarkable in this sentence is the demonstration it gives that Mr. Romanes, in spite of the pains he has taken to read and reply to what his opponents have written, has so utterly failed to apprehend the most essential point of their whole contention. If we were Nominalists ; if we were disciples of Locke ; if we did not, in unison with the whole Aristotelian school, give to the word "idea" a fundamentally different meaning from what Mr. Romanes gives it ; if we did not assert an essential difference of *kind* between recepts and concepts ; and if we did not affirm that reasoning consists in drawing inferences, not in the detection of ratios—

---

* p. 77.

† "The region of Symbolism" is an odd name for the active intellect of man !

‡ p. 80

H

then there would be no essential difference between us, and Mr. Romanes's book, so far as we are concerned, need never have been written. We are, however, very thankful that it has been written, and we rejoice to note every point of agreement which it shows to exist between its author and ourselves. One such point concerns the present relation of thoughts to words, his remarks as to which seem to us to be very useful and very true.

He says,* "On reading a letter, for instance, we may instantaneously decide upon our answer, and yet have to pause before we are able to frame the propositions needed to express that answer. Or, while writing an essay, how often does one feel, so to speak, that a certain truth stands to be stated, although it is a truth which we cannot immediately put into words," etc. † Mr. Romanes, however, makes a singular mistake in the use of the expression "*verbum mentale.*" He employs it ‡ as if it meant a mental utterance of words, instead of (as it does mean) the thought which accompanies whatever words, or other external signs, may be made use of.

Towards the end of this chapter he says, "On the whole, therefore, I conclude that, although language is a needful condition to the *original construction* of conceptional thought, when once the building has been completed, the scaffolding may be withdrawn, and yet leave the edifice as stable as before." But why should he deem that language was thus prior and originally necessary? If thought can *now* exist

---

* p. 82.   † As to this, see further, "On Truth," p. 230.
‡ p. 82.

without it, why may it not have done so *earlier?*
Surely *experience* points to the origin of thought from a
direction opposite to that indicated by Mr. Romanes.
If, as he affirms, Friedrich Müller is right in affirming
the plain truth, " Sprechen ist nicht Denken, sondern es
ist nur Ausdruck des Denkens," then Herr Geiger's dictum : " So ist denn überall die Sprache primar, der
Begriff entsteht durch das Wort " must be a dictum not
only untenable, but absurd, as we have already endeavoured * to show.

* See " On Truth," pp. 230–234. Mr. Romanes refers (in a
note on p. 83) to a brief correspondence which took place between
ourselves and Prof. Max Müller in this connection. Therefore we
think it may as well be reproduced here. It was as follows :—

[*Nature*, February 2, 1888.]
Letter from Prof. F. Max Müller to an American Friend.

" Oxford, January 22.
" YOU tell me that my book on the ' Science of Thought ' is
thoroughly revolutionary, and that I have all recognized authorities
in philosophy against me. I doubt it. My book is, if you like,
evolutionary, but not revolutionary ; I mean it is the natural outcome of that philosophical and historical study of language which
began with Leibnitz, and which during our century has so widely
spread and ramified as to overshadow nearly all sciences, not
excepting what I call the science of thought.

" If you mean by revolutionary a violent breaking with the
past, I hold, on the contrary, that a full appreciation of the true
nature of language and a recognition of its inseparableness from
thought will prove the best means of recovering that unbroken
thread which binds our modern schools of thought most closely
together with those of the Middle Ages and of Ancient Greece.
It alone will help us to reconcile systems of philosophy hitherto
supposed to be entirely antagonistic. If I am right—and I must
confess that with regard to the fundamental principle of the identity of reason and language I share the common weakness of all
philosophers, that I cannot doubt its truth—then what we call the
history of philosophy will assume a totally new aspect. It will

Although Mr. Romanes thus (p. 81) contends against that identification of thought with language which Pro-

reveal itself before our eyes as the natural growth of language, though at the same time as a constant struggle of old against new language—in fact, as a dialectic process in the true sense of the word.

"The very tenet that language is identical with thought—what is it but a correction of language, a repentance, a return of language upon itself?

"We have two words, and therefore it requires with us a strong effort to perceive that behind these two words there is but one essence. To a Greek this effort would be comparatively easy, because his word *logos* continued to mean the undivided essence of language and thought. In our modern languages we shall find it difficult to coin a word that could take the place of *logos*. Neither *discours* in French, nor *Rede* in German, which meant originally the same as *ratio*, will help us. We shall have to be satisfied with such compounds as thought-word or word-thought. At least, I can think of no better expedient.

"You strongly object to my saying that there is no such thing as reason. But let us see whether we came honestly by that word. Because we reason—that is, because we reckon, because we add and subtract—therefore we say that we have reason; and thus it has happened that reason was raised into something which we have or possess, into a faculty, or power, or something, whatever it may be, that deserves to be written with a capital R. And yet we have only to look into the workshop of language in order to see that there is nothing substantial corresponding to this substantive, and that neither the heart nor the brain, neither the breath nor the spirit, of man discloses its original whereabouts. It may sound violent and revolutionary to you when I say that there is no such thing as reason; and yet no philosopher, not even Kant, has ever in his definition of reason told us what it is really made of. But remember, I am far from saying that reason is a mere word. That expression, 'a mere word,' seems to me the most objectionable expression in the whole of our philosophical dictionary.

"Reason is something—namely, language—not simply as we now hear it and use it, but as it has been slowly elaborated by man through all the ages of his existence on earth. Reason is the growth of centuries, it is the work of man, and at the same time an instrument brought to higher and higher perfection by the lead-

fessor Max Müller rightly declares to be "the inevitable
conclusion of Nominalism," he, none the less, very

ing thinkers and speakers of the world.   No reason without
language—no language without reason.   Try to reckon without
numbers, whether spoken, written, or otherwise marked ; and if
you succeed in that I shall admit that it is possible to reason or
reckon without words, and that there is in us such a thing or such
a power or faculty as reason, apart from words.

"You say I shall never live to see it admitted that man cannot
reason without words.   This does not discourage me.   Through
the whole of my life I have cared for truth, not for success.   And
truth is not our own.   We may seek truth, serve truth, love truth ;
but truth takes care of herself, and she inspires her true lovers
with the same feeling of perfect trust.   Those who cannot believe
in themselves, unless they are believed in by others, have never
known what truth is.   Those who have found truth know best how
little it is their work, and how small the merit which they can claim
for themselves.   They were blind before, and now they can see.
That is all.

"But even if I thought that truth depended on majorities, I
believe I might boldly say that the majority of philosophers of all
ages and countries is really on my side (see ' Science of Thought,'
pp. 31 *et seq.*), though few only have asserted the identity of reason
and language without some timorous reserve, still fewer have seen
all the consequences that flow from it.

"Some people seem to resent it almost as a personal insult that
what we call our divine reason should be no more than human
language, and that the whole of this human language should have
been derived from no more than 800 roots, which can be reduced
to about 120 concepts.   But if I had wished to startle my readers
I could easily have shown that out of these 800 roots one-half
could really have been dispensed with, and has been dispensed
with in modern languages (see ' Science of Thought,' p. 417), while
among the 120 concepts not a few are clearly secondary, and owe
their place in my list (*ib.* p. 619) merely to the fact that in Sanskrit
they cannot be reduced to any more primitive concept.   To dance,
for instance, cannot be called a primitive concept ; perhaps not
even to hunger, to thirst, to cook, to roast, etc.   Only it so happens
that in Sanskrit, to which my statistical remarks were restricted, we
cannot go behind such roots as NART, KSHUDH, TARSH, PAK,
etc.   It is in that limited sense only that such roots and such

strangely says (p. 84), " Since the time when the ancient
Greeks applied the same word to denote the faculty of

concepts can be called primitive. The number of really primitive
concepts would be so alarmingly small that for the present it
seemed wiser to say nothing about it. But so far from being
ashamed of our modest beginnings, we ought really to glory rather
in having raised our small patrimony to the immense wealth now
hoarded in our dictionaries.

" When we once know what our small original patrimony consisted in, the question how we came in possession of it may seem
of less importance. Yet it is well to remember that the theory of
the origin of roots and concepts, as propounded by Noiré, differs,
not in degree, but *toto cælo* from the old attempts to derive roots
from interjections and imitations of natural sounds. That a certain
number of words in every language has been derived from
interjections and imitations no one has ever denied. But such
words are not conceptual words, and they become possible only
after language had become possible—that is, after man had realized
his power of forming concepts. No one who has not himself
grappled with that problem can appreciate the complete change
that has come over it by the recognition of the fact that roots are
the phonetic expressions of the consciousness of our own acts.
Nothing but this, our consciousness of our own repeated acts,
could possibly have given us our first concepts. Nothing else
answers the necessary requirements of a concept, that it should be
the consciousness of something manifold, yet necessarily realized
as one. After the genesis of the first concept, everything else
becomes intelligible. The results of our acts become the first
objects of our conceptual thought ; and with conceptual thought,
language, which is nothing if not conceptual, begins. Roots are
afterwards localized, and made the signs of our objects by means
of local exponents, whether suffixes, prefixes, or infixes. What
has been scraped and shaped again and again becomes as it were
' shape-her',' *i.e.* a shaft ; what has been dug and hollowed out by
repeated blows becomes 'dig-her',' *i.e.* a hole. And from the
concept of a hole dug, or of an empty cave, there is an uninterrupted progress to the most abstract concepts, such as empty
space, or even nothing. No doubt, when we hear the sound of
cuckoo, we may by one jump arrive at the word 'cuckoo.' This
may be called a word, but it is not a conceptual word, and we
deal with conceptual words only. Before we can get at a

language and the faculty of thought, the philosophical propriety of the identification has become more and

single conceptual word, we have to pass through at least five stages :—

"(1) Consciousness of our own repeated acts.

"(2) *Clamor concomitans* of these acts.

"(3) Consciousness of that *clamor* as concomitant of the act.

"(4) Repetition of that *clamor* to recall the act.

"(5) *Clamor* (root) defined by prefixes, suffixes, etc., to recall the act as localized in its results, its instruments, its agents, etc.

"You can see from my preface to the 'Science of Thought' that I was quite prepared for fierce attacks, whether they came from theologians, from philosophers, or from a certain class of scholars. So far from being discouraged, I am really delighted by the opposition which my book has roused, though you would be surprised to hear what strong support also I have received from quarters where I least expected it. I have never felt called upon to write a book to which everybody should say *Amen*. When I write a book, I expect the world to say *tamen*, as I have always said *tamen* to the world in writing my books. I have been called very audacious for daring to interfere with philosophy, as if the study of language, to which I have devoted the whole of my life, could be separated from a study of philosophy. I have listened very patiently for many years to the old story that grammar is one thing and logic another ; that the former deals with such laws of thought as are observed, the latter with such as ought to be observed. No, no. True philosophy teaches us another lesson— namely, that in the long-run nothing is except what ought to be, and that in the evolution of the mind, as well as in that of Nature, natural selection is rational selection ; or, in reality, the triumph of reason, the triumph of what is reasonable and right ; or, as people now say, of what is fittest. We must learn to recognize in language the true evolution of reason. In that evolution nothing is real or remains real except what is right ; nay, in it even the apparently irrational and anomalous has its reason and justification. Towards the end of the last century, what used to be called *Grammaire Générale* formed a very favourite subject for academic discussions ; it has now been replaced by what may be called *Grammaire Historique*. In the same manner, *Formal Logic*, or the study of the general laws of thought, will have to make room for *Historical Logic*, or a study of the historical growth of

more apparent.   Obscured as the truth may have become for a time through the fogs of Realism [!], dis-

thought.   Delbrück's essays on comparative syntax show what can
be done in this direction.   For practical purposes, for teaching the
art of reasoning, formal logic will always retain its separate existence ; but the best study of the real laws of thought will be hereafter the study of the real laws of language.   If it was really so
audacious to make the identity of language and reason the foundation of a new system of philosophy, may I make the modest request
that some philosopher by profession should give us a definition of
what language is without reason, or reason without language?

" F. M. M."

[*Nature*, February 16, 1888.]

REASON AND LANGUAGE.

" PROF. MAX MULLER has been so kind as to favour the readers
of *Nature* with his views on language and reason, concisely expressed in a letter to an American friend.   As one grateful reader,
I must desire both to express my thanks, and also to beg for yet a
little further information with respect to matters of such extreme
interest.

"The Professor says, 'Because we reason—that is, because we
reckon, because we add and subtract—therefore we say that we
have reason.'   Now, in the first place, I should be glad to be told
why 'reason' is to be regarded as identical with such 'reckoning'?   I have been taught to distinguish two forms of intellectual
activity : (1) Acts of intuition, by which we directly apprehend
certain truths, such as, *e.g.*, our own activity, or that A is A ; and
(2) Acts of inference, by which we indirectly apprehend others,
with the aid of the idea 'therefore'—evolving into explicit recognition a truth previously implicit and latent in premisses.   The
processes of addition and subtraction alone, seem to me to constitute a very incomplete representation of our mental processes.

"The Professor also identifies language and reason, denying to
either a separate existence.   As to 'reason,' he says, 'We have
only to look into the workshop of language in order to see that
there is nothing substantial corresponding to this substantive, and
that neither the heart nor the brain, neither the breath nor the
spirit, of man discloses its original whereabouts.'   The expression
'whereabouts' would seem to attribute to those who assert the existence of 'reason,' the idea that it possesses the attribute of

cussion of centuries has fully cleared the philosophical atmosphere so far as this matter is concerned "!

extension ? In order to understand clearly the passage quoted, we should learn what Prof. Max Müller really means by the term ' spirit,' which here figures as one species of a genus also comprising the breath, the brain, and the heart. Reason, however, is not represented as being simply language 'as we now hear it and use it,' but ' as it has been slowly elaborated by man through all the ages of his existence upon earth.' Thus understood, the Professor 'cannot doubt' 'the identity of reason and language.' Never- theless he immediately proceeds to point out a striking want of identity between them. He says, quite truly, ' We have two words, and therefore it requires with us a strong effort to perceive that behind these two words there is but one essence'—namely, that denoted by the Greek word, *logos*—'the undivided essence of language and thought.' Now, the intimate connection of lan- guage (whether of speech or gesture) with thought, is unquestion- able ; but intimate connection is not 'identity.' If thought and language are '*identical*,' how came two words not to have two meanings, or two thoughts to be expressed by one word? The plain fact that we have different words with one meaning, and dif- ferent meanings with one word, seems to demonstrate that thought and language cannot be 'identical.'

" ' No reason without language—no language without reason,' is a statement true in a certain sense, but a statement which cannot be affirmed absolutely. Language (meaning by that term only *intellectual* expression by voice or gesture) cannot manifestly exist without reason ; but no person who thinks it even *possible* that an intelligence may exist of which ours is but a feeble copy, can venture dogmatically to affirm that there *is* no reason without lan- guage, unless he means by reason mere 'reasoning,' which is evidently the makeshift of an inferior order of intellect unable to attain certain truths save by the roundabout process of inference.

" But I demur to the assertion that truly intellectual processes cannot take place in us apart from language. In such matters our ultimate appeal must be to our own reflective consciousness. Mine plainly tells me that I have every now and then apprehensions which flash into my mind far too rapidly to clothe themselves even in mental words, which latter require to be sought in order to ex- press such apprehensions. I also find myself sometimes express- ing a voluminous perception by a sudden gesture far too rapid even

Mr. Romanes tells us, further on in his book,* that
"within the four corners of human experience a self-

for thought-words, and I believe that other persons do the same.
A slight movement of a finger, or the incipient closure of an eyelid,
may give expression to a meaning which could only be thought in
words by a much slower process.

"It is the more remarkable that Prof. Max Müller should deny
the existence of reason, since he unequivocally affirms, in rather
lofty language, the existence of truth. Yet surely the existence of
truth, in and by itself, is inconceivable. What can truth be, save a
conformity between thought and things? I affirm, indeed, the
certain existence of truth, but I also affirm that of reason, as existing anteriorly to language—whether of voice or gesture. What is
the teaching of experience? Do men invent new concepts to suit
previously coined words, or new words to give expression to freshly
thought-out concepts? The often referred to jabber of Hottentots
is not to the point. No sounds or gestures which do not express
concepts would be admitted by either Prof. Max Müller or myself
to be 'language.'

"The Professor speaks of the 'alarmingly small' number of
primitive concepts ; but who is to be thereby alarmed? Not men
who occupy a similar standpoint to mine. I fully agree with
Prof. Max Müller in saying, 'After the genesis of the first concept,
everything else becomes intelligible.'

"We come now to the supreme question of the origin of language.
As to this the Professor observes, 'No one who has not himself
grappled with that problem can appreciate the complete change
that has come over it by the recognition of the fact that roots are
the phonetic expressions of the consciousness of our own acts.
Nothing but this, our consciousness of our own repeated acts, could
possibly have given us our first concepts. Nothing else answers
the necessary requirements of a concept, that it should be the consciousness of something manifold, yet necessarily realized as one.'
. . . The results of our acts become the first objects of our conceptual thought.' The truth of these statements I venture to question,
and after noting the dogmatic nature of the assertion, 'Nothing but
this *could,*' etc., I must object to the statement of fact as regards
human beings now. I do not believe that the infant's first object of thought is 'the results of its own acts.' In the first place,

* p. 397.

conscious personality cannot be led up to in any other way than through the medium of language." But ex-

no object of our early thoughts is merely 'the results of our own acts,' but a combined result of our own activity and of the action on us of our environment. Secondly, my observations lead me to believe that the infant's first thoughts relate to things external, and certainly not to the results of its own activity as such, which is a highly complex and developed thought. It may be that the Professor, when he says, 'The results of our acts *become* the first object of our conceptual thought,' means that such acts in remote antiquity *became* the objects of man's first thought. This is probably the case, since, with respect to the origin of thought and language, Prof. Max Müller has adopted Noiré's crude notion that they sprang from sounds emitted by men at work, conscious of what they were doing, in the presence of others who beheld their actions and heard the sounds; the result being the formation of a conceptual word, to attain which five stages had to be gone through as follows :—

"'(1) Consciousness of our own repeated acts.

"'(2) *Clamor concomitans* of these acts.

"'(3) Consciousness of our *clamor* as concomitant to the act.

"'(4) Repetition of that *clamor* to recall the act.

"'(5) *Clamor* (root) defined by prefixes, suffixes, etc., to recall the act as localized in its results, its instruments, its agents, etc.'

"But if language and reason are identical, reason could not exist before a single conceptual word existed. Nevertheless, to attain to this first single word, we see, from the above quotation, that man must have had the notion of his own acts as such; the notion of their repetition; the notions of clamour, action, and the simultaneity of clamour and action; the will to recall the act (yet *nihil volitum quin præcognitum*); and, finally, the notions of consequence, instrumentality, agency, or whatever further notions the Professor may intend by his 'etc.'

"Thus he who first developed language must be admitted to have already had a mind well stored with intellectual notions! But can it for one instant be seriously maintained, close as is the connection of language with reason, that their genesis (miracle apart, of which there is no question) was *absolutely* simultaneous? He must be a bold, not to say a rash, man who would dogmatically affirm this. But if they were not *absolutely* simultaneous, one must have existed, for however brief a space, before the other. That

perience abundantly refutes the notion that speech, whether as uttered or understood, is thus antecedently

intellectual language could have existed without reason 'is absurd. Reason, then, must, for however short a period, have preceded language.

"In conclusion, I desire to point out a certain misrepresentation with respect to natural selection. The Professor says, 'In the evolution of the mind, as well as in that of Nature, natural selection is rational selection ; or, in reality, the triumph of reason, the triumph of what is reasonable and right ; or, as people now say, of what is fittest.' But we may ask in passing, if reason has no existence, how can it 'triumph?'   The misrepresentation of natural selection, however, lies in his use of the word ' fittest.' When biologists say that the ' fittest' survives, they do not mean to say that that survives which is the most 'reasonable and right,' but that that survives which *is able to survive.*   What there is less ' reasonable and right' in a Rhytina than in a Dugong, or in a Dinornis than an Apteryx, would, I think, puzzle most of our zoologists to determine ; nor is it easy to see a triumph of reason in the extermination of the unique flora of St. Helena by the introduction of goats and rabbits.

"St. George Mivart."

[*Nature*, March 1, 1888.]

LANGUAGE = REASON.

"Prof. St. George Mivart has read my letter on 'Language = Reason' in *Nature* of February 2 (p. 393) with very great care, and I feel grateful to him for several suggestive remarks. But has he read the heavy volume to which that letter refers—my ' Science of Thought'?   I doubt it, and have of course no right to expect it, for I know but too well myself how difficult it is for a man who writes books to read any but the most necessary books. I only mention it as an excuse for what might otherwise seem conceited—namely, my answering most of his questions and criticisms by references to my own book.

"Prof. Mivart begins by asking why I should have explained reasoning by reckoning.

" Now, first of all, from an historical point of view—and this to a man who considers evolution far more firmly established in language than in any other realm of Nature is always the most important—the Latin *ratio*, from which came *raison* and our own

necessary. This will appear later on * from the case of
Laura Bridgman and the still more remarkable one of

reason, meant originally reckoning, casting up, calculation, computation, long before it came to mean the so-called faculty of the
mind which forms the basis of computation and calculation, judgment, understanding, and reason.

"Secondly, I began my book on the 'Science of Thought' with
a quotation from Hobbes, that all our thinking consisted in addition
and subtraction, and I claimed the liberty to use the word 'thinking' throughout my own book in the sense of combining. Such a
definition of thinking may be right or wrong, but, provided a word
is always used in the sense in which from the beginning it has
been defined, there can at all events be no misapprehension nor
just cause of complaint on the part of the critic.

"What I meant by combination, or by addition and subtraction
being the true character of thinking, I explained very fully.
'Any book on logic,' I said, 'will teach that all our propositions
are either *affirmative* or *negative*, and that in acquiring or com-
municating knowledge we can do no more than to say that A is B,
or A is not B. Now, in saying A is B, we simply add A to the
sum already comprehended under B, and in saying A is not B, we
subtract A from the sum that can be comprehended under B. And
why should it be considered as lowering our high status, if what we
call thinking turns out to be no more than adding or subtracting?
Mathematics in the end consist of nothing but addition and subtraction, and think of the wonderful achievements of a Newton
or a Gauss—achievements before which ordinary mortals like
myself stand simply aghast.'

"Prof. Mivart holds that there are but two forms of intellectual
activity: (1) Acts of intuition, by which we directly apprehend
certain truths, such as, *e.g.*, our own activity, or that A is A; and
(2) Acts of inference, by which we indirectly apprehend others,
with the aid of the idea 'therefore.'

"There is a wide difference between our apprehending our own
activity and our apprehending that A is A. Apprehending our
own activity is inevitable, apprehending that A is A is voluntary.
Besides, the 'therefore' on which Prof. Mivart insists as a distinguishing feature between the two forms of thought is present in
the simplest acts of cognition. In order to think and to say,

---

* See below, chapter iii.

Martha Obrecht.   He also says, " It is only by means
of marking ideas by names that the faculty of conceptual

'This is an orange,' I must implicitly think and say, 'This is
round, and yellow, has a peculiar skin, a sweet juice, etc.; *therefore* it is an orange.'   The 'therefore' represents, in fact, the
justification of our act of addition.   We have by slow and repeated
addition formed the concept-name, 'orange,' and by saying, 'This is
an orange,' we say no more than that we feel justified, till the
contrary is proved, in adding this object before us to the sum of
oranges already known to us.   If the contrary is proved, we subtract, and we add our present object either to the class and name
of lemons, citrons, etc., or to a more general class, such as apples,
fruit, round objects, etc.   We ought really to distinguish, as I have
tried to show, not only two, but four phases in every act of cognition, viz. sensation, perception, conception, and naming ; and I
contend that these four phases, though distinguishable, are not
separable, and that no act of cognition is perfect without the last
phase of naming.

"But how is it, Prof. Mivart continues, that different words in
our language have one meaning, and different meanings one word?
Does not this show that thought and language cannot be identical?

"It has been the principal object of all my mythological studies
to account not only for the origin of *polyonymy* and *homonymy*,
but to discover in them the cause of much that has to be called
mythology, whether in ancient tradition, religion, philosophy, or
even in modern science.   I must therefore refer Prof. Mivart to
my earlier writings, and can only mention here a few well-known
cases of mythology arising from polyonymy and homonymy.

"We can easily understand why people should have called the
planet Venus both the morning and the evening star ; but we
know that in consequence of these two names many people have
believed in two stars instead of one.   The same mountain in
Switzerland is called by the people on the south side *Blackhorn*,
by the people on the north side *Whitehorn*, and many a traveller
has been misled when asking his way to the one or the other.
Because in German there are two words, *Verstand* and *Vernunft*,
originally meaning exactly the same thing, German metaphysicians
have changed them into two distinct faculties, and English philosophers have tried to introduce the same distinction between the
understanding as the lower and reason as the higher faculty.

"Nothing is really easier to understand, if only we consult the

thought is rendered possible." But a manual sign for a
horse is no more a picture of a horse than is the written

ancient annals of language, than why the same object should
have had several names, and why several objects should have had
the same name. But this proves by no means that therefore the
name is one thing and the concept another. We can distinguish
name and concept as we distinguish between the concave and con-
vex sides of a lens, but we cannot separate them, and in that sense
we may call them inseparable, and, in one sense, idéntical.

"Lastly, Prof. Mivart starts the same objection to my system of
psychological analysis which was raised some time ago in these
columns with so much learning and eloquence by Mr. Francis
Galton. He appeals to his own experience, and maintains that
certain intellectual processes take place without language. This
is generally supposed to put an end to any further argument, and
we are even told that it is a mistake to imagine that all men are
alike, so far as their psychological processes are concerned, and
that psychologists should study the peculiarities of individuals
rather than the general character of the human intellect. Now,
it seems to me that *l'un n'empêche pas l'autre*, but that in the end
the object of all scientific inquiry is the general, and not the
individual. The true life of language is in the dialects, yet the
grammarian aims at a general grammar. In the same way the
psychologist may pay any amount of attention to mere individual
peculiarities and idiosyncrasies ; only he ought never to forget
that in the end man is man.

"But it does not even seem to me that intellectual processes
without language, as described by Mr. Galton and Prof. Mivart,
are at all peculiar and exceptional. I have described similar
cases, and tried to account for them, in different parts of my book.
If Prof. Mivart says that 'a slight movement of a finger may give
expression to a meaning which could only be thought in words
by a much slower process,' I went much further by saying that
'silence might be more eloquent than words.'

"Mr. Galton asked me to read a book by Alfred Binet, 'La
Psychologie du Raisonnement,' as showing by experiments how
many intellectual acts could take place without language. I read
the book with deep interest, but great was my surprise when I
found that M. Binet's observations confirmed in the very strongest
way my own position. I had shown how percepts—that is, images
—could exist with a mere shadow of language, and that nothing

or spoken word "horse." It is an intellectual sign, the
efficiency of which proves the radical independence of

was more wonderful than what Leibnitz called the algebra of
thought. Now, what do M. Binet's experiments prove? That
there are two kinds of images, the *consecutive*, reproduced spontaneously and suddenly, and the *memorial*, connected with an association of ideas. The *consecutive* image, a kind of impression *avant la
lettre*, may reappear long after the existing sensation has ceased to
act, and it reappears without any rhyme or reason. But how are
the memorial images recalled, seen by people, such as M. Binet
describes, in a state of hypnotism? Entirely by the word. Show
a hypnotized patient her portrait, and she may or may not recognize
it. But tell her, in so many words, ' This is your portrait,' and
she will see her likeness in a landscape of the Pyrenees (pp.
56–57). M. Binet is fully aware of what is implied by this. Thus,
on p. 58, he writes, ' *L'hallucination hypnotique est formée d'un
image suggérée par* la parole.' So, again, when describing the
simplest acts of perception, M. Binet explains how much is added
by ourselves to the mere impressions received through the senses
by ' *ce qu'on croit voir,*' by ' *ce qu'on croit sentir,*' and by ' *le nom
qu'on croit entendre prononcer.*' The facts and experiments, therefore, contained in M. Binet's charming volume seem to me entirely
on my side, nor do I see that thoughtful observer has ever denied
the necessity of language or signs of some sort for the purpose of
reasoning, nay, even of imagination.

. " I find it difficult to answer all the questions which the Professor
has asked, because it would seem like writing my own book over
again. However, I shall confess that I have laid myself open to
some just criticism in not renouncing altogether the metaphorical
poetry of language. I ought not to have spoken of Truth as a kind
of personal being, nor of Reason as a power that governs the universe. But no astronomer is blamed when he uses the old terminology of sunrise and sunset ; no biologist is misunderstood when
he speaks of mankind ; and no philosopher is denounced when he
continues to use the big I instead of ' succession of states of consciousness.' If, therefore, I said that I recognized in evolution the
triumph of reason, I meant no more than that I could not recognize in it the triumph of mere chance. Prof. Mivart imagines
that I misunderstood what the biologist means by the survival of
the fittest. Far from it, I understand that phrase, and decidedly
reject it. For, either the survival of the fittest means no more than

speech which thought possesses. A sign of some kind is necessary because, since we each have both an

that that survives which is able to survive,—this would be a mere truism and a patent tautology,—or, if we take in the whole circumstances of Nature, the survival of the fittest implies some kind of inherent fitness and reasonableness. Prof. Mivart writes : ' What there is less reasonable and right in a Rhytina than in a Dugong, or in a Dinornis than in an Apteryx, would, I think, puzzle most of our zoologists to determine ; nor is it easy to see a triumph of reason in the extermination of the unique flora of St. Helena by the introduction of goats and rabbits.'   No doubt, it is not easy to see this. But need I remind Prof. Mivart that many things may be true, though it is not easy to see them ? We often do what we think is reasonable and right, though we seem to see nothing but mischief to ourselves and others arising from our acts. Why do we do this ? Because we believe in the ultimate triumph of reason and right, though it may take millions of years to prove that right is right.   I have the same faith in Nature ; and, taking my stand on this scientific faith, I believe that natural selection must in the end prove rational selection, and that what has been vaguely called the survival of the fittest will have to be interpreted in the end as the triumph of reason, not as the mere play of chance.

" F. MAX MÜLLER.

" Oxford, February 21."

[*Nature*, March 15, 1888.]

REASON AND LANGUAGE.

"THE kindness of Prof. Max Müller's reply I recognize with pleasure, but without surprise, since those who know him know him to be as remarkable for his courtesy as his great learning.

" In answer to his first question, I must say that I made a point of attending his Royal Institution lecture on the day his ' Science and Thought' was published, and was greatly disappointed that illness hindered my attending the others. But I immediately obtained his book, and applied myself to understand what seemed to me its essence, though I have not read it from cover to cover. Should I have to review it, of course I shall conscientiously peruse the whole of it.

" Before replying further, it may be well to restate my position as follows :—

" Man is an intellectual being, able to apprehend certain things

I

intellect and a body forming one absolute unity (one embodied intelligence), some bodily activity must, as

directly and others indirectly. Normally, his conceptions clothe themselves in vocal sounds, and get so intimately connected therewith, that the 'word' becomes practically a single thing composed of a mental and an oral element. But these elements are not *identical*, and the *verbum mentale* is anterior and superior to the *verbum oris* which it should govern and direct. Abnormally, conceptions do not clothe themselves in oral expressions at all, but only in manual or other bodily signs, and this shows that concepts may be expressed (however imperfectly) in the language of gesture without speech. One consequence of these relations is that neither the utterance of sounds (articulate or inarticulate) nor bodily movements could have generated the intellect and reason of man, and Noiré's hypothesis falls to the ground. On the other hand, beings essentially intellectual, but as yet without language, would immediately clothe their nascent concepts in some forms of bodily expression by means of which they would quickly understand one another.

"As to the expressions 'reason' and 'reckoning,' I would observe that a study of an organism's embryonic development is a most valuable clue to its nature, and no doubt a similar utility attends historical investigations in Prof. Max Müller's science. Nevertheless, we cannot understand the nature of an animal or plant by a mere knowledge of an early stage of its existence ; an acquaintance with the outcome of its development is even more important. Similarly, I venture to presume, the ultimate meaning of a word is at least as much its true meaning as is some archaic signification which may have grown obsolete. The word 'spirit,' if it once meant only the breath, means more now—as we see from the Professor's first letter. Similarly, if 'reason,' in its Latin form, once only meant 'reckoning,' that is no 'reason' why it should only mean reckoning now. Here it would seem as if we had an instance of the *verbum mentale* having acted upon and modified the *verbum oris*. I cannot but regard the representation that affirmative and negative propositions are mere cases of addition and subtraction, as an incorrect and misleading representation, save when they refer to mathematical conceptions. I am compelled also to object to another of the Professor's assertions. He says, 'There is a wide difference between our apprehending our own activity and apprehending that A is A. Apprehending our own

before said,* accompany our every thought ; but that sign need not be now, nor need it ever have been, any form of speech.

activity is inevitable, apprehending that A is A is voluntary.' It is true there is a great difference between these apprehensions, though they both agree in being instances of apprehensions which are not inferences, and as such I adduced them (*Nature*, February 16, p. 364). Nevertheless in my judgment the difference between them is not the difference which the Professor states. Both are alike voluntary, regarded as deliberate reflex cognitions, and both are alike inevitable, regarded as indeliberate, direct perceptions. The labourer inevitably perceives that his spade is what it is, though the nature of that perception remains unnoticed, just as he inevitably perceives his own continuous being when he in no way adverts to that fact.

"I must further protest against the assertion that the idea 'therefore' is 'present in the simplest acts of cognition'—that every perception of an object is an inference. This I regard as one of the fundamental errors which underlie all the madness of idealism. Akin thereto is the notion that a philosopher who desires to speak with the very strictest accuracy ought, instead of using 'the big I,' to say, 'a succession of states of consciousness.' To me it is certain that even one state of consciousness (to say nothing of 'a series') is no more immediately intued by us than is the substantial ego ; each being cognized only by a reflex act. What I intue is my 'self-action,' in which intuition, both the 'ego' and the 'states' are implicitly contained, and so can be explicitly recognized by reflection. I was myself long in bondage to these two errors, from which it cost me severe mental labour to escape by working my way through philosophical subjectivism. These questions I cannot here go any further into, and I only mention them in consequence of Prof. Max Müller's remarks. I will, however, in turn, refer him to my 'Nature and Thought,' as well as to a larger work which I trust may before long be published, and which, I venture to hope, he will do me the honour to look at.

"My object in calling attention to the fact that one word may have several meanings, and several words one meaning, was to show that there could not be 'identity' between thought and language. This point the Professor seems practically to concede,

---

* See above, p. 53.

Our author further observes * that when thoughts which have coexisted with words come to be thought

since he now only calls them 'inseparable, and in one sense identical.' I do not understand degrees of identity. No mere closeness of resemblance or connection can make two things absolutely identical. I did not, however, content myself with denying this 'identity' on account of polyonymy and homonymy ; I also referred to common experience (which shows us that men do not invent concepts for preformed words, but the reverse), and I appealed to certain facts of consciousness. To my assertions about consciousness the Professor replies : 'The object of all scientific inquiry is the general and not the individual.' But this is a quite inadequate reply, since our knowledge of general laws is based on our knowledge of individual facts, and if only one man could fly, that single fact would be enough to refute the assertion that flight is impossible to man.

"With respect to evolution, I never said that Prof. Max Müller misunderstood 'natural selection,' but only that he misrepresented it—of course unintentionally. It is of the essence of natural selection not to affirm teleology as formerly understood, although, of course, it can say nothing (for the whole of physical science can say nothing) about a primordial teleology at the foundation of the entire cosmos. I, in common with the Professor, look forward to 'the ultimate triumph of reason and right,' but my confidence is not due to any 'faith' I have in 'Nature' or anything else. I profoundly distrust 'faith' as an ultimate basis for any judgment ; I regard my conviction as a dictum of pure reason—the certain and evident teaching of that science which underlies and gives validity to every other. I therefore agree with Prof. Max Müller in regarding it as a lesson which 'true philosophy teaches us.'

"St. George Mivart."

In the number of the *Nineteenth Century* for March, 1889, Prof. Max Müller has published an article, entitled, "Can we think without Words?" Therein (p. 401, note 2) he in a truly wonderful manner concedes all that we demand—at least, he represents himself as having done so in a previous work. His words are : "When I speak of words I include other signs likewise, such as figures, for instance, or hieroglyphics, or Chinese or Accadian symbols. All I

---

* p. 83.

of without words, "concepts become, as it were, degraded into recepts, but recepts of a degree of complexity of organization which would not have been
possible but for their conceptional parentage." Now,
it is quite true that thoughts, as well as words, are very
often made use of without our adverting to the full
meaning we give them (and, indeed, the full implications
of our thoughts are hardly ever noted), so that they
are used as intellectual counters or symbols in reasoning. * Nevertheless, we are always conscious of what
they are, and can direct our attention at will to their
full intellectual significance. Thus they are widely
different from "recepts," and never become (what they
never originally were) a mere bundle of feelings. We
therefore deny in the strongest terms that a concept
can ever be degraded into a recept.

Mr. Romanes once more very surprisingly declares †

maintain is that thought cannot exist without signs, and that our
most important signs are words." Of course this is true, and this
is what we have always maintained. But if it is true, then thought
can exist without words. The Professor quotes from p. 58 of a
work published by Longmans, entitled, "Three Introductory Lectures
on the Science of Thought, delivered at the Royal Institution,
London." At p. 405 of the *Nineteenth Century* he asks, "What
else can the elements of thought be, if not words, the embodiment
of concepts?" But if "words" are "the embodiment of concepts,"
the concepts must exist before they are embodied. The "elements
of thought," then, must be something else than words. The
Professor cannot mean that people by merely uttering unmeaning
articulate sounds, get thought into them.

* Our power of thus temporarily disregarding the significance
of concepts is a great help to us in our intellectual progress, as an
economy of labour. As to this, see "On Truth," p. 363.

† pp. 83, 397. This is almost enough to make an opponent
despair of enabling him to understand his (the said opponent's)
position.

that he anticipates no opposition, from any school, to his analysis of mental states, and, he adds, that if his classification of them is accepted, it follows that the question of the origin of the human intellect is thrown back upon that of "the faculty of language." He also concludes his fourth chapter (which ends his main analysis of mental states) by affirming * that the only question "presented to the evolutionist is—Why has no mere brute ever learnt to communicate with its fellows? Why has man alone of animals been gifted with the Logos?"

Some questions concerning language, the reader will observe, have already been touched upon by Mr. Romanes, and therefore necessarily by us. Further elucidation of his views as to "mental states" will also become evident in his treatment of speech. But in his next five chapters he mainly applies himself to questions concerning language, and to that also our own next chapter will be devoted, although we have by no means accepted his classification of mental states, so that we cannot admit that the main question is really "thrown back" upon that of the origin of speech.

The distinction between the views expressed by Mr. Romanes and those held by his opponents—with respect to the question of mental states, to which his five first chapters are mainly devoted—may be briefly summarized as follows: Mr. Romanes ignores that distinction between our own higher and lower mental powers which we regard as probably the most fundamental and important of all the distinctions to be made

* p. 84.

in the study of mind. Instead of dividing the mental faculties, as Mr. Romanes does, into "percepts," "recepts," and "concepts," we divide them into two fundamental categories: (A) sensuous affections, and (B) ideas. Amongst the former we class all those which Mr. Romanes distinguishes as "recepts," while "percepts," instead of being at the root of all (where we place "sencepts"), are by us held to be intellectual activities, beyond the scope of all our sensitive faculties.

CHAPTER III.

REASON AND LANGUAGE.

MR. ROMANES having in the first section of his work (first five chapters) assumed that animals have perceptions (not merely sensitive affections) similar to our own, tries in his next section (chapters v.–ix.) to show that there is no essential difference between the language of man and that of animals. He tries to show this by representing not only that words, but that special modes of expressing them, were necessary antecedents for self-conscious expression on the one hand, and on the other, that the brute creation by sounds and gestures can express ideas, and truly communicate a knowledge of the facts to which their ideas relate.

In his fifth chapter, on Language, Mr. Romanes does us the honour to adopt our own classification * of its various categories, adding a seventh category for all

* Taken from our "Lessons from Nature," p. 83. It may be convenient to our readers to present here the same classification as more recently expressed by us ("On Truth," p. 235), which is as follows :—

Language consists of two kinds—the language of feeling, and the language of the intellect. Of the mere language of the emotions and of feeling we may have—

(1) Sounds which are neither articulate nor rational, such as cries of pain, or the murmur of a mother to her infant.

(2) Sounds which are articulate but not rational, such as many

kinds of written signs which we willingly adopt for greater clearness, and to avoid all divergence which does not seem to us absolutely necessary.

Of these seven categories we regard the first three as being common to us and to animals, and hold that the last four—as external manifestations of internal intellectual conceptions—are absolutely peculiar to mankind.*

Mr. Romanes begins by saying,† "Now, the first thing to be noticed is, that the signs made may be made either intentionally or unintentionally; and the next is, that the division of intentional signs may be conveniently subdivided into two classes—namely, intentional signs which are natural, and intentional signs which are conventional."

oaths and exclamations, and the words of certain idiots, who will repeat, without comprehending, every phrase they hear.

(3) Gestures which do not answer to rational conceptions, but are the bodily signs of pain or pleasure, of passion or emotion.

Of the language of the intellect we may have—

(4) Sounds which are rational but not articulate, such as the inarticulate ejaculations by which we sometimes express assent to, or dissent from, given propositions.

(5) Sounds which are both rational and articulate, constituting true "speech."

(6) Gestures which give expression to rational conceptions, and are therefore "external" but not "oral" manifestations of abstract thought. Such are many of the gestures of deaf-mutes, who, being incapable of articulating words, have invented or acquired a true gesture-language.

We will here add—

(7) A special external manifestation of abstract thought in the form of written or pictorial signs.

* As to language and the fundamental distinction which exists between its emotional and intellectual forms, see further, "On Truth," chap. xvi., pp. 351–355.

† p. 86.

Here we must be on our guard against an ambiguous employment of the terms "intentional" and "conventional." Nothing can be *really* "intentional" that is not done consciously, and "consciousness," as opposed to "consentience," is admitted to be now the exclusive prerogative of man. But no action which is not "intentional" can really be a sign.* Nevertheless, a distinction is to be drawn between two kinds of acts, neither of which is *really, i.e.* "formally," intentional, as, *e.g.*, would be the contact between our hand and a cat's back which we had intentionally began to stroke.

Thus, one animal, on rounding some corner, may come in contact with another, of which it had had no sense-perception; or it may come in contact with another which it has seen, and which it has pursued and caught. The latter contact may be loosely spoken of as "intentional," though it is not, of course, "formally" so. It may be well to distinguish an act which is thus but "materially intentional" by the term "*impulsional*"—to mark it off, both from what is fully conscious and volitional † or "formally" intentional, and from what is merely accidental.

As to the second ambiguous term, "conventional," Mr. Romanes applies it, in part, to denote a movement which animals have learnt to make by sensuous association,‡ or have acquired simply by imitation; and we

---

* See above, p. 65.

† Of course what is *really* "intentional" is also "impulsional." It is that and more.

‡ That is, by the association of sounds heard or movements seen, with the making of sounds or gestures by themselves. It is thus that the ordinary tricks of animals are acquired.

know that human idiots, devoid of consciousness, learn movements in the same way. But we also know that fully conscious men and women often adopt through distinct agreement (it may be tacitly) certain special movements as "signs." These latter are, of course, truly conventional signs, but not the former, which—as having been nevertheless acquired—may be distinguished as "*acquisitional*" signs.

Mr. Romanes continues : * "The subdivision of conventional signs may further be split into those which are due to past associations, and those which are due to inferences from present experience. A dog which 'begs' for food, or a parrot which puts down its head to be scratched, may do so merely because past experience has taught the animal that by so doing it receives the gratification it desires ; here is no need for reason— *i.e.* inference—to come into play. But if the animal has had no such previous experience, and therefore could not know by special association that such a particular gesture, or sign, would lead to such a particular consequence, and if under such circumstances a dog should see another dog beg, and should imitate the gesture on observing the result to which it led ; or if under such analogous circumstances a parrot should spontaneously depress its head for the purpose of making an expressive gesture,—then the sign might strictly be termed a rational one."

Now, there is, proverbially, great virtue in an "if," and much unequivocal evidence would be needed to show that such acts ever occur in animals. Granting,

* p. 86.

however, that they do occur—even every day—that tendency to imitation which we know many animals and human idiots possess, would amply account for them without the intervention of "inference." They may, therefore, be distinguished as "*imitational*" actions. Animals, by the association of sensations, often, as everybody knows, perform actions which serve as means to a practical end, without either "ends" or "means" being apprehended as such. "Imitational" actions of the kind may well take their place in this category. If animals had a true power of inference, they would not perform the very unreasonable actions * they often do—*e.g.*, building a nest in a house in full course of being taken down, or in a water-pipe, etc.

In a note † Mr. Romanes observes : " In the higher region of recepts both the man and the brute attain in no small degree to a perception of analogies or relations : this is inference or ratiocination in its most direct form, and differs from the process as it takes place in the sphere of conceptual thought, only in that it is not itself the object of knowledge. But, considered as a process of inference or ratiocination, I do not see that it should make any difference in our terminology whether or not it happens itself to be an object of knowledge."

We have already given—we trust sufficient—reasons for denying to brutes any real power of intellectual perception, while if man has, as we affirm, an intellectual nature distinct in kind, such a difference of nature may well hinder even his recepts from being absolutely the

* See " On Truth," p. 355.   † p. 87.

same as those of any brute.* We have also pointed out the essential nature of ratiocination and its distinctness from mere sensuous inference, as also that to suppose a reflex act necessary in order that a mental act should be conceptual and truly intellectual, is a mistake. Nothing more is needed for mental conception than direct consciousness, such, *e.g.,* as that we have of our own existence when least adverting to the fact of our existence. We are therefore far indeed from affirming that the nature of a psychical process is altered by becoming known. That it is so altered is one of those things which Mr. Romanes has to prove.† Nevertheless, the presence or absence of *a power* to know a psychical process performed, serves as an indication of a difference in nature and kind between the being that has, and one that has not, such a power.

Mr. Romanes next presents us ‡ with a scheme to show, in diagrammatic form, the classification which he has himself " arrived at, and which," he tells us, " follows closely the one given by" ourselves. " Indeed," he adds, "there is no difference at all between the two, save that I have endeavoured to express the distinction between signs as intentional, unintentional, natural, conventional, emotional, and intellectual." This shows how Mr. Romanes has failed to appreciate our position. There is a great and fundamental distinction " between the two ;" and this I will endeavour also to express in diagrammatic form.

* See above, p. 94.
† Since he says that a recept is changed into a concept by becoming known.
‡ pp. 88, 89.

Mr. Romanes's scheme is as follows :—

LANGUAGE, OR SIGN-MAKING.

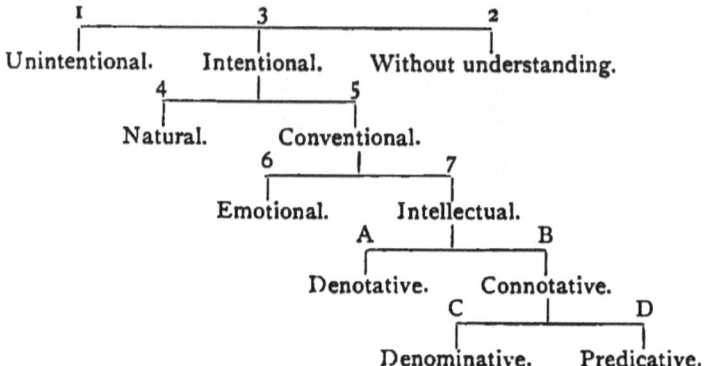

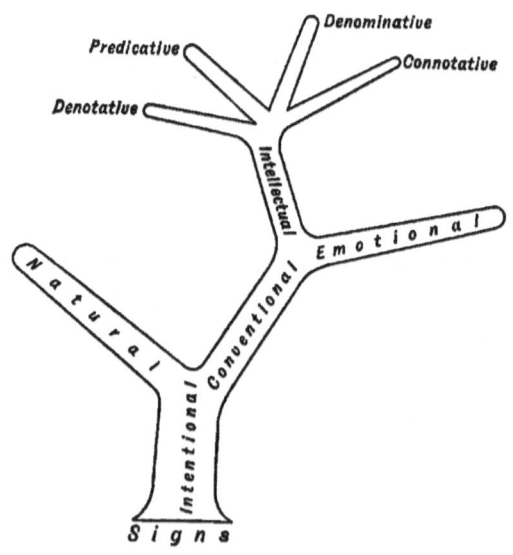

We, on the other hand, express ourselves thus :—

LANGUAGE, OR SIGN-MAKING.

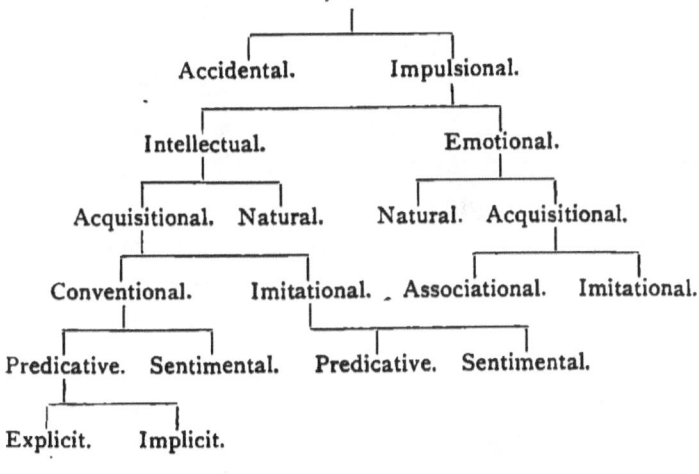

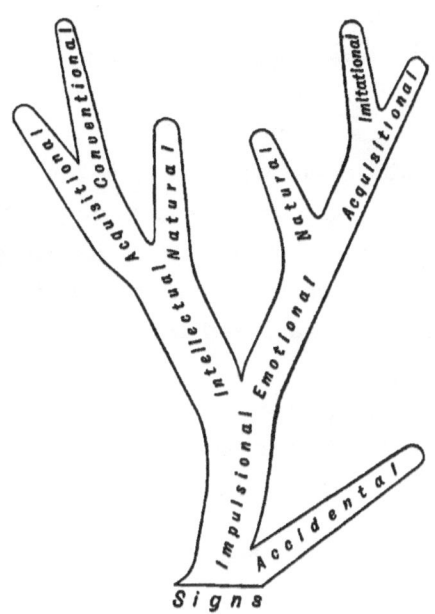

Conventional, and therefore acquired, intellectual language, may express either sentiments * or thoughts, and such thoughts may be signified with or without explicit statement—as we may or may not add the words, "and therefore equal," to a statement that two angles are angles at the base of an isosceles triangle.

As to animals, Mr. Romanes affirms † that we may take "as beyond the reach of question the important fact that they do present, in an unmistakable manner, a *germ* of the sign-making faculty." He tells us also that "the fact is so important in relation to" his subject, that he will "pause to consider the modes and degrees in which the faculty is exhibited by animals."

Here the expression "germ of the sign-making faculty" is ambiguous. That animals possess not only "a germ" of emotional language, but have it fully matured and developed, is certain; but that they have the minutest germ of an intellectual sign-making faculty is a thing we most strenuously deny. A sign, as before said,‡ is a token depicting ideas it is thereby intended to communicate; and we have already pointed out § in what sense alone actions can truly be called "signs." Let us now consider the actions of animals which Mr. Romanes brings forward, and see how far they indicate any use of "signs."

A wasp, finding a store of honey, "returns to the nest and brings off in a short time a hundred other wasps." What is there wonderful in this? It is surely

---

* As to the distinction between animal emotions and our higher sentiments, see "On Truth," pp. 186, 221.

† p. 88.   ‡ See above, p. 7.   § See above, p. 65.

well within the compass of instinct. There is no need to suppose an intellectual communication by gesture, but merely an instinctive stimulation inducing an instinctive response. In some of the tales given by Mr. Romanes, the language used plainly shows how the narrator is saturated with prejudice. It is impossible to place confidence in the narration of one to whom dispassionate consideration has evidently been impossible. We are told of a queen bee, which, when laying eggs, in company with workers, in the cells of the comb, missed four of the cells, and was thereupon pushed back by the workers till she had traversed the cells again more than once in vain. Thereupon the comment is made: "Thus the workers knew how to advise the queen that something was yet to be done; but they knew not how to show her where it had to be done." In another instance we read that a hive having been divided into two chambers by means of a partition, great excitement was caused in the half where the queen was not; but when Huber used a trellis-work partition, through the openings of which the bees could pass their antennæ, then there was no disturbance, because the bees in the half of the hive where the queen was "were able to inform the others that the queen was safe." Now, we do not deny that the excited feelings of the bees could be thus appeased, but there is no proof of it. The less complete separation made by the trellis-work partition might have sufficed for this; but the hasty inference to the contrary, and the expressions used, show plainly the animus of the narrator.

K

The tales told of ants are most remarkable for the mode in which they are told.   Certain mining ants do not lose time by carrying the earth they excavate to the surface,* "but pass the pellets to those above ; and the ants on the surface, when they receive the pellets, carry them—with an appearance of forethought which quite staggered Mr. Bates—only just far enough to insure that they shall not roll back again into the shaft, and, after depositing them, immediately hurry back for more."   Why Mr. Bates should have been "staggered" by so very simple a phenomenon, we are quite at a loss to conceive.

With respect to certain other ants, Mr. Belt is quoted as saying, † "I noticed *a sort of assembly* of about a dozen individuals that *appeared* in consultation.   Suddenly one ant left the *conclave*, and ran with great speed up the perpendicular face of the cutting without stopping."   Shortly, "information was communicated to the ants below, and a dense column rushed up in search of prey."   What possible right could Mr. Belt have to call a dozen ants in proximity "a sort of assembly" or "a conclave," or to declare that they "appeared in consultation"?   If persons who describe such things would simply content themselves with describing that they actually see, great would be the gain.   Even Mr. Bates speaks of "news of a disturbance" being "quickly communicated," as if he was stating an observed fact instead of drawing an uncertain inference.   Again, we have a statement as follows concerning ants induced by terror to change

* p. 92.   † The italics are ours.

an habitual route: One day some ants had been crushed on a mantel-shelf; "the effect of this was immediate and unexpected. As soon as those ants which were approaching arrived near to where their fellows lay dead or suffering, they turned and fled with all possible haste. In half an hour the wall above the mantel-shelf was cleared of ants. During the space of an hour or two the colony from below continued to ascend until reaching the lower bevelled edge of the shelf, at which point the more timid individuals, although unable to see the vase,* somehow became aware of the trouble, and turned without further investigation; while the more daring advanced hesitatingly just to the upper edge of the shelf, when, extending their antennæ and stretching their necks, they *seemed to peep* cautiously over the edge until they beheld their suffering companions, when they too turned and followed the others." This conduct is so unlike that of ants with which we are familiar, that we cannot help suspecting some (of course, quite un-intentional) inaccuracy in the anecdote; the animus with which it is related being again betrayed by the words we have italicized.

We will give yet another quotation† as to these ants: "A curious and invariable feature of their behaviour was that when an ant, returning in fright, met another approaching, the two would always communi-cate; but each would pursue its own way, the second ant continuing its journey to the spot where the first ant had turned about, and then following that example."

* A vase of flowers which the ants sought.
† From p. 94.

This was certainly not a rational proceeding, while it quite resembles instinctive action.

Sir John Lubbock's experiments with glasses and tapes * are interesting, but only go to prove the presence of those faculties of sense-perception which no one denies to insects or other animals.

That birds utter different tones, † according as their feelings are stimulated by different circumstances, is what no one thinks of denying. The same is true of apes, dogs, and cats; and if barking or mewing in a peculiar way, with the pulling of a maid's apron towards a door which denies an exit, could prove the presence of intellect in such animals, then no one could be so insane as to deny it. These matters, however, are quite beside the question. Such actions, instead of being considered as true signs, may be accounted for as mere means unconsciously employed for a practical end. ‡

Whether an animal can "point," might seem to be so simple a question that no mistake could be made about it. Nevertheless, so great is the confusion introduced into this simple matter, that it becomes necessary to distinguish different significations of that term.

When we say a dog "points," we do not mean that it points as a man would. It halts in a peculiar way, and onlookers know the reason why. But it does not necessarily follow that the dog has any feeling of relation between its actions and those of the sportsman

---

* *Loc. cit.*   † p. 96.

‡ See above, p. 124. When we say "unconsciously employed," we, of course, do not intend to imply the absence of "consentience."

with it, though it may possess such feelings. We have not the least objection to suppose it does possess them. But if it has them that does not prevent the action being a radically different one from the pointing of man—it does not make it a "sign." * All persons interested in these questions have probably read or heard of the card tricks of Sir John Lubbock's dogs. They have really no novel significance, and are fundamentally but what "Toby the learned pig" did in the days of our early childhood.

The anecdote of the cat who got help for a parrot up to its knees in dough; those of cats jumping on chairs, etc., are interesting, but not in the least inconsistent with our view of animal faculties being distinct in kind from those of man. We have ourselves elsewhere furnished anecdotes of the same kind.†

But the small value of the many marvellous tales told us about "animal intelligence," the credulity of observers or narrators, and Mr. Romanes's own need of a keener critical faculty, may all, we think, be made clear to readers of ordinary impartiality and intelligence by the following citations.

Mr. Romanes says,‡ "Concerning the use of gesture-signs by monkeys, I give the remarkable case recorded by James Forbes, F.R.S., of a male monkey begging the body of a female which had just been shot.

---

* As to this and other feelings of relation, see "On Truth," pp. 188–200, and 344–356.

† See "The Cat" (John Murray), p. 367. Animals which from past sense-experiences have associated feelings of relief with the presence of a certain person, may be thus led to seek the presence of such a person when fresh painful feelings are excited in them.

‡ p. 100.

'The animal came to the door of the tent, and, finding threats of no avail, began a lamentable moaning, and by the most expressive gestures seemed to beg for the dead body. It was given him; he took it sorrowfully in his arms and bore it away to his expecting companions.'" Successful, like Priam, it would be interesting to know what the monkeys did with the corpse. Mr. Romanes calls this tale "remarkable." It is so, indeed, but not in the sense which he intends. Had the apes made gestures, such as are used in ballets, stronger words could not have been used to describe them than "*most expressive.*" It was, perhaps, but an accident which prevented the subsequent movements of the apes being seen and interpreted as "truly funereal;" seeing that Professor Büchner * has credited insects with the performance of pious funereal rites. He describes to us two bees flying out of a hive, "carrying between them the corpse of a dead comrade," who, after they had found a suitable hole, "carefully pushed in the body head foremost, and placed above it two small stones [!]. They then watched for about a minute before they flew away"!

Mr. Romanes cites, with analogous credulity, an account of a monkey shot by Captain Johnson, which "instantly ran down to the lowest branch of a tree, as if he were going to fly at me, stopped suddenly, and coolly put his paw to the part wounded, covered with blood, and held it out for me to see."

We are yet further told † of a "closely similar case," recorded by Sir William Hoste, as follows :—

* In his sensational romance, entitled, "Mind in Animals," p. 249.
† p. 101.

"One of his officers, coming home after a long day's shooting, saw a female monkey running along the rocks, with her young one in her arms. He immediately fired, and the animal fell. On his coming up, she grasped her little one close to her breast, and with her other hand pointed [!] to the wound which the ball had made, and which had entered above her breast. Dipping her finger in the blood, and holding it up, she seemed to reproach him with having been the cause of her pain, and also of that of the young one, to which she frequently pointed."

Now, that these relations repose on a basis of truth is not to be doubted, neither is the perfect good faith of the narrators to be suspected. That the mother hugged her young one, that the wounded apes made gestures due to anger, pain, terror, or distress, no reasonable critic would question. It is, however, quite evident that these kind-hearted sportsmen read into such movements, motives and meanings due to their own fertile imaginations. Such mistaken inferences are not to be wondered at on the part of military men, possibly unskilled either in scientific observation or philosophic reflection; but it is strange indeed to see their delusions shared by a professed psychologist.*

But we reach the climax of absurdity in a tale which is gravely quoted from a correspondent by Mr. Romanes,† as evidence of exceptional capacity on the

---

* For an absurd tale about a gorilla, quoted by a writer who distinguished himself in "moral philosophy" at the London University, see "On Truth," p. 349.

† p. 190.

part of a talking bird. It concerns a cockatoo which had been ill, and the words are :—

"A friend came the same afternoon, and asked him how he was. With his head on one side and one of his cunning looks, he told her that he was 'a little better;' and when she asked him if he had not been very ill, he said, 'Cockie better; Cockie ever so much better.' . . . When I came back (after a prolonged absence) he said, 'Mother come back to little Cockie : mother come back to little Cockie. Come and love me, and give me pretty kiss. Nobody pity poor Cockie. The boy beat poor Cockie.' He always told me if Jes scolded or beat him. He always told me as soon as he saw me, and in such a pitiful tone."

After this we feel with Mr. Romanes that "enough has now been said." For if what he represents as facts and valid inferences were truly such, we should not say with our author that "animals present the germ of the sign-making faculty," but that animals plainly have and exercise the very same intellectual powers that we possess and exercise, and that nothing but a series of accidents can have prevented some bird, such as this Cockie, from having discovered the law of gravitation or dictated a treatise like the ethics of Aristotle !

Mr. Romanes concludes the chapter we are examining as follows : "It is certain that . . . . no distinction between the brute and the man can be raised on the question of the kind of signs which they severally employ as natural or conventional. This distinction, therefore, may in future be disregarded, and natural and conventional signs, *if made intentionally as signs,* I shall consider as *identical.*"

This treatment of the subject is indeed a convenient one for Mr. Romanes's purpose, but it is a quite unjustifiable treatment. At the beginning of this chapter we were careful to point out the really fundamental distinction which exists with respect to the different classes of actions thus conveniently confounded together under this ambiguous and misleading use of the terms "natural" and "conventional," and we think it only necessary now to refer to what we have before said.* Not one tittle of credible evidence has been adduced that any mere animal ever made, or was able to make, any real sign whatever.

In his sixth chapter the author applies himself to the consideration of "tone and gesture," as being the most natural and least conventional form of the sign-making faculty, and that which, in his opinion, comes first "in the order of its probable evolution." He says,† truly enough, that animals express their feelings by "hissings, spittings, growlings, screamings, cooings, etc.," as well as by bodily movements, and that, "even in fully developed speech, rational meaning is largely dependent for its conveyance upon slight differences of intonation."

He observes, and we entirely agree with him, "that an infant makes considerable advance in the language of tone and gesture before it begins to speak; and, according to Dr. Scott, who has had a very large experience in the instruction of idiotic children, 'those to whom there is no hope of teaching more than the merest rudiments of speech, are yet capable of receiving a con-

* See, once more, above, pp. 65, 122.   † p. 104.

siderable amount of knowledge by means of signs, and of expressing themselves by them.'"

The following interesting remarks are quoted * from Colonel Mallery: "The wishes and emotions of very young children are conveyed in a small number of sounds, but in a great variety of gestures and facial expressions. A child's gestures are intelligent long in advance of speech ; although very early and persistent attempts are made to give it instruction in the latter, but none in the former, from the time when it begins *risu cognoscere matrem*. It learns words only as they are taught, and learns them through the medium of signs which are not expressly taught. Long after familiarity with speech, it consults the gestures and facial expressions of its parents and nurses, as if seeking thus to translate or explain their words. . . . The insane understand and obey gestures when they have no knowledge whatever of words. . . . Sufferers from aphasia continue to use appropriate gestures."

Colonel Mallery also says that "Indians who have been shown over the civilized East [of the United States] have often succeeded in holding intercourse by means of their invention and application of principles, in what may be called the voiceless mother utterance, with white deaf-mutes, who surely have no semiotic code more nearly connected with that attributed to the Indians than is derived from their common humanity. They showed the greatest pleasure in meet-

---

* p. 105. From his "Sign-language among the North American Indians" (First Annual Report of the Bureau of Ethnology) : Washington, 1881.

ing deaf-mutes, precisely as travellers in a foreign country are rejoiced to meet persons speaking their language."

Gesture-language is declared * by Mr. Tylor to be "substantially the same all the world over," and Colonel Mallery has affirmed † that "the sign-language of the Indians is not, properly speaking, one language; but it and the gesture-systems of deaf-mutes, and of all peoples, constitute one language—the gesture-speech of mankind—of which each system is a dialect." This shows plainly how all men are of one intellectual nature.

Mr. Romanes also gives ‡ at length a very interesting account of a conversation held between two Indians of different races, and carried on entirely in gesture-language. It began with the questions and answers: "Which of the North-Eastern tribes is yours? Mountain river men. How many days from Mountain river? Moon new and full three times." The dialogue was continued through a great variety of detail.

A deaf-mute at Washington is said § to have related to some Indians that "when he was a boy, he went to a melon-field, tapped several melons, finding them to be green or unripe; finally, reaching a good one, he took his knife, cut a slice and ate it. A man made his appearance on horseback, entered the path on foot, found the cut melon, and, detecting the thief, threw the melon towards him, hitting him in the back, whereupon he ran away crying. The man mounted and rode off in an opposite direction." There is also given ‖ "the

* See p. 107. † See p. 111. ‡ p. 108.
§ p. 112. ‖ p. 113.

narrative of a boy going to an apple-tree, hunting for ripe fruit, and filling his pockets, being surprised by the owner and hit upon the head with a stone." This anecdote was much appreciated by the Indians and completely understood.

The amount of abstract thought thus expressed and apprehended by means of gesture only, shows that it must be a matter of difficulty to lay down any hard and fast line beyond which intellectual intercourse by gesture only should be absolutely impossible.

As to the effect of spoken language on gesture, Mr. Romanes observes : * "As all the existing races of mankind are a word-speaking race, we are not able to eliminate this factor, and to say how far the sign-making faculty, as exhibited in the gesture-language of man, is indebted to the elaborating influence produced by the constant and parallel employment of spoken language. We can scarcely, however, entertain any doubt that the reflex influence of speech upon gesture must have been considerable, if not immense." This seems to us to be very questionable ; for the use of so rapid and very serviceable an agent as spoken language, must have tended to starve out and replace the relatively slow and much less serviceable language of gesture. No doubt, speech has greatly aided the elaboration of ideas, and so enriched the conceptual *material* for gesture-expression, without at all facilitating or developing *gesture expression itself.* We have no evidence of its having done the latter, and do not see how it could have had that effect. Mr. Romanes continues :

* p. 113.

" Even the case of the deaf-mutes proves nothing to the contrary ; for these unfortunate individuals, although not able themselves to speak, nevertheless inherit in their human brains the psychological structure which has been built up by means of speech ; their sign-making *faculty* is as well developed as in other men, though, from a physiological accident, they are deprived of the ordinary means of displaying it. Therefore we have no evidence to what level of excellence the sign-making faculty of man would have attained, if the race had been destitute of the faculty of speech."

But deaf-mutes never inherited the extraordinary manual dexterity they show in manifesting their ideas. Such special nervous connections, or hypertrophied condition of nerves and ganglia as may be supposed to have been induced by long descent through speaking ancestors, they might have inherited. Such an inheritance, however, could never have aided their gesticulations. We must rather suppose that the nervous conditions of abundant gesticulation must have been going through a process of atrophy for ages, during all the many generations of their loquacious fathers. Moreover, as we shall see almost directly, deaf-mutes do not express their ideas in the order and sequence followed in the spoken language of their fellows, but have a special construction of their own. Yet this construction could never have been inherited from their speaking forefathers. *À fortiori*, then, their modes of gesticulation could not be the outcome of their speaking forefathers. As no amount of gesture-capacity could possibly by itself have initiated the beginning of speech, so no speaking capacity could by itself have initiated the bodily movements of gesture-language.

We may further observe that no nervous developments of either kind (those subserving oral, and those subserving manual expression) could have constituted a faculty of conception generally, since such things are but differences in degree in the material accompaniments of a corresponding physiological activity; while the first introduction of a power of conception is the initiation of a psychical difference of kind. Mr. Romanes is not always careful enough about such distinctions, since, in the passage last quoted, he speaks of a "psychological structure" of "brain" being inherited, instead of speaking of an anatomical condition accompanying a certain psychological activity. Some definite structural conditions and physiological activities must —in a creature at once corporeal and intellectual as we are—accompany all thinking. Nevertheless, the phenomena exhibited by deaf-mutes and gesticulating Indians, serve abundantly to prove that neither the anatomical nor the physiological conditions need be such as are indispensable for speech. They show that such highly abstract ideas as "ripeness," "appearance," "detection," "direction," "surprise," etc., can be both entertained and plainly signified in the absence of such anatomical and physiological conditions.

Mr. Romanes next calls our attention * to some details concerning the syntax of gesture-language. Thus the construction † of the sentences of deaf-mutes is said to be uniform "in different countries, and wholly

* p. 114.   † See also "On Truth," p. 229.

independent of the syntax which may happen to belong
to the language of their speaking friends." They do
not say, "'black horse,' but 'horse black;' not 'Bring a
black hat,' but 'Hat black bring;' not 'I am hungry,
give me bread,' but 'Hungry me, bread give.'" We
need hardly observe that these modes of construction
answer every practical purpose, while, as we recently
remarked, they could never by any possibility have been
inherited from speaking ancestors. Thus we have here
absolute proof positive of the independent and spontaneous activity of the human intellect in forming and
expressing its own concepts or abstract ideas—entities
at the opposite pole of psychical, cognitive life, to sense-
perceptions and sensuous universals.

This innate intellectuality, this spontaneous, purposive, voluntary expression of concepts in manual
language, is made specially clear in the following passage,* which shows how the deaf and dumb first give
expression to that part of their communication which
they are most anxious to impress on their hearer : " If
a boy had struck another boy, and the injured party
came to tell us, if he was desirous to acquaint us with
the idea that a particular boy did it, he would point to
the boy first. But if he was anxious to draw attention
to his own suffering, rather than to the person by whom
it was caused, he would point to himself and make
the act of striking, and then point to the boy." Mr.
Romanes quotes † an answer given by a deaf and dumb
pupil to the Abbé Sicard. But the answer is far more
remarkable for the highly abstract conception it ex-

* p. 115. † p. 116.

pressed than for the order of its expression. To the question, "Who made God?" he replied, "God made nothing." This was the same construction as he employed for affirming that a shoe was made by the shoemaker, *i.e.* "The shoe made the shoemaker." Thus, by "God made nothing," he meant, God was not made by anything, *i.e.* is self-subsisting!

The deaf and dumb, we are told,* express a conjunctive sentence "by an alternative or contrast; ' I should be punished if I were lazy and naughty,' would be put, ' I lazy, naughty, no!—lazy, naughty, I punished, yes!' Obligation may be expressed in a similar way ; ' I must love and honour my teacher,' may be put, ' Teacher, I beat, deceive, scold, no!—I love, honour, yes!'"

Of course this is a roundabout form of language, compared with oral expression ; but, though longer, it is fully as complete logically.

As an example of extremely elaborated gesture-language, we may cite Colonel Mallery's version † of a narration of the parable of the Prodigal Son by signs : "Once, man one, sons two. Son younger say, Father property your divide : part my, me give. Father so.— Son each, part his give. Days few after, son younger money all take, country far go, money spend, wine drink, food nice eat. Money by-and-by gone all. Country everywhere food little : son hungry very. Go seek man any, me hire. Gentleman meet.' Gentleman son send field swine feed. Son swine husks eat, see— self husks eat want—cannot—husks him give nobody. Son thinks, say, father my, servants many, bread enough,

* p. 117.   † p. 118.

part give away can—I none—starve, die. I decide: Father I go to, say I bad, God disobey, you disobey—name my hereafter *son*, no—I unworthy. You me work give servant like. So son begin go. Father far look: son see, pity, run, meet, embrace. Son father say, I bad, you disobey, God disobey—name my hereafter *son*, no —I unworthy. But father servants call, command robe best bring, son put on, ring finger put on, shoes feet put on, calf fat bring, kill. We all eat, merry. Why? Son this my formerly dead, now alive: formerly lost, now found: rejoice."

Colonel Mallery's testimony is also priceless as showing that these unfortunates have and can give plain expression to the most abstract of all concepts—that of "being" or "existence." He tells us that the sign used by deaf-mutes to express it is "stretching the arms and hands forward, and then adding the sign of affirmation."

The abstract cognition, "time," is also clearly signified * in such ways as the following: "Sleep done, I river go;" meaning, "When I have had my sleep, I will go to the river."

The idea of equality is also signified by deaf-mutes by extending the index fingers side by side—as when repeating that expression in the Lord's Prayer, "As in Heaven." We see, then, how intellectual concepts and distinct statements may be made with the copula remaining latent and implicit, while the most lofty abstractions, even such a supremely abstract idea as existence, may be intellectually conceived and clearly expressed by this wonderful language of gesture.

* p. 119.

L

In his next (seventh) chapter Mr. Romanes applies himself to the consideration of articulation.

He begins by referring, as we have before done,* to the occasional meaningless articulations of idiots, some birds, young children, and certain savages and lunatics. He tells us † of one of his own children who was very late in beginning to speak, but who " at fourteen and a half months old said once, and only once, ' Ego.' " This fact is cited as one instance out of many, to show (what we also affirm) that meaningless articulation is " spontaneous and instinctive, as well as intentionally [and we say, also unintentionally] imitative." He also quotes from Mr. Tylor, to the effect "that even born-mutes, who never heard a word spoken, do of their own accord and without any teaching make vocal sounds more or less articulate, to which they attach a definite meaning, and which, when once made, they go on using afterwards in the same unvarying sense."

This, we may be told, is simply the result of inheritance from many generations of speaking ancestors. But we may reply, How about those who first articulated? Why are we not to suppose such actions to have been instinctive? We know that instinct is a radically distinct faculty,‡ not to be explained by either lapsed or actual intelligence, or by mere reflex action, but rather as a special modification of that *sensori-motor* power which we know also exists in us now. How else could the language of gesture have arisen? And if we allow an instinctive activity to primitive gesture, why not also

* See " On Truth," p. 197.   † p. 122.
‡ See " On Truth," pp. 358–366, 515–518.

to primitive articulation? When once any one has a meaning to convey, he must, if he can succeed in conveying it, convey it by *some* visible, audible, or tactile sign. The employment of any one must be due to an internal impulse, and the employment also of any one kind of sign is fundamentally as wonderful as are either of the others. If existent dumb sign-making is due to ancestral speech, and ancient speech due to still more ancient gesture—as Mr. Romanes represents—to what was the original gesture due?

As we have already pointed out,* the nervous anatomical conditions which favoured and were further developed by one kind of expression, could never have favoured the other.

We are quite sure that Mr. Romanes is entirely sincere and honest, and does not see the equivocal nature of his argument. Nevertheless, to represent that the origin of each kind of language was developed from the other, and to withdraw whichever conception of origin an inquirer may seem disposed to select, is practically to shuffle with ideas in a way which reminds us not a little of the well-known "three-card trick." To this question we shall, however, be compelled to revert† when we come to examine Mr. Romanes's eighth chapter—that on "the relation of tone and gesture to words."

Our author candidly makes the noteworthy admission‡ that it would "be wrong to say that a higher faculty is required to learn the arbitrary association between a particular verbal sound and a particular act

---

* See above, p. 141. † See below, pp. 163.
‡ p. 123.

or phenomenon, than is required to depict an abstract idea in gesture ;" and adds, with much truth : "This only shows that where higher faculties are present, they are able to display themselves in gesture as well as in speech." With this we entirely agree. Where intellect exists it can manifest itself either by speech or gesture and where it does not exist, mere consentience may associate (as in apes, dogs, and learned pigs) definite articulate sounds, as well as definite gestures, with particular motions.

Mr. Romanes affirms that "the higher animals unquestionably do understand the meaning of words." This is ambiguous. If we employ the word "understand" in a loose and popular sense, every one would admit the truth of what he says, but not if we use it in its human sense. Therein, as we have shown,[*] the ideas of "existence" and "truth" are latent, and if animals understood words in that human sense of the term "understand," they would certainly be able to converse, at least in gesture. Such anecdotes as those of terrier dogs holding food on their muzzle till the words "Paid for" are uttered, or collie dogs being roused by hearing "Cow in the potatoes," are easy enough to understand on the very principle which we have just quoted Mr. Romanes as admitting.[†] As we are told,[‡] "numberless other anecdotes of the same kind might be quoted," but their value is far from being in proportion to their number. The mere titles of such books as Watson's "Reasoning Power in Animals," and

---

[*] See "On Truth," p. 103, and above, p. 45.
[†] p. 123.   [‡] p. 125.

Mennier's "Les Animaux Perfectibles," afford us reason to regard their contents with grave suspicion. Mr. Chambers, Professor Bain, and the late Mr. G. H. Lewes agree as to this tendency to exaggeration, declaring it to be "nearly as impossible to acquire a knowledge of animals from anecdotes, as it would be to obtain a knowledge of human nature from the narratives of parental fondness and friendly partiality," and affirming that the researches of various eminent writers on animal intelligence have been "biassed" by a secret desire to establish the identity of animal and human nature !

This "secret desire" goes further still, as Mr. Darwin himself has shown by naïvely declaring :* "It always pleases me to exalt plants in the organic scale ! "

Mr. Romanes thinks it difficult to overrate the significance of this power which animals have of associating actions with sounds. "The more," he tells us,† "my opponents maintain the fundamental nature of the connection between speech and thought, the greater becomes the importance of the consideration that the higher animals are able in so surprising a degree to participate with ourselves in the understanding of words. From the analogy of the growing child we well know that the understanding of words precedes the utterance of them, and therefore that the condition to the attainment of conceptual ideation is given in this higher product of receptual ideation. Surely, then, the fact that not a few among the lower animals (especially elephants, dogs, and monkeys) demonstrably share

* See "Life and Letters," vol. iii. p. 333.   † p. 126.

with the human infant this higher excellence of receptual capacity, is a fact of the largest significance. For it proves at least that these animals share with an infant those qualities of mind, which in the latter are immediately destined to serve as the vehicle for elevating ideation from the receptual to the conceptual sphere: the faculty of understanding words in so considerable a degree brings us to the very borders of the faculty of using words with an intelligent appreciation of their meaning."

But Mr. Romanes's opponents who agree with us, by no means maintain the "fundamental nature of the connection between speech and thought," in Mr. Romanes's sense, which is, the dependence of thought on speech. They maintain, indeed, the "fundamental" necessity of the presence of "thought" in whoever uses either words or gestures to express ideas, but they deny the existence of any fundamental connection between thought and articulate utterance. Not only, indeed, do they deny this, but they affirm that there is a fundamental severance between thought and many articulate utterances; such as those of parrots, jackdaws, and abnormal human beings, such as talking idiots. They also deny, on the grounds previously stated, *, the presence of "thought" in that associative, consentient apprehension of words which we meet with in dogs and

---

* Because the facts can be well explained by the mere existence of associations between feelings and emotions, and because were brutes thoughtful as to such words, their thoughtfulness would be displayed in other, less equivocal, modes, such as no one (save such persons as the anonymous narrator of the before-cited tale of the cockatoo) pretends they do display it in.

various other animals. To say, therefore, that brutes "participate with ourselves in the understanding of words" is a false—because ambiguous, and therefore misleading—assertion. We might as truly say that a cat walking over the keys of a piano "participates" with the skilled pianist in "a power of eliciting musical sounds by instrumental agency"! To assert that "participation" which Mr. Romanes asserts, is, once more, to beg the very question his work is professedly devoted to prove.

We deny the existence of any real analogy between brutes and the growing child, beyond that which necessarily follows from their common "animality," the existence of which we, of course, affirm as strongly as Mr. Romanes does, and the consequences of which we pointed out in our introductory chapter. Words are understood by a child before it speaks, because it already possesses intellect, and the use of significant oral expressions normally and naturally follows. But brutes which are physically able to articulate, do not utter words which they may have associated with antecedent sensuous affections as significant expressions, just because they have no veritable understanding power before, during, or after, hearing the words in question.

Therefore we altogether deny the consequence which (as we have just seen) Mr. Romanes draws—namely, that "the condition to the attainment of conceptual ideation is given in this highest product of receptual ideation." A psychical power of sensuous, consentient apprehension is, of course, in us, a necessary antecedent condition for the attainment of conceptual ideation; just as is a power of sensation, a sufficient integrity of nervous structure, a sufficient supply of healthy, nutritious blood, and life itself. But neither in life, nor healthy blood, nor an unimpaired nervous system, nor sensitivity, and consentient apprehension, is "given" the "condition to the attainment of conceptual ideation," unless an intellectual nature is already present. Elephants, dogs, and monkeys do not "*demonstrably* share with the human infant" its powers of apprehension. For it is impossible to "demonstrate" that the infant has not already that intellectual nature, the presence of which soon becomes undeniable. Neither can any one "demonstrate" that the infant's merely receptual powers are not modified by the latent presence of a truly intellectual nature. Mr. Romanes tells us that the power of "understanding words" to the extent that dogs, elephants, and apes understand them, "brings us to the very borders of the faculty of using words with an intelligent appreciation of their meaning." But this is quite a mistake. Words, apart from their intellectual employment, are merely bodily movements of parts accessory to respiration, accompanied by sound. There is, then, no *à priori* reason why a dog, were it physically capable of articulation,* should not use words to denote its "feelings," instead of wagging or stiffening its tail as the case may be. Did it so articulate, the careless observer would be very apt to interpret its words as declarations of facts, instead of being (as on the hypothesis they would be) nothing but signs of feelings. Mr. Romanes himself says,† "If these animals were able to articulate,

* And it is by no means absolutely certain it is not so capable.
† pp. 127, 128.

they would employ simple words to express simple ideas. I do not say, nor do I think, that they would form propositions; but it seems to me little less than certain that they would use articulate sounds, as they now use tones or gestures. . . . For instance, it would involve the exercise of no higher psychical faculty to say the word 'Come,' than it does to pull at a dress or a coat . . . or to utter the word 'Open,' instead of mewing before a closed door; or, yet again, to utter the word 'Bone,' than to select and carry a card with the word written upon it."

With a protest against the employment here of the term "idea," we can express our entire and cordial agreement * with this passage. Words so used need have no meanings beyond those expressed by the various movements which animals do make.

Mr. Romanes next proceeds to relate certain anecdotes about articulating birds, and make certain reflections there anent. We have already seen † how easy is Mr. Romanes's credulity on this subject; and we should bear this credulity in mind, in every attempt to estimate justly the value of his deductions.

---

* See "On Truth," p. 352, where we have already pointed out these considerations.

† See above, p. 136. At p. 130 he also tells us, in a note : " I have received numerous letters detailing facts from which I gather that parrots often use comical phrases when they desire to excite laughter, pitiable phrases when they desire to excite compassion, and so on ; although it does not follow from this that the birds understand the meanings of those phrases, further than that they are as a whole appropriate to excite the feelings which it is desired to excite." Such phenomena he also believes himself to have observed.

He begins by telling us,* "It is unquestionable that many parrots know perfectly well that certain names belong to certain persons, and that the way to call these persons is to call their appropriate names." Here, again, we meet with that ambiguous use of the verb "to know" which we have before objected to here and elsewhere.† He then decorates with the term "very proper" a flagrant statement he quotes from Houzeau, affirming that the way in which "some parrots habitually use certain words shows an aptitude correctly to perceive [!] and to name [!] qualities as well as objects."

These statements are either due to a confusion of thought, or to a want of care to avoid playing fast and loose with terms, and so—practically, however unconsciously—throwing dust into the eyes of readers not careful to protect their mental vision. Thus, he next tells us,‡ very properly, that "the apposite use of words or phrases by talking birds are found on inquiry to be due, as antecedently we should expect that they must, to the principle of association. The bird hears a proper name applied to a person, and so, on learning to say the name, henceforth associates it with that person. And similarly with phrases. These with talking birds are mere vocal gestures, which in themselves present but little more psychological significance than muscular gestures. The verbal petition, 'Scratch poor Poll,' does not in itself display any further psychological development than the significant gesture of depressing the head against the bars of the cage." This is precisely what we insist upon, and such articulations, like such movements,

* p. 129. † See "On Truth," p. 189. ‡ p. 131.

can be fully accounted for without the presence of any real "understanding" or "knowledge" at all. Such associations (cited from remarks made by Dr. Samuel Wilks, F.R.S.) as those between the sight of certain persons and sounds or phrases such a bird has heard them utter, or between the sight of the coachman and the words "half-past two," generally said to him when he comes for orders, or between the sound of drawing a cork with a corkscrew and the sight of a bottle, etc. —all such phenomena of association are most easy to understand and are fully to be accounted for without the presence of any faculty higher than that of consentience.

But after thus admitting the position we contend for, Mr. Romanes proceeds to retract his admissions,* without saying or appearing to be the least aware that he is so doing. He says, "In designating as 'vocal gestures' the correct use (acquired by direct association) of proper names . . . and short phrases, I do not mean to disparage the faculty which is displayed. On the contrary, I think this faculty is precisely the same [!] as that whereby children first learn to talk. . . . The only difference is that, in a few months after its first commencement in the child, this faculty develops into proportions far surpassing those which it presents in the bird, so that the vocabulary becomes much larger and more discriminative. But the important thing to attend to is that at first, and for several months after its commencement, the vocabulary of a child is always designative of particular objects, qualities, actions, or

* p. 133.

desires, and is acquired by direct association." This is really, though not formally, contradictory to what Mr. Romanes has earlier most truly said,* that the nascent intelligence first apprehends general characters, and not particulars, which latter are only subsequently detected by a process of mental analysis. Of course we utterly deny that the first talking of a parrot and a child is, or can be, due to a faculty which is "*precisely the same*," as we also deny that "in this stage language is nothing more than vocal gesticulation." † It may or it may not be "more," according to the circumstances.

"Therefore," concludes Mr. Romanes, "we may now, I think, take the position as established *à posteriori* as well as *à priori*, that it is, so to speak, a mere accident of anatomy that all the higher animals are not able thus far to talk ; and that, if dogs or monkeys were able to do so, we have no reason to doubt that their use of words and phrases would be even more extensive and striking than that which occurs in birds."

This is true enough, and thus such emotional language need mean no more in the case of a gorilla than it does in that of a cockatoo.

It would be an altogether different matter if animals were really able to use names, knowing what they were about, or could point out groups of objects understood as such. This, however, is what Mr. Romanes does not hesitate to say they can do. He tells us : 'There still remains one feature in the psychology of talking birds to which I must now draw prominent attention. So far as I can ascertain, it has not been mentioned by any previous writer, although I should think it is one that can scarcely have escaped the notice of any attentive observer of these animals. I allude to the aptitude which intelligent parrots display of extending their articulate signs from one object, quality, or action, to another which happens to be strikingly similar in kind. For example, one of the parrots which I kept under observation in my own house learnt to imitate the barking of a terrier, which also lived in the house. After a time this barking was used by the parrot as a denotative sound, or proper name, for the terrier— *i.e.*, whenever the bird saw the dog it used to bark, whether or not the dog did so. Next, the parrot ceased to apply this denotative name to that particular dog, but invariably did so to any other, or unfamiliar, dog which visited the house. Now, the fact that the parrot ceased to bark when it saw my terrier after it had begun to bark when it saw other dogs, clearly showed that it distinguished between individual dogs, while receptually perceiving their class resemblance. In other words, the parrot's name for an individual dog became extended into a generic name for all dogs."

Now, as Mr. Romanes very often refers back to this example, we must criticize the passage with some pains and at some length. In the first place, as Mr. Romanes has before remarked *—citing Dr. Wilks—it is common enough for parrots to imitate on seeing a visitor some words or noise he habitually makes, as it may imitate the sound of cork-drawing on seeing a bottle. Barking at the sight of the terrier is, then (as Mr. Romanes would

* pp. 131, 132.

be the first to say), quite a simple matter. But it is notorious, and admitted on all hands, that animals become impressed so as to identify particulars with particulars—as to form what I have elsewhere * termed "sensuous universals." A sheep does not dread this particular wolf, but any other wolf also. Therefore it must have a corresponding plexus of feelings ; and as the parrot easily can form an association between a plexus of visual feelings and a sound, so it may easily form an association between a similar sound and a plexus' of visual feelings closely resembling the former one. There is no more difficulty in one case than in the other, and no more need of attributing to it any superior cognitive power or *intention* of extending the meaning of the sound first used. In the first there was no real or intentional meaning, though there was a spontaneous activity excited by certain sense-impressions, and the same cause suffices to account for the second case just as well as the first. There is, of course, a certain spontaneity and a certain "meaning" in the sounds, but the meaning is not an intended one. A weather-cock veering east intends to make known the meaning which is, of course, present in its automatic indication "materially," though not "formally." As to the parrot discontinuing to employ its vocal gesture for the terrier after it had began to apply

* See "On Truth," pp. 191, 206. They have only been so termed by a remote analogy with true "universals," for there is nothing which can be truly called universal in such sense-affections. "Sense" is really ignorant, though the practical outcome of its affections may resemble perceptions in the material, external effects which follow. See above, p. 44, note †.

the same gesture to other dogs, it is a singular fact,
which we are inclined to be sceptical about. We doubt
whether Mr. Romanes can be sure that the parrot did
so entirely drop the use of this sign. But whether it did
or not does not matter in the slightest degree for the
argument. The dropping of it could be no indication
of intellect. The recognition by a really intellectual
nature, of other dogs as being " dogs," would not make
the first known dog a bit less a dog, or cause it to be
considered less a dog. That the parrot could practically
distinguish between the familiar terrier and strange
dogs no person can doubt. Every dog who lives with
a cat in the house knows his friend " Tom " from all
other cats, and generally shows a disposition to treat the
latter very differently from the way in which " Tom " is
treated by him. In this anecdote, if we accept without
question all the facts stated, there is not a scintilla
of evidence of the possession by the parrot of an intellectual nature ; there is nothing but what may be
entirely accounted for by that power of association and
consentient apprehension which we all allow that
animals possess.

Mr. Romanes distinguishes * " four divisions of the
faculty of articulate sign-making—namely, meaningless
imitation, instinctive imitation, understanding words as
irrespective of tones, and intentional use of words as
signs." We do not quite understand how " understanding words " can be a division of " sign-making," and
we object to his remark that the understanding of words
" implies, *per se*, a higher development of the sign-

* p. 137.

making faculty than does the understanding of tones and gestures." Such an understanding of words as is shown by a parrot, dog, or chimpanzee, is, as Mr. Romanes himself allows, but the understanding of a "vocal gesture," and it is acuteness of the senses, and not intellect, which enables animals to apprehend such gestures. Mr. Romanes himself has said * (as we have seen) that "the verbal petition, 'Scratch poor Poll,' does not in itself [*i.e.* "*per se*"] display any further psychological development than depressing the head against the bars of the cage."

Speaking of what he calls "the intentional use of words as signs," he says,† "Talking birds show themselves capable of correctly using proper names, noun-substantives, adjectives, verbs, and appropriate phrases, although they do so by association alone, or without appreciation of grammatical structure." Grammatical structure! Why, the immense majority of mankind speak with true intellect and perfect logic, "without appreciation" of grammatical structure! That birds use such words of different kinds "correctly," is a mere accident resulting from circumstance of association, as Mr. Romanes would himself assert. Nevertheless, by this use of the adverb "correctly," a flavour of intellectuality is insinuated, and this requires to be noted. The faculty of vocal articulation, he further tells us, "is exhibited by talking birds in so considerable a degree, that the animals even invent names." But to "invent" is something much higher than spontaneously to associate sounds with sights, and Mr. Romanes has declared that "association"

* p. 131.   † p. 138.

does account for these performances. Whether he admits this or not is, however, quite indifferent to us, as we ground our whole argument, not on authority, but on evidence. To say "half-past two" at the sight of a coachman on whose appearance those words have constantly been heard, is not "to apply words to designate an object," but to emit sounds with which the sight of that object has become accidentally associated.

Mr. Romanes next makes an altogether unwarrantable assertion which shows great confusion of thought ; he tells us that such inventions on the part of parrots "often clearly have an onomatopoetic origin." Now, onomatopœia is a term used to denote the voluntary employment of an imitation of sounds heard, to denote the conception of the object which makes the sound —as when a child calls a duck " quack-quack," or when the word "hiss," or something like it, has been employed to express the idea of a hissing snake. Now, when a parrot, which has often seen and heard corks drawn, makes the sound of the drawing of a cork at the sight of a bottle, such is no true case of onomatopœia, as there is no evidence of intention on the part of the bird to use the sound as a name.

Mr. Romanes ends the chapter by detailing evidence to show the extent to which, under favourable circumstances, young children will invent arbitrary signs, mostly of an articulate kind. Had we space we would gladly cite these, as they are much to our purpose. We maintain that man possesses, and always has possessed, an instinct of language, whereby to express, and wherein to incarnate, his spontaneously arising concepts. We

M

quite accept what Mr. Romanes says,* that such speech may attain an astonishing degree of fulness and efficiency, and that though such words have sometimes an onomatopoetic origin, they, as a rule, have not such ; that they are far from being always monosyllabic ; that they are sufficiently numerous and varied to constitute a not inefficient language without inflections, and that its syntax has an affinity to that of gesture-language.

The eighth chapter is devoted to a consideration of the relation borne by tone and gesture to words. We have but little to object to its contents. No reasonable person could, or would wish to dispute the great superiority of speech over gesture-language, as a medium for the communication of thought. Obviously thought can thus be much more easily and rapidly expressed ; it can be used in the dark, and while the hands are otherwise occupied. Nevertheless, Mr. Romanes very properly observes † that he is speaking of gesture-language as we actually find it. What the latent capabilities of such language may be is another question. He adds later on,‡ "I doubt not it would be possible to construct a wholly conventional system of gestures which should answer to, or correspond with, all the abstract words and inflections of a spoken language. . . . This, however, is a widely different thing from supposing that such a perfect system of gesture-signs could have grown by a process of natural development ; and, looking to the essentially ideographic character of such signs, I

---

* p. 144.   † p. 147.
‡ p. 148. See also above, p. 141 ; and see, below, the case of Martha Obrecht.

greatly question whether, even under circumstances of the strongest necessity (such as would have arisen if man, or his progenitors, had been unable to articulate), the language of gesture could have been developed into anything approaching a substitute for the language of words." So also do we. But we are certain, nevertheless, that such a dumb community of essentially rational animals would have evolved a natural and instinctive language of gesture, capable of making known the concepts they had formed, and of aiding them by the "recognitions" of their thus expressed concepts to evolve ever more and more abstract concepts, though probably never attaining to nearly the height that man has attained to by the aid of speech. We are certain they would have done this both on the *à priori* ground of the necessary consequence of the presence of animality and rationality in one absolute unity of existence, and also on *à posteriori* grounds, from the evidence afforded by such extraordinary examples of defective existence, as the blind, deaf, and dumb Laura Bridgman,* and the still more striking case of Martha Obrecht, which we will describe a little later.

* With how little reason has Professor Huxley said ("Man's Place in Nature," p 52, quoted by Mr. Romanes, p. 134), "A race of dumb men, deprived of all communication with those who could speak, would be little indeed removed from the brutes. The moral and intellectual differences between them and ourselves would be practically infinite, though the naturalist should not be able to find a single shadow even of specific structural difference." Mr. Romanes, in a note (pp. 134, 135), refers to recent discoveries in cerebral physiology as to a "material organ of speech." Such discoveries in no way effect our position, or can do so, as they relate merely to the instrument whereby the *verbum mentale* is able to manifest itself externally, and everybody knows that various

To such *à posteriori* evidence * Mr. Romanes opposes
certain assertions respecting "the psychological *status*
of wholly uneducated deaf-mutes," in spite of the fact
that each such mute "inherits a human brain, the structure of which has been elaborated by the speech of his
ancestors," and "is also surrounded by a society the
whole structure of whose ideation is dependent upon
speech." Such mutes, he tells us, † "grow up in a state
of intellectual isolation, which is almost as complete as
that of any of the lower animals." But, in the first
place, their state is an abnormal one, and therefore they
might (according to what we laid down in our introductory remarks) be expected to seem to fall even *below*
the condition of animals in a normal state. Secondly, we
cannot draw valid conclusions as to the essential nature
of our intellect from human beings who are avowedly
mentally deficient, and every deaf-mute must be so, either
essentially or accidentally. It would be obviously as
absurd to judge of the nature of the human rational
faculty from an absolute idiot, as it would be to study
the power of flight in a bird the wings of which had
been cut.

But let us accept Mr. Romanes's instances as valid,
without further protest, and see whether they "can
never rise to any ideas of higher abstraction than those
which the logic of feelings supplies." He cites ‡ the
Rev. S. Smith as telling him of a deaf-mute who

forms of aphasia coexisting with a complete power of thinking,
and sometimes even of manifesting thoughts by appropriate
gestures, have been observed and recorded.

 * As to some of which, see above, pp. 138–146.
 † p. 149.   ‡ p. 150.

"*previous to education*, supposed the Bible to have been printed by a printing-press in the sky, which was worked by printers of enormous strength—this being the only interpretation the deaf-mute could assign to the gestures whereby his parents had sought to make him understand that they believed the Bible to contain a revelation from a God of power who lives in heaven." But, surely, here we have, "previous to education," a manifest intellectual faculty, and a power of abstraction of a most unequivocal kind. The deaf-mute had formed concepts of "a Bible," "printers," a "printing-press," "superterrestrial existence," "power," "beings of superhuman power," and a "descent from the sky to earth following upon their activity." Also, of course, in this concept there were implicitly contained ideas of time, space, reality, truth, and existence. This is something considerably above the "logic of feelings," and rather different from the psychical state of "any of the lower animals." Moreover, we should never forget the constant necessity under which all men labour (from the lowest to the highest) to make use of analogy, and to express by analogy in terms of sensitivity, thoughts which are altogether beyond sense. We must also recollect that all such expressions are inadequate, and that we are constantly tempted to despise expressions which we do not use, and fancy that our own terms (though really as sensuous, fundamentally) must be a great deal better. The image of a printing-press worked in the sky by beings of superhuman strength is for us grotesque. But it might, none the less, serve to image forth in some minds, that same conception of "inspired expression in the Bible," which a very different set of mental images helps us to conceive of.

But we have other instances we can bring forward which plainly show the essential intellectuality of such unfortunates.

The case of Laura Bridgman is a well-known one, and referred to by our author. She was blind as well as deaf, and had half lost the power of smell, and had become thus afflicted so early that she had no recollection of seeing or hearing. Yet she learned to apprehend abstract relations and qualities, and to read and write. A similarly afflicted child, named Meystre,* at Lausanne, gained an idea of God as "thought enthroned somewhere." Such instances surely demonstrate the existence of wonderful innate capacities in the human mind.

A still more noteworthy case is that (before referred to) of Martha Obrecht.† She was deaf, dumb, and blind, and was confided to a convent at Larnay (Poitiers) when she was eight years old.‡ There, by

---

* See "On Truth," p 232.

† See "Apologie Scientifique," by Canon F. Duilhé de Saint-Projet, *Ed. Privat*, Toulouse, 1885, pp. 374–387.

‡ The following are some of the details given in the work referred to :—

"C'etait comme une masse inerte, ne possédant aucun moyen de communication avec ses semblables, n'ayant pour traduire ses sentiments qu'un cri joint à un mouvement de corps, cri et mouvement toujours en rapport avec ses impressions.

"La première chose à faire était de lui donner un moyen de communiquer ses pensées et ses désirs. Dans ce but, nous lui faisions toucher tous les objets sensibles, en faisant sur elle le signe de ces objets ; presque aussitôt elle a établi le rapport qui existe entre le signe et la chose. . . ." (They thought to try steel

intelligent and very patient instruction, the poor child was enabled gradually to acquire the power of appré-

letters, but it was too soon ; imitation signs were first necessary.) " Ici, le sens du toucher (la main) à joué un rôle qui nous a jetés maintes fois dans le plus grand étonnement. . . . Dès le début, lorsque nous lui présentions un morceau de pain, nous lui faisions faire de la main droite l'action de couper la main gauche, signe naturel qui font tous les sourd-muets. La petite élève ayant remarqué que chaque fois qu'on lui présentait du pain, en lui faisait ce signe ou qu'on le lui faisait faire, a dû *raisonner* et se dire : Quand je voudrai du pain je ferai ce signe. En effet, c'est ce qui a en lieu. Quand à l'heure du repas, on a tardé, tout exprès, à lui donner du pain, elle a reproduit l'action de couper la main gauche avec la main droite. Il en a été de même pour les autres choses sensibles ; et du moment qu'elle a eu la clef du système, il a suffi de lui indiquer une seule fois le signe de chaque objet. . . . Les objets qu'elle touche . . . sont des choses sensibles, les signes correspondants qu'on lui fait ou qu'on lui fait faire sont également choses sensibles ; mais le lieu, le rapport qui unit chaque objet à son signe, l'idée générale de ce rapport, *la clef du système*, n'a rien de commun avec la matière.

"Nous sommes passées ensuite aux choses intellectuelles . . . afin de lui donner, sur le fait même, le signe de l'idée ou du sentiment qui se révélait en elle. La suprenait on impatiente, ou livrée à un mouvement de mauvaise humeur, vite on lui faisait faire le signe de l'impatience, et on la repoussait un peu pour lui faire comprendre que c'était mal. Elle s'était attachée à une sourde-muette déjà instruite et qui s'est dévouée avec beaucoup de zèle à son éducation. Souvent elle lui témoignait son affection en l'embrassant en lui serrant la main. Pour lui indiquer une manière plus générale de traduire ce sentiment de l'âme, nous avons posé sa petite main sur son cœur en l'appuyant bien fort. Elle a compris que ce geste rendait sa pensée, et elle s'en est servie toutes les fois qu'elle a voulu dire qu'elle aimait quelqu'un ou quelque chose ; puis, par *analogie*, elle a repoussé de son cœur tout ce qu'elle n'aimait pas.

" C'est ainsi que peu à peu nous sommes parvenues à la mettre en possession du langage mimique en usage chez les sourds-muets. Elle s'en est facilement servie dès la première année. . . .

" La puissance de réflèchir, de généraliser, de raisonner se mani-feste de plus ; ce sont là des opérations essentiellement intellectu-

hending and expressing intellectual conceptions, and highly abstract and lofty ideas, with distinct and clear

elles, absolument incompatibles avec la substance matérielle, inerte, inactive, composée de parties, etc.

"Dès la première année, la jeune Marthe se sert facilement du langage mimique dont la nature est d'être idéologique. Les idées, les notions qu'elle possède—notions de choses sensibles ou intellectuelles—ne sont pas représentées, suscitées dans son esprit par des mots, par des combinaisons de sons articulés ou figurés,—elle n'entend pas, elle ne voit pas—mais par des impressions du toucher, impressions de formes et de mouvements transitoires, qui expriment directement, immédiatement la notion ou l'idée. L'âme intelligente apparaît ici d'autant plus distinctement qu'elle se meut, vit et agit dans une région tout immatérielle.

"De ces opérations de l'esprit aux premières révélations de la conscience la gradation est insensible et facile. Déjà dans le courant de la première année nous avons pu lui donner quelques leçons de morale. Comme tous les enfants elle manifestait assez souvent des penchants à la vanité et à la gourmandise.

"Lorsque des dames visitaient l'établissement, la petite enfant se plaisait à faire l'examen de leur toilette. Le velours, la soie, la dentelle, éveillaient en elle un sentiment d'envie. Aussi, lorsque quelque découpure lui tombait sous la main, elle s'en faisait ou un voile ou une cravate. Pour la guérir de ce penchant naturel à la vanité, il a suffi de lui faire comprendre que, sa mère n'étant pas ainsi vêtue, il ne fallait pas désirer ces choses.

"Pour la corriger de ses petites gourmandises, on lui a dit que les personnes à qui elle reconnaît une supériorité—les Sœurs, la supérieure, le Père aumônier—avaient aussi ces défauts dans leur enfance, mais que leur mère leur ayant dit que c'était mal, elles s'étaient corrigées. Ces raisonnements ont eu sur l'enfant un grand empire, et ces légers défauts ont disparu. Il est aisé de reconnaître dans ces quelques traits, la distinction du bien et du mal le discernement de ce qui est permis et de ce qui est défendu ; l'idée d'autorité morale—sa mère, ses supérieurs—l'idée d'obligation et de loi morale. Il est aisé de constater des actes de volonté libre ; des actes de commandement à soi-même, de réaction vertueuse contre les impressions extérieures contre les appétits naturels—la gourmandise, la vanité. On peut enfin constater également une perception confuse du beau, des symptômes du sentiment esthétique, véritablement etranges chez un être privé

moral and religious apprehensions, and not only to read, but also to write perfectly well.

des deux sens esthétiques par excellence, des deux sens révélateurs de l'harmonie des lignes, des couleurs ou des sens,—de la vue et de l'ouïe. Le velours, la soie, la dentelle révèlent à son toucher manuel des qualités *sui generis;* elle a compris que le vêtement ne sert pas seulement de protection pour le corps, mais aussi de parure. N'insistons pas ; nous sommes en présence d'un plus étonnant prodige : dans cette enfant de dix ans à peine, hier encore 'masse inerte,' en apparence bien au-dessous de la bête, nous allons voir se former ou s'eveiller nous allons voir eclater l'idée de Dieu.

"Vers la fin de la deuxième année, nous avons cru pouvoir aborder les questions religieuses l'enfant ne savait encore ni lire ni écrire ; le langage mimique était le seul moyen de communication entre elle et nous. Nous sommes passées des choses visibles aux invisibles. Pour lui donner la première idée d'un être souverain, nous lui avons fait remarquer la hiérarchie des pouvoirs dans l'établissement. Elle avait déjà compris, dans ses rapports avec nous, que les Sœurs étaient au dessus des élèves, etc. Quand Mgr. l'évêque vint nous visiter, nous lui fîmes comprendre qu'il était encore au dessus des personnes qu'elle était habituèe à respecter, et que bien loin, là bas, il y avait un premier évêque qui commandait à tous les autres : évêques, prêtres et fidèles. De cette souveraineté qui lui paraissait bien grande, nous sommes passées à celle du Dieu créateur et souverain seigneur.

"Impossible de décrire l'impression produite chez l'enfant par la connaissance de cette première verité d'un ordre supérieur. L'immensité de Dieu l'a aussi beaucoup frappée. La pensée que ce Dieu souverain voit tout, même nos plus secrétes pensées, l'a beaucoup émue. Et maintenant, quand on veut arrêter chez elle quelque petite saillie d'humeur, il suffit de lui dire que le bon Dieu la voit. . . . Cependant l'instruction scolaire de Marthe, engagée dans une voie nouvelle, va progresser comme par bonds et se produire pour la première fois par le langage alphabétique, par la dactylologie, qui est l'équivalent de la parole articulée et enfin par les divers genres d'écriture.

"Avant d'apprendre à l'enfant à lire et à écrire comme les aveugles, nous avons dû lui enseigner la dactylologie. Nous avons commencé dans le courant de la troisième année. Ici encore le sens du toucher a été le grand moyen de communication et de

But to all such instances as these, Mr. Romanes
would object that the children thus developed were the

convention. Lorsque recevant un morceau de pain, elle en a fait,
le signe, nous lui avons dit qu'il y avait un autre moyen de désigner
le pain, et à l'aide de la dactylologie, nous avons figuré dans sa
main la suite des lettres qui composent le mot *pain.* Ce nouveau
système, cette révélation-nouvelle a été pour cette jeune intelligence ce qu'est un rayon de soleil pour une fleur naissante, après
une sombre et froide nuit. Elle a demandé elle même le nom
de chacun des objets dont elle savait le signe ; le nom des personnes de la maison, qu'elle reconnaissait très bien d'ailleurs en
leur touchant la main.

"Marthe Obrecht ne voyant pas, n'entendant pas, avait donc
assez de finesse de tact dans la main, assez de puissance de
mémoire pour démêler et retenir une série d'impressions succes-
sives très variées, dont l'ensemble formait le nom de chaque objet,
de chaque personne. Elle avait assez d'énergie active dans l'intelligence pour isoler chacune de ces impressions particulières, de
ces formes fugitives que lui révélait sa main, pour discerner vingt-
quatre types différents correspondant aux vingt-quatre lettres de
l'alphabet, pour saisir leurs combinaisons indefiniment variées et
le plus souvent arbitraires. . . .

"Lorsque notre élève nous a paru suffisamment exercée à la
dactylologie, allant toujours à petits pas du connu à l'inconnu
nous lui avons fait toucher l'alphabet et l'écriture des aveugles, lui
faisant comprendre que c'était encore là un moyen de transmettre
et de fixer sa pensée et de s'instruire comme ses compagnes privées
de la vue. Nouveau rayon de soleil, nouvelles émotions fécondes,
et révélatrices pour cette chère petite âme. . . . L'enfant s'est mise
au travail avec une ardeur incroyable ; elle a très bien saisi la
convention établie entre l'alphabet manuel et l'alphabet pointé des
aveugles ; et bientôt elle a pu lire et écrire des mots et de petites
phrases. . . .

    "'MA BONNE MÈRE,
        "Je suis fâchée vous part vite embrasser rien, parce
que je vous aimé beaucoup. Je vous remercie oranges. Les
sourdes-muettes contentes manger oranges. La bonne Mère
supérieure est très malade, elle tousse beaucoup. Monsieur
médécin défend la bonne Mère se promener, je suis très fâchée. . . .
Je bien savante, prie pour vous bien portante. Sœur Blanche

children of parents and of a line of ancestors who could speak, and must therefore have an inherited tendency to language, with "a human brain, the structure of which has been elaborated by the speech of his ancestors." *
But, as we have already pointed out,† such an inherited nervous structure could not have facilitated either the beginning or the development of gesture-language. Yet it was *exclusively* by gesture-language that the latent intelligence of Martha Obrecht was developed.

We altogether repudiate, therefore, and utterly deny the alleged ‡ "important fact" that "thought is quite as much the effect as it is the cause of language." When we call to mind how intellectual gesture may not only exist without speech, but arise independently of inherited aptitude and quite spontaneously, we cannot but regard as absurd the asserted probability that "in the absence of articulation, the human race would not have

est mère pour Marthe, je prie pour Sœur Blanche. Je désir vous embrasser.

'MARTHE OBRECHT.'

"... Depuis deux ans Marthe a appris à écrire comme nous ; je vous envoie un second spécimen de son travail.

" Dans ces pages, ecrites comme nous écrivons, et qui me sont adressées, la jeune fille sourde-muette et aveugle me dit. . . .

"Quand je suis venue ici pour m'instruire, j'étais seule, je ne pensais rien, je ne comprenais rien, pour dire : il faut toucher tout pour bien comprendre, faire des signes et apprendre l'alphabet pendant deux ans. Après, pendant un an j'ai appris pointer comme les aveugles, maintenant je suis bien heureuse de bien comprendre tout. Depuis deux ans j'ai voulu apprendre écrire comme les voyantes, j'écris bien un peu. Quand je suis venué ici ma maman est partie ; j'ai été très colère et crié fortement. Les chères Sœurs m'ont caressé beaucoup, j'ai été moins colère, je les aime bien, elles sont toujours bonnes pour moi."

* p. 140.   † See above, p. 141.   ‡ p. 151.

made much psychological advance upon the anthropoid apes"!

We have no desire to quarrel with Mr. Romanes's further contention that gesture may aid speech, and speech give a higher degree of perfection and distinctness to gesture. Nevertheless, it is also true (as we have already remarked) that speech may starve gesture, and also elaborate gesture may diminish the fulness of speech. There appears, therefore, to be here no certain foundation whereon to build an *à priori* structure of inferences. But whether gesture favours or mars the development of speech, it is certain the latter could never have been originated by it. There must have been an innate, spontaneous tendency to articulate, or articulation could never have taken place. Our author, moreover, always writes as if mere motions by themselves could generate thoughts, yet nothing but thought already existing could ever generate those intentionally significant motions (gestures) whereby ideas can be readily expressed and easily understood.

Mr. Romanes next endeavours to meet the very obvious difficulty that, had reason and language the simple and accidental origin he assigns them, we ought to find other animals plainly on the road to reach the high level which man has obtained, and we ought not to find that great gulf which all parties admit actually exists between the speaking man and the dumb brute. He tries to do away with this objection by appealing * to what he calls "a fair analogy"—that of flight. He says, "Flying is no doubt a very useful faculty to all

* p. 156.

animals which present it," and yet only certain animals, and only bats amongst the class of beasts, have attained to it, though they all possess structures which might be modified into organs of flight. "Similarly," he tells us, "'the flight of thought' is a most useful faculty," but "it has only been developed in man." The analogy we do not admit. The utility of flight is as nothing compared with the utility of thought—as the experience of each autumn abundantly demonstrates in every county of England. A multitude of unfavourable conditions might check the development of wings, which would also be of little service to a whale, an ant-eater, or a mole. But as regards "thought," the case is not "*similar*," but quite *otherwise*. Not only can we see no reason why anything (disease or mutilation apart) should hinder its manifestation if it existed ; but we can also see that its possession must be the greatest possible gain. Nevertheless there is no animal which shows a sign of possessing it. Mr. Romanes himself says, "it has only been developed in man"! Much mistaken, then, was he when he wrote : "So far, then, as we have yet gone, I do not anticipate that opponents will find it prudent to take a stand." *

Hereupon follow statements of the "exact meanings" severally given by our author to what he terms (1) indicative, (2) denotative, (3) connotative, (4) denominative, and (5) predicative language. †

---

* p. 157.

† He tells us (pp. 161, 162), "By an *indicative* sign I will understand a significant tone or gesture intentionally expressive

Since our author does not, however, discriminate between material and formal understanding, making known, denominating, etc., his distinctions are useless, and cannot be accepted by us. As critics, we need only attend to them as far as may be necessary to apprehend fully the author's meaning, and to scrupulously avoid doing him a shadow of injustice.

His ninth chapter, that on speech, is the one for which, he tells us, * all his preceding chapters were arranged, adding, *mirabile dictu,* "Therefore, as already remarked, I have thus far presented material over which I do not think it is possible that any dispute can arise"!

As Mr. Romanes has adopted our classification of language, we regret, for the sake of convenience, that he did not, as we did, restrict his use of the term "speech" to denote rational expression which is exclusively oral. Mr. Romanes also includes under that term, rational expression by gesture. Nevertheless, he truly says,†

of a mental state; but yet not in any sense of the word denominative.

"By a *denotative* sign I will understand the receptual marking of particular objects, qualities, actions, etc.

"By a *connotative* sign I will understand the classificatory attribution of qualities to objects named by the sign, whether such attribution be due to receptual or to conceptual operations of the mind.

"By a *denominative* sign I will understand a connotative sign consciously bestowed as such, or with a full conceptual appreciation of its office and purpose as a name.

"By a *predicative* sign I will mean a proposition, or the conceptual apposition of two denominative terms, expressive of the speaker's intention to connote something of the one by means of the other."

* p. 163.   † p. 164.

"The distinction resides in the intellectual powers ; not in the symbols thereof. So that a man *means*,* it matters not by what signs he expresses his meaning : the distinction between him and the brute consists in his being able to *mean a proposition*," that is, "to make an act of judgment."

Mr. Romanes unintentionally misrepresents, and quite needlessly censures us for having said † that the simplest element of thought is a judgment. He evidently thinks we meant an *explicit*, instead of an *implicit*, judgment. Yet as an "explicit" judgment is manifestly made up of concepts, it is strange that he should have deemed us capable of an absurdity at once so outrageous and so evident. That the simplest element of thought is an implicit judgment, Mr. Romanes himself states ‡ plainly enough.

* See also "On Truth," p. 280. It is curious that Mr. Romanes criticizes Prof. Huxley's exceedingly sophistical remark about a machine which marks likeness and unlikeness, saying ("Critiques and Addresses," p. 281), "Whatever does this reasons ; and if a machine produces the effects of reason, I see no more ground for denying it the reasoning power, because it is unconscious, than I see for refusing Mr. Babbage's engine the title of a calculating machine on the same grounds." This remark Mr. Romanes declares absurd, but he excuses the Professor on the ground that "he must have been writing in some ironical sense, and therefore purposely threw his criticisms into a preposterous form." It was, however, by no means ironical, but a very serious work, which first appeared in the *Contemporary Review*, 1871, as a criticism of our "Genesis of Species," and an article in the *Quarterly Review*, on Darwin's "Descent of Man."

† In an address to the Biological Section of the British Association, in 1879.

‡ Thus at p. 168 he says, "Given the power of conceiving, and the germ of judgment is implied, though not expanded into the blossom of formal predication. For whenever we bestow a name

He further objects * to our remark † that when the mind perceives the truth expressed in the principle of contradiction, its intuition, or perception, is aided by "images" or "phantasmata" answering respectively to "a thing being" and "a thing not being," "at the same time" and "in the same sense," observing that such images "must indeed be vague." There is here an imperfect description. The "images" are not the direct, but only the indirect, support of the intuition. Its direct support consists of "recognitions" of past perceptions as to coexistences, and the recollections of the past perceptions themselves repose upon reminiscences (phantasmata) of the sensuous affections which first accompanied them.

Thus, as we said, such sensuous images or phantasmata by no means *constitute* the intuition, though without such sensuous elements underlying it and indirectly supporting it, no such judgment or intuition could take place.

Mr. Romanes, having misunderstood us to so extraordinary an extent, very naturally objects ‡ that the

we are implicitly judging that the thing to which we apply the name presents the attributes connoted by that name. . . . To utter the name Negro . . . is to form and pronounce at least two judgments . . . to wit, that it is a man, and that he is black." Again, he observes (p. 173) about our assertion that "the simplest element of thought is a judgment," as follows : " Of course, if it were said that these two faculties are one in kind—that in order to conceive we must judge, and in order to name we must predicate—I should have no objection to offer." Mr. Romanes could hardly justify our assertion more completely than by such statements as these. As to what is implied in the term "negro," see " On Truth," p. 137.

* p. 166 (note).
† Made in the same address to the British Association.
‡ p. 168.

distinction between animal and human intelligence lies in the power of "bestowing a name known as such" and forming a *concept*. In this we quite agree with our author, as also in his remark * that "in the very act of naming we are virtually predicating existence of the thing named," and that "the power to 'think is,' is the power concerned in the formation of a concept;" while it is also concerned (in spite of Mr. Romanes's denial) "in the apposing of concepts when formed."

Mr. Romanes denies† that the predication of existence is the essential or any *important* part of a full, formally expressed proposition. Rather, he tells us, "it is really the least essential or the least important. For existence is the category to which everything must belong if it is to be judged about at all." But because it is a category to which every actual thing must belong, it by no means follows that it is an *unimportant* category. Mr. Romanes might be deprived of objects and conditions belonging to various categories which might not matter much to him, but he could hardly say it was unimportant to him whether or not he was deprived of *existence!* He continues, "Merely to judge that *A is* and *B is*, is to form the most barren (or least significant) judgment that can be formed with regard to A and B." Of course it is manifest that so to affirm is to give the minimum of information about A and B; but though it tells little as to extent, it tells us a truth of the most profound and intensely important kind. Existence is an attribute which clings to everything to the very last, and clings to it in a certain form even when it has ceased actually to

* pp. 171, 172.   † p. 172.

N

be, since possible existence may still remain to it—as a fine head of hair to a man who has just had his head shaved. He says,* next : " When we bring these two judgments (concepts) together in the proposition *A is B*, the new judgment which we make has nothing to do with the existence either of A or of B, nor has it really anything to do with existence as such.   The existence both of A and of B has been already presupposed in the two concepts, and when these two existing things are brought into apposition, no third existence is thereby supposed to have been created."   Most certainly not.   What madman ever thought that by saying, " A cat *is* a carnivorous beast," he *created* even one existence ?   But, assuming that Mr. Romanes means, " No third existence is thereby supposed to have been affirmed," we may again ask, what madman ever thought that by saying, " A cat is a carnivorous beast," he *affirmed* a " third existence " ?   What is affirmed in such a predication is, that a cat is a real creature which possesses those attributes which distinguish the class of animals termed carnivorous.   Herein   actual   being   or   existence   is implied.   But the assertion might have been, " A mermaid is a creature half a woman and half a fish," and here   again   being   or   existence   is   implied.   But it is no longer actual, material existence, but *ideal* existence. Nevertheless, such ideal existence is really existence of a kind.   There is such an idea : my mind possesses it while I write, and whatever I actually possess must at least be.   Such reality in ideal existence must be admitted by Mr. Romanes, since   he   tells   us   " the

* p. 172.

existence of both A and B has been already presupposed in the two concepts." But the two things thus coupled can only be distinct ideally, since no two materially distinct existences can really be identically the same. We cannot say of two leaves the most alike to be found in a whole forest, that one *is* the other.

Mr. Romanes further contradicts himself expressly when he says that "the proposition A is B" has nothing to do with existence. For he has told us, "The existence both of A and B has been already presupposed in the two concepts." But if "existence" is supposed in each of the two concepts by itself, surely their conjunction cannot immediately drive such existence out of both of them ; and if not, at least as much existence as was in them separately, must be present in the express judgment their conjunction produces ! Mr. Romanes will hardly try to explain this confusion of thought by referring to his qualification "as such" in his phrase, "The proposition *A is B* has really nothing to do with existence *as such.*" Of course, no one is so absurd as to pretend that when we say A is B, our main intention is to call attention to, and to insist upon, the fact that A exists and B exists. No one could possibly mean that when we say, "A cat is a carnivorous beast," our main intention is to call attention to, and insist upon, the fact that a cat exists and a carnivorous beast exists. The meaning of the predication we have just stated, and we have truly stated also that existence is implied therein.

Every judgment, therefore, and every concept also, implies existence. That each judgment, indeed, does so must be admitted by every disciple of John Stuart Mill, who tells us * that the apprehension of the truth of any judgment we make is not only an essential part, but the essential part, of it as a judgment : " Leave that out, and it remains a mere play of thought on which no judgment is passed."   But if this is correct, every judgment must have to do with existence ; for how can anything be true which may not " be" at all !   When Mill denies, in the passage cited by Mr. Romanes,† that the copula in the affirmation, " Socrates is just," does not signify existence, he either contradicts himself (which is nothing new),‡ or he means that the signification of existence lies not in the " is," but exclusively in one or both of the two words, " Socrates," and "just "—which would be a very singular assertion.   The quotation from Hobbes (so highly approved by Mill), to the effect that " the placing two names in order may serve to signify their consequence, if it were the custom, as well as the words " *is, to be*, and the like " is very true, but tells in no way against our position.   The word " is," is full, indeed, of significance when it is used ; but it may be perfectly well understood, and its meaning truly exist, in sentences wherein no distinct word is set apart for its expression.

We repeat that we quite agree with Mr. Romanes in saying that the distinction between man and brute consists not in verbal predication, but in mental affirmation or conception.   " The subsequent working up of names into propositions is merely a further exhibition of the

* In his " Examination of Sir W. Hamilton's Philosophy," p. 346.
† " Logic," vol. i. p. 86.   ‡ See " On Truth," p. 247.

self-same faculty." * But, then, we do not mean by naming, what Mr. Romanes means ; because we are not, as he is, followers of "Nominalism." We read with amazement his remark about Realism, "which," he tells us, "neither those who think with Mr. Mivart nor any other psychologists with whom I have to do are likely nowadays to countenance."

He goes on, "If I do not apologize for having occupied so much space over so obvious a point, it is only because I believe that any one who reads these pages will sympathize with my desire to avoid ambiguity, and thus to reduce the question before us to its naked reality." We gladly take this opportunity to say we are sure not only that Mr. Romanes has tried to be clear, but also that he has succeeded. Ambiguous terms we have noted, but their ambiguity is due to no carelessness on Mr. Romanes's part, but to the fact that he has not yet succeeded in fully understanding the position of his opponents. "So far," he continues, "it will be observed, this question has not been touched. I am not disputing that an immense and extraordinary distinction obtains, and I do not anticipate that either Mr. Mivart or any one else will take exception to this preliminary clearing of the ground, which has been necessitated only on account of my opponents having been careless enough to represent the Proposition as the simplest exhibition of the Logos." As to this we have already remarked enough.

"Wherein," he then asks,† "does this distinction truly consist? It consists, as I believe all my opponents

* p. 174.   † p. 175.

will allow, in the power which the human being displays of *objectifying ideas*, or of setting one state of mind before another state, and contemplating the relation between them." To this we reply, it truly consists in the power of " objectifying ideas " in the sense of perceiving objects as real external existences, and so forming ideas or concepts: not, be it observed, in recognizing their objectivity; that is a further and a reflex act. We mean only that direct ideal apprehension which an ordinary child (who hardly yet reflects at all) enjoys when objects present themselves to his senses while his consciousness is not absorbed in other ways. Again, we deny that " objectifying ideas " is equivalent, as Mr. Romanes says, to " setting one state of mind before another state, and contemplating the relation between them." That is another very special kind of reflex mental act, and its presence is by no means necessary for the existence of true conception.

He adds, " The power to ' think is '—or, as I should prefer to state it, the power to think at all—*is the power which is given by introspective reflection in the light of self-consciousness.*" But the power " to think at all " must exist before " introspective reflection," or else the latter could never come into existence. If we never had any conscious ideas directly, how could we ever know by reflection that we had them ? Such a reflex act is strictly a *re*cognition, or a " consciously knowing over again " what we have " consciously known before." We could never learn by reflection that we had known what we had never been conscious of; for had we been unconscious of it, we could not have known it. It is true that we can know by reflection that we have had sense-impressions which did not, when we received them, rise into consciousness; but such impressions were not and could not be knowledge, but only some of the *conditions of knowledge.* Consciousness must accompany knowledge, but it need only be direct consciousness, and need by no means be reflex *self*-consciousness.

Mr. Romanes fully admits "that no animal *can possibly* attain to these excellencies of subjective life," but this he assures us we shall find to be due to " the absence in brutes of the needful *conditions* to the occurrence of these excellencies as they obtain in ourselves. From which," he tells us,* "it follows that the great distinction between the brute and the man really lies behind the faculties both of conception and predication : it resides in the conditions to the occurrence of either."

These conditions Mr. Romanes thinks to find in external circumstances, while we see clearly they reside in difference of kind or innermost nature. According to him, as we shall see, mere animals may give names, and his Nominalism tells him that whatever creature possesses names, possesses concepts also; since the latter are, for him, nothing but names.

But if a non-speaking, poorly-gesturing, unintellectual creature said " Di " when it saw a bear, how could that utterance, accompanying its plexus of sense-impressions, give it a power of " objectifying " that plexus ? But a creature endowed with an intellectual faculty, yet unable to say even " Di," would be able by gesture to

* pp. 175, 176.

make known its intellectual perception and conception of a bear, and these, as we shall see later on, might perfectly exist before the mind—by the help of imagined bodily motions—without the need of the imagination of any word. Apart from the intellectual faculty, the vocal gestures would be as conceptually meaningless as any other bodily gesture. They would remain simple recepts, and could never become " concepts." According to Mr. Romanes,* however, "concepts differ from recepts in that they are recepts which have themselves become objects of knowledge ; " and he adds, in a note, that some concepts "may be the knowledge of other concepts." But even as to the first kind, he tells us that the condition of their existence " is the presence of self-consciousness in the percipient mind." Here Mr. Romanes suffers from his failure to distinguish between direct "consciousness" and reflex " self-consciousness." Concepts, we affirm, are never recepts, though they are elicited by groups of sense-impressions ; and what he calls concepts of concepts, are concepts due to our conscious recognition (but not reflection on the fact of *re*cognition) of former perceptions of our intellectual faculty.

Mr. Romanes next states his reasons for denying a difference of kind between the psychical powers of man and brute, by "a careful analysis of conceptual judgment."

First, he addresses himself to the task of doing away with any distinction as regards naming. He tells us,† " When a parrot calls a dog *bow-wow* (as a parrot, like a child, may easily be taught to do), the parrot may be said, in one sense of the word, to be *naming* the dog ;

* p. 176. † p. 179.

but it is not *predicating* any characters as belonging to a dog, or performing any act of *judgment* with regard to a dog. Although the bird may never (or but rarely) utter the name save when it sees a dog, this fact is attributable to the laws of association acting only in the receptual sphere. . . . Therefore, all my opponents must allow that in one sense of the word there may be names without concepts : whether as gestures or as words (vocal gestures), there may be signs of things without these signs presenting any vestige of predicative value. Names of this kind I have called *denotative :* they are marks affixed to objects, qualities, actions, etc., by receptual association alone." We freely concede that in such a mere analogical sense vocal or motor phenomena of the kind may be termed " names," and they are to a certain sense signs, as smoke may be a sign of internal heat in a volcano.

He follows this by observing that such a name may be "extended to denote also another thing, which is seen [!] to belong to the same class or kind," when they become what he has called "*connotative*," and in this connection he refers back to his instance of the parrot and the dog, which we have already * criticized, saying,† " Even my parrot was able to extend its denotative name for a particular dog to any other dog which it happened to see—thus precisely resembling my child, who habitually extended its first denotative name *Star* to a candle." ‡ But this we altogether deny, and must

---

* See above, p. 157.   † p. 180.

‡ At p. 159 he had said, " One of my children learnt to say the word *Star*. Soon after having acquired this word, she extended its signification to other brightly shining objects, such as candles, gas-

defend Mr. Romanes's infant from its parent's unjust depreciation. The child did not, of course, think of the term "as a term," or set "the term before the mind as an object of thought;" that would be a highly complex reflex act. But it distinctly perceived (by a *direct* mental act) that there was a similarity of brightness, and so formed at once its concept, "bright things," of which concept, *Star* was the oral expression. It consciously made this (though not with reflex consciousness), and so its perception differed *toto cœlo* from the mere senception and materially felt likeness which caused the parrot to give forth, as the result of its plexus of similar feelings, the dog's name again. To say, with Mr. Romanes, that the parrot's utterance takes place because "another thing *is seen*" to resemble a preceding one, is ambiguous. That it is seen with the parrot's corporeal eyes, and impresses its consentience, is, of course, true; but we have no reason to suppose that because it is seen and felt, it is also *perceived*. Therefore, instead of "precisely resembling" the act of the child, the act of the parrot is something fundamentally different from it.

He continues, "Connotation, then, begins in the purely receptual sphere of ideation."

Now, by "connotation," as we have seen, Mr. Romanes means,* attributing "qualities to objects by means of a name," and this, he says, may be receptual or conceptual. But the parrot cannot be said to "attribute

lights, etc. Here there was plainly a perception of likeness or analogy."

* p. 162.

qualities," although by the unconscious use of a name
it may make us, who are conscious, recognize the fact
that certain qualities are present. He tell us * that
" it is obviously most imperative for the purposes of
this [his] analysis to draw a distinction between connotation as receptual and conceptual." It is, indeed, *most*
imperative, and the distinction consists in this : that receptual connotation is connotation improperly so called,
while conceptual connotation alone deserves the name.
The uniting together of these two psychical activities
under one general generic term is most misleading, and
again practically begs the question which Mr. Romanes
has to prove. However, he draws a further distinction,
which we are anxious to give him the full benefit of. He
says, " This distinction I have drawn by assigning the
word *denomination* to all connotation which is of a truly
conceptual nature—or to the bestowing of names *consciously recognized as such*." If by " as such " he does not
mean a reflex cognition that the name is a name, and so
intended ; but only that there is a direct consciousness
of naming, as of every other act, then we accept this
very cordially. Thus, as he truly says,† " the whole
question is narrowed · down to a clearing up of the
relations which obtain between connotation as receptual
and conceptual—or between connotation that is, and
connotation that is not, denominative."

He begins by considering what he calls " an instance
of undenominative or receptual connotation in the case
of a young child." Of course it is obvious that a child
at birth is not able to form judgments, as also that its

* p. 180. † p. 180.

latent intellectual nature is called forth into manifesta-
tation by the incidence of sense-impressions. This we
all agree in asserting. We say, however (as we laid
down in our introduction), that the ultimate outcome
proves the intellectual energy to have been latent from
the first.

Mr. Romanes truly asserts that * "analogies which do
not strike animals strike men." A child will say *Bow-
wow* successively of the house-dog, all other dogs, toy-
dogs, models of dogs, and pictures of dogs. He adds †
that in this "we have a clear exhibition, in a simple
form, of the development of a connotative name within
the purely receptual sphere." But this we altogether
deny. Such naming by the child is truly and formally
conceptual. Instead, then, of its being "absurd to suppose
that the child was thus raising the name *Bow-wow* to
any conceptual value," it would be absurd to suppose it
was not the sign of a direct universal ‡ and a perfect
concept. It is true that for this purpose, as Mr.
Romanes says,§ "there is no need for any introspective
regarding of the name as a name;" there is, indeed,
no need of any such reflex action, in order that a perfect
concept may exist. All that is needed is that direct consciousness which accompanies all our ordinary mental
activity, without our at all adverting to it. Truly may
Mr. Romanes say, "Nevertheless, it is evident that
already the child has done more than the parrot."

"Names," indeed, "may be . . . connotative in the
absence of self-consciousness," that is, of reflex con-

* p. 181.   † p. 181.
‡ See "On Truth," p. 206.   § p. 182.

sciousness, but direct consciousness there must be, otherwise the names only connote practically and materially
—as a sieve* practically and materially sorts. Such sorting, however, is fundamentally different from the sorting
performed by a man. Mr. Romanes urges,† "If we say
that a child is connoting resemblances when it extends
the name *Bow-wow* from a particular dog to dogs in
general, clearly we say the same thing of a parrot when
we find that thus far it goes with the child." No assertion could well be less warranted than this one. The
material resemblance between the two cases need mean
no more than the material resemblance between, say, a
sentence as spoken by a parrot, and the same sentence
as spoken by a grown man.

To serve his purpose and explain his meaning fully,
Mr. Romanes distinguishes‡ four classes of psychical
acts as follows :—

"(1) *Lower Recepts*, comprising the mental life of all
the lower animals, and so including such powers of receptual connotation as a child when first emerging from
infancy shares with a parrot.

"(2) *Higher Recepts*, comprising all the extensive
tract of ideation that belongs to a child between the
time when its powers of receptual connotation first
surpass those of a parrot, up to the age at which
connotation, as merely denotative, begins to become also
denominative.

"(3) *Lower Concepts*, comprising the province of
conceptual ideation where this first emerges from the

---

* See above, pp. 64, 67.   † p. 183.
‡ pp. 184, 185.

higher receptual, up to the point where denominative connotation has to do, not merely with the naming of recepts, but also with that of associated concepts.

"(4) *Higher Concepts*, comprising all the further excellencies of human thought."

For us, as before said,* the first of these four categories belongs to merely sensitive, consentional life. All the other three are fully and truly conceptual. Mr. Romanes seems to have some inkling of this from the fact that he proposes † to term his Higher Recepts, *Pre-concepts*, although he deems that they mark a stage of psychical life anterior to the advent of concepts and consciousness. He asks where else can he place the limit between brute and man except at the point "where the naming powers of a child demonstrably excel those of a parrot or any other brute," and he adds,‡ "If this place happens to be before the rise of conceptual powers, I am not responsible for the fact." Nor, of course, is he. He is only responsible for making the mistake of considering such children as being "below the use of the conceptual powers," when they are nothing of the kind.

Having made this statement as to concepts, Mr. Romanes naturally proceeds to extend his distinction to judgments, and classifies them § "as receptual, pre-conceptual, and conceptual." By the first, he says,‖ he means the "practical inferences" allowed by us to animals. "Also," he tells us,¶ "if a brute which is able to name each of two recepts separately

* See above, pp. 56, 59.   † p. 185.   ‡ p. 186.
        § p. 189.   ‖ p. 191.   ¶ p. 189.

(as is done by a talking bird), were to name the two
recepts simultaneously when thus combined in an act
of 'practical inference,' although there would then be
the outward semblance of a proposition, we should not
be strictly right in calling it a proposition. It would,
indeed, be the statement of a truth *perceived ;* but not
the statement of a truth perceived *as true.*" · But in a
true and formal judgment we need by no means distinctly advert to its truth, though it must *implicitly* contain the idea of truth, as Mill says. And if such a judgment of a brute did this, which it must do if it stated
a truth *perceived*, it would be a true, formal, conceptual
judgment.   But the junction of two things felt as
related, is by no means what we mean by a "practical
inference." As we before pointed out,* such an inference is only the revival of certain sensuous elements in
the imagination, occasioned by the fresh occurrence of
certain actual sensations, whereof such imagined ones
were, in past experience, the complement. We are confident, moreover, that no brute ever united vocal or
other gestures so as to form the semblance of a proposition. Mr. Romanes, indeed, tells us " that this possibility of receptual predication on the part of talking
birds is not entirely hypothetical, and then proceeds to
cite, as evidence in his favour, the absurd tale about
the cockatoo "Cockie" which was before † quoted and
commented on.

We find it thus quite easy " to meet " Mr. Romanes's
contention, although he thinks we shall not find it ‡ an
easy task so to do. We also venture to think that we

* See above, p. 63.　　† See above, p. 136.　　‡ p. 191.

have made good our complaint by showing that "there *is* something wrong in " his "psychological analysis."

He finally tells us,* " In the result, I claim to have shown that if it is possible to suggest a difference of kind between any of the levels of ideation which have now been defined, this can only be done where the advent of self-consciousness enables a mind, not only to *know*, but *to know that it knows ;* not only to *receive* knowledge, but also to *conceive* it ; not only to *connotate*, but also to *denominate ;* not only to *state a truth*, but also to state that truth *as true*." The advent of the faculty of intellect does, we hold, enable the mind to do all this, but it is enough to show its presence if this be done with direct consciousness ; a reflex act of consciousness not being necessary to prove the presence of intellect.

To make our relative position clear, Mr. Romanes's views and our own may be contrasted in a tabular form as follows :—

His	*Our*
Percepts, Perception	= Sencepts, Senception.
Lower Recept	= Sensuous cognitions.
Higher Recept	= Concepts and percepts as made known by the gestures of young children.
Lower Concepts	= Concepts and percepts as made known by speech or the gestures of adults.
Higher Concepts	= Conceptions concerning matters previously apprehended.
Receptual naming	= The mere unintentional, accidental making known of facts to intellectual onlookers.
Pre-conceptual judgments	= Judgments as made known by the gestures of young children.
Conceptual judgments	= Judgments of more developed minds, as expressed by either speech or voiceless gesture.

* p. 192.

CHAPTER IV.

REASON AND CONSCIOUSNESS.

IN our author's tenth chapter we at last come upon a consideration of that question which, in our opinion, as we before said,* ought to have been the first one treated of. The question to which Mr. Romanes's whole book is devoted, is the question whether the mind of man could have been developed from the psychical faculties of brutes, or whether it is fundamentally different—different in kind and origin.† In considering this question up to the point at which we have now arrived, he has again and again affirmed ‡ that the intellectual knowledge of self, or "self-consciousness" is the distinctive character of the human mind, and his task is to show that the difference thus admitted to exist is one not of kind but of degree. Almost at his first page § (in describing the scope and purpose of his book), he declares his intention to "examine" that "question of the deepest importance"—"the question whether the mind of man is essentially the same as the mind of the lower animals." An examination like this is, and must, of course be, an examination into the

---

* See above, p. 36. † p. 3, note †
‡ See, *e.g.*, p. 175. § p. 3.

essential nature of the psychical faculty in man and brute. Yet when he comes at last to apply himself to this fundamental question, he lays down his arms and proclaims his utter inability to attack it. "I am as far as any one can be," he tells us, * "from throwing light upon the intrinsic nature of that the probable genesis of which I am endeavouring to trace "!

But if he can throw no light on "the intrinsic nature" of the "mind of man," how can he pretend to decide whether or not it is "essentially the same" as what he calls "the mind of the lower animals"?

If, as he affirms,† "the problem of self-consciousness" is one which, however profoundly reflected on, "does not admit of solution," by what right does he venture to affirm that "self-consciousness" *is nothing more* than the further developed sensitivity of an ape or of an amœba?

He seeks to protect himself from the consequences of this confession of inability to attack the one only question of real importance for his cause, as we noted before,‡ by a profession of Idealism. With respect to such a profession we have a few words to say, and they are not at all intended to apply to Mr. Romanes himself, for we are firmly persuaded that he is honest and sincere. We are, however, no less persuaded that there are others who are not so, but who disingenuously seek to hide their really crass materialism behind a carefully painted Idealistic mask. A solemn profession of Idealism, made with the tongue in the cheek, enables its professors to throw dust in the eyes of anyone who may approach to inspect their proceedings too closely.

* p. 195.   † p. 194.   ‡ See above, p. 37.

Such men are enabled, by assuming the snowy fleece of an Ovine philosophy, to ravage the student flock very much at their own sweet will. It is easy for some materialists to profess Idealism. Let us assume, for argument's sake, that consciousness really is nothing more than the temporary accompaniment of a certain kind of matter under certain conditions. A man fully persuaded of the truth of such a system could none the less affirm : "Consciousness must be more certain about itself than anything else, can only know other things through itself, and may therefore regard itself as the most real of realities, or as the only reality." He may really hold and, by insinuations, inculcate materialism, while thus making a profession of Idealism all the time.*

In his profession of Idealistic faith Mr. Romanes

* In our work "On Truth" (p. 135) we have called attention to this double-dealing, and the whole second section of the book (pp. 71–141) is devoted to a consideration of Idealism. Some reviews of this section have afforded curious examples of the effects of prejudice and one-sidedness. We have been reproached for ignoring Green, Caird, Wallace, Bradley, and others, as if our contention had not been directed to a question much more fundamental than any with which the various schools of existing Idealists respectively deal. A man who saws through the trunk of a tree just above the root, may be dispensed from the task of lopping its individual branches. We have been absurdly accused of asserting that modern science cannot be accepted by sincere Idealists. What we have contended is that the ultimate analysis and interpretation of the facts of consciousness—our conscious experience—so indubitably affirms the action of efficient causation between bodies which exist independently of all human thought, as to render the fundamental position of every form of Idealism logically untenable. The carelessness or dishonesty of one reviewer has actually gone so far as to represent our definition of true or intellectual perception (given at p. 223) as being that which we have given (at p. 201) as our definition of mere *sense* perception.

declares * "that in the datum of self-consciousness we each of us possess, not merely our only ultimate knowledge, or that which only is 'real in its own right,' but likewise the mode of existence which alone the human mind is capable of conceiving as existence, and therefore the *conditio sine quâ non* to the possibility of an external world."

This is going too far: it is impossible, with reason, to affirm absolutely that the self-consciousness known to us by introspection is the only entity which is "real in its own right." Neither is it true to say that we cannot conceive of a world without self-consciousness. Of course, being always self-conscious when thinking, we cannot think of a world without consciousness, save by the help of consciousness—in other words, we cannot think without thought. To say this, however, is trivial. Although we cannot think without thought, we can none the less conceive of the absence of self-consciousness from the world, as is shown by the fact that there have been and are thinkers who profess materialism ; as well as Idealists who, with Hegel, held that God becomes conscious of Himself in man.

We have already referred to a mistake made by Mr. Romanes as to what are the necessary conditions and effects of self-consciousness. This error appears most plainly developed in the present chapter. Therein he most truly observes that it is only in man that we can study the gradual manifestation of consciousness, but it is especially unfortunate that he seems here to

* p. 194. Readers should study Prof. Veitch's excellent work, "Knowing and Being," recently published.

identify it with reflex mental action. He says,* " It will, I suppose, on all hands be admitted that self-consciousness consists in paying the same kind of attention to internal or psychical processes as is habitually paid to external or physical processes—a bringing to bear upon subjective phenomena the same powers of perception as are brought to bear upon the objective."

But this is an utter mistake. If we could not be self-conscious directly, or without holding up a previous mental act and recognizing it, we could never be self-conscious at all. For whatever consciousness we have of an act performed, must itself be either direct or reflex. If it be affirmed to be direct, why should we deem it more difficult to have been directly conscious of the first mental act than of the second? If it be affirmed to be necessarily reflex, then how can we ever obtain any knowledge of it? If reflex consciousness is absolutely necessary in the first case, it must be so likewise in the second, and so again for the second act, and so on *ad infinitum.* We must be able to know with consciousness, directly, or we can never consciously know at all !

He says,† next, "Again, I suppose it will be further admitted that in the minds of animals and in the minds of infants there is a world of images standing as signs of outward objects ; and that the only reason why these images are not attended to unless called up by the sensuous associations supplied by their corresponding objects, is because the mind is not yet able to leave the ground of such association, so as to

* pp. 195, 196.   † p. 196.

move through the higher and more tenuous medium of introspective thought." We object to the above expression, "standing as signs of outward objects." We admit the existence in animals of groups and groups of groups of imaginations, and that they have a material relation to the objects which produced them and may result in exciting various results ; but we deny that any animal ever recognizes any objects in the same sense as children do, therefore we would keep clear of the suspicious word, " sign "—particularly suspicious as used by Mr. Romanes, who has never defined the meaning he gives to that term.

He next proceeds to observe * that " the foundations of self-consciousness are largely laid in the fact that an organism is one connected whole. . . . Hence a brute, like a young child, has learnt to distinguish its own members, and likewise its whole body from all other objects." Here we must explain : It has, of course, feelings of activity and passivity, self and not-self,† but need not on that account have a scintilla of consciousness. Similarly it may, by a loose analogy, be said to "know how to avoid sources of pain " and to "seek those of pleasure." But Mr. Romanes himself says, " Such knowledge and such experience all belong to the receptual order," and this order, as we have several times pointed out, is no case of true knowledge. He continues,‡ "But this does not hinder that they play a most important part in laying the foundations of a consciousness of individuality." Of course not! All sensation " plays a most important part in laying the

* p. 197.   † See " On Truth," p. 190.   ‡ p. 197.

foundations" for intellectual action, just as all mere vegetative vitality "plays a most important part in laying the foundations" for the exercise of sensitivity, and just as the power of chemical action, or even of physical energy, "plays a most important part in laying the foundations" for vegetative vital activity. But this relation does not reduce vital action to mere physics, or sensitivity to mere vitality. These faculties remain distinct, and we have no reason to suppose a real transition or a fundamental identity to exist between them in any case. Neither, then, because sensitivity serves as a foundation upon which embodied intellect may act, does that fact give us any ground for concluding that sensitivity *is* intellect.

Mr. Romanes asserts,* as still more important, the fact that brutes can apprehend (have "recepts" in "reference to") *"the mental states of other animals."* This we deny. We admit they are acted upon by, and respond to, the sensations they receive through the *actions* of animals, due to psychical states of such animals ; but that is a very different matter. Our author cites Wundt as giving his opinion that "the most important of all conditions to the genesis of self-consciousness is given by the muscular sense in acts of voluntary movement." Mr. Romanes himself, while agreeing with Wundt "that this is a highly important condition," thinks that the others he has mentioned are "quite as much, or even more so." All these are, no doubt, as we have said, important or indispensable *antecedent conditions* to the evocation of consciousness,

* p. 197.

as fire is an important, indispensable antecedent condition to enable the genius of a distinguished *chef* to
furnish forth an artistic dinner. "That is to say," he
continues,* "the logic of recepts, even in brutes, is
sufficient to enable the mind to establish true analogies
between its own states (although these are not yet the
objects of separate attention, or of what may be termed
subjective knowledge), and the corresponding states of
other minds." This sentence, in spite of the words in
the parenthesis, is a most misleading one. We might
with as much justice and propriety represent a match
coated with a certain phosphoric compound, as capable of
establishing "a true analogy between its own" dynamic
state and the dynamic state of a lighted candle! He
goes on, "I take it to be a matter of general observation
that animals habitually and accurately interpret the
mental states of other animals, while they also well
know that other animals are able similarly to interpret
theirs—as is best proved by their practising the arts of
cunning, concealment, hypocrisy, etc." We take it for
granted that the "general observation" of a multitude
of persons interested in animals, but not experts in the
study of their own mental processes, does often lead
them to form such mistaken inferences. But they are
inferences which the facts do not suffice to prove, and
which, if true, would overthrow the infinitely wider basis
of experiment and observation which has convinced
serious thinkers since Aristotle, that animals are not
rational. That they act in many respects so as to lead
the careless or prejudiced observer to think they really

* p. 198.

have such perceptions and intuitions as those here attributed to them, is, of course, most obvious; but their actions, nevertheless, do not afford us any proof that they ever experience "perception" or form an "intuition" of any sort or kind whatever. Mr. Romanes quotes M. Quatrefages's relation, of an experience such as we are all more or less familiar with—namely, a dog playing with his master, and only biting him most tenderly. As to this M. Quatrefages says, "In reality it played a part in a comedy, and we cannot act without being conscious of it." To this assertion we reply, "*We*, indeed, cannot, but a mastiff may, and nothing in the tale appears to us in the least to indicate a faculty higher than that consentience we assign, in different degrees, to a mastiff and an earth-worm." Mr. Romanes follows up this citation with another extraordinary, gratuitous assertion. He says, "It is of importance further to observe that at this stage of mental evolution the individual—whether an animal or an infant—so far realizes its own individuality as to be informed by the logic of recepts that it is *one of a kind*. I do not mean that at this stage the individual realizes its own or any other individuality as such; but merely that it recognizes the fact of its being one among a number of similiar though distinct forms of life." This we strenuously deny. There is no shadow of reason for asserting that any animal "recognizes" any "fact," though, of course, it is manifest that their various feelings lead them to act in ways to a certain superficial extent similar to the ways in which creatures like ourselves would act. Many very lowly animals go in troops, and, of course, their movements are guided by feelings which differ according as such movements relate to themselves, to organisms of the same kind or to organisms of other kinds. "In this way," he tells us,* "there arises a sort of 'outward self-consciousness,' which differs from true or inward self-consciousness only in the absence of any attention being directed upon the inward mental states as such." But true self-consciousness by no means needs for its existence that it should be "directed upon the inward mental states at all," and, *à fortiori*, it does not need that it should be "directed upon the inward mental states *as such*." He goes on,† "This outward self-consciousness is known to us all, even in adult life—it being but comparatively seldom that we pause in our daily activities to contemplate the mental processes of which these activities are the expression." In order to avoid confusion, it may be well here to enumerate the states of consciousness that really exist. We have :—

(1) Reflex consciousness concerning our mental processes as such, as, *e.g.*, that in thinking, "That man is probably a thief," we are making an "act of judgment."

(2) Reflex consciousness as to what we think, but not as to the nature of our mental process itself, as when we say, "*I do* think that man is a thief."

(3) Direct consciousness, as when we think a man a thief, without adverting to the fact that we think so at all, and still less advert to the fact that in so thinking we are making a judgment.

But besides these states of consciousness, we may

* p. 199.   † Ibid.

also perform a variety of movements, often complex, owing to the incidence of sensations in the arousing of emotions without consciousness, and such mere results of sensitivity have been distinguished by Mr. Lewes and ourselves * as *consentience*, which we freely allow to animals, and deem amply sufficient to account for all their highest psychical states and the various external manifestations thereof.

Mr. Romanes, on the other hand, fails to distinguish between direct self-consciousness and consentience, saying, † "Receptual or outward self-consciousness, then, is the practical recognition of self as an active and a feeling agent; while conceptual or inward self-consciousness is the introspective recognition of self as an object of knowledge, and, therefore, as a subject." We repeat, direct consciousness is *not* introspective. It does not think without knowing what it thinks about, but without expressly directing its attention to what it is doing. In a note Mr. Romanes quotes from Wundt as replying "to the objection that there can be no thought without knowledge of thought," by saying, "that before there is any knowledge of thought there must be the same order of thinking as there is of perceiving, prior to the advent of self-consciousness." But we deny that there is any "perception" without consciousness other than mere "sense-perception;" which is only called perception by analogy. Probably Wundt means that before reflex thought, there must be direct thought, which is true; as well as that before we can think even directly, there must be antecedent sensitivity in exercise, which is also

* See "On Truth," pp. 183, 354.   † pp. 199, 200.

truc. But sensitivity in exercise is not "thought." If animals had consciousness they would make for themselves conceptual signs of one kind or another, and not merely emotional expressions.

Our author next says,* "I take it, then, as established that true or conceptual self-consciousness consists in paying the same kind of attention to inward psychical processes as is habitually paid to outward physical processes." This error we have already forestalled† in our preceding distinction of "direct" from "reflex" consciousness.

He then tells us,‡ "All observers are agreed that for a considerable time after a child is able to use words as expressions of ideas, there is no vestige of true self-consciousness."

This is an amazing assertion. Children often exhibit their self-consciousness in an unmistakable manner, long before they can use words. A boy may very likely have "bitten his own arm"—as Professor Preyer is quoted as relating; but that does not show an absence of self-consciousness. Even a grown man has struck his own head and inflicted other injuries on his body without thereby giving us the least reason to suppose he did not know full well that it *was* his own body. Mr. Romanes makes,§ as we have before noted, the fact of a child's speaking of itself in the first person the sign of the advent of self-consciousness and conceptual power.‖ But when a child speaks of himself

* p. 200.   † See above, pp. 197, 202.
‡ p. 200.   § p. 201.
‖ At p. 230, "self-consciousness" is explicitly stated to be "the very condition to the occurrence of conceptual ideation."

as "Jimmy," it is absurd to suppose he does not understand that *he* is Jimmy, and that Jimmy is himself.

Mr. Romanes really attaches an altogether absurd
importance to the saying of "I." We cannot, of
course, intelligently say it without having a concept
of self, but we cannot intelligently say anything else
without having a concept thereof. The idea of self
is by no means so exceptionally gifted that it alone
of all things is able to evoke mental conception. Any
object indicated by either voice or gesture as being
one of a kind, or being in any particular state, is the
result of a concept, and the index of the presence of
"conceptual ideation." If a thing is not known to be of
any kind or in any state at all, it is not known, but if it
is understood, it must be understood by the medium of
a concept. Any object whatever will serve to give rise
to a concept equally well with the object "self," to which
Mr. Romanes thus attributes such factitious importance.

He further observes,* "It will no doubt be on all
hands freely conceded, that at least up to the time when
a child begins to speak it has no beginning of any
true or introspective consciousness of self."

We concede nothing of the kind, but rather think
that in all cases self-consciousness precedes, and may
for a long time † precede, speech.

Anecdotes of child-language will be more conveniently considered in our next chapter, but we cannot

---

* p. 202.

† Amongst my own friends I know a very striking instance in
confirmation of this. A youth (now a very distinguished medical
man) was long unable to speak after he was able to express most
plainly by gesture-language, what related to his own individuality.

refrain altogether from noticing here some instances quoted from Mr. Sully, as follows :—

"When a child of eighteen months on seeing a dog exclaims, 'Bow-wow,' or on taking his food exclaims, 'Ot' (Hot), or on letting fall his toy says, 'Dow' (Down), he may be said to be implicitly framing a judgment : 'That is a dog,' 'This milk is hot,' 'My plaything is down.' . . . The boy . . . we will call C., was first observed to form a distinct judgment when nineteen months old, by saying, 'Dit ki' (Sister is crying)."

But we deny that any distinction as to explicitness or implicitness is conveyed by the distinction between the utterances of these children of eighteen months and nineteen months respectively. Indeed, we regard the attempt to draw such a distinction as a most absurd attempt. "Dit ki" is admitted to be the expression of a distinct judgment. Now, in what respect does the utterence of the monosyllable "Ot" differ from "Dit ki"? It merely differs in the emission of two sounds instead of one, but the one sound, "Ot," means as much as do the two sounds "Dit ki." The sound "Ot" was understood by those present to predicate heat of the food, and no one, out of Bedlam, can question that the child meant to convey the notion that its food was hot. But, as Mr. Romanes has most truly observed,* it is what is *meant*, not what is *said*, which is the really important matter.† It comes to this, then—that a sentence is conveyed in the one instance by two sounds,

---

* p. 164.

† Even adults often express a full judgment by a single word. Suppose two men are watching birds not distinctly to be seen, and trying to make out what they are. When one man, having made

and in the other by the utterance of a monosyllable. The latter mode is only inferior in so far as it seems incapable of being adapted to express the complex ideas of later life.   If it were only possible to follow out that mode without confusion, then the use of mono-syllables to express whole sentences, instead of being inferior, would be the very highest ideal of language.

Of course, as children grow up, they more and more conform to their environment and imitate the adults about them, and it is, as we have said, practically much more convenient to use distinct articulate sounds to express the several ideas involved in a sentence.   Thus it is natural enough that a child somewhat older should say, "Ka in milk (Something nasty in the milk); milk dare now (There is still some more milk in the cup)," and so on; also that a child, "towards the end of the second year," should say, "Dat a big bow-wow (That is a large dog); Dit naughty * (Sister is naughty)," and " Dit dow ga (Sister is down on the grass)."

It was with little short of amazement that we read Mr. Romanes's comment † on these facts :—

"Were it necessary, I could confirm all these state-ments from my own notes . . . but I prefer . . . to quote such facts from an impartial witness.   For *I conceive that they are facts of the highest importance*‡ in relation to our present subject."

---

sure, cries out "Grouse !" is that less truly the expression of a judgment than saying, " They are grouse " ?

* It is very difficult to see what important difference exists between the nineteen months expression, " Dit ki," and the nearly two year old expression, " Dit naughty."

† p. 203.   ‡ The italics are ours.

He then proceeds to "show" their importance, observing—

"We have now before us unquestionable evidence
that in the growing child there is a power, not only of
forming, but of expressing a pre-conceptual judgment,
long before there is any evidence of the child presenting
the faintest rudiment of internal, conceptual, or true
self-consciousness."

We have now before us, to our judgment, unquestionable evidence that in the growing child there is
consciousness and a power of conception, long before
there is any power of speech whatever; as also that
clearly conceived judgments are explicitly made known
sometimes by the utterance of two sounds, and sometimes by a mere monosyllable, as is frequently the case
with adults also—even Fellows of the Royal Society.
Therefore, instead of saying with Mr. Romanes [*] that
expressions of children are *not* examples of "true predication in the sense of being the expression of a true
or conceptual judgment," because the child using them
has not yet spoken of itself as "I," we say that, being
at once true predications—true conceptual judgments—
they prove that self-consciousness preceded them, in
spite of the very unnecessary habit of using the term
"I" not having come into use.   He tells us [†] that the
child's expression, "Mama pleased to Dodo," would have
no meaning as spoken by a child, unless the child knew
"what is the state of mind he thus attributes to another."
So when the child Dodo further says, "Dodo pleased
to mama," he is conscious that he is pleased.   Mr.

[*] p. 205.   [†] p. 206.

Romanes says, "Thus the child is enabled to fix these states before his mental vision as things which admit of being denoted by verbal signs." We do not say this : The child thinks nothing of "signs," or his own mental states *as such.* To do that would be to make acts of reflex consciousness. But he knows well enough he is pleased, and means to make it known ; and this he could not do had he not self-consciousness.

Mr. Romanes quotes the late Mr. Chauncey Wright as saying, "It does not appear impossible that an intelligent dog" may be aided by purposely directing its attention to the accessories of a spot where a lost bone may have been buried.

Attention, in the sense of what we have called "sensuous attention"* (or the intensifying of the looking, by some object associated with the lost bone striking the senses), is one thing, but true or intellectual attention is quite another thing.

With respect to the development of self-consciousness, Mr. Romanes affirms it to be "gradual," because "the process is throughout of the nature of a growth."

In this connection, however, comes a passage † to which we think it desirable to call special attention. It is as follows :—

"Nevertheless, there is some reason to think that when this growth has attained a certain point, it makes, so to speak, a sudden leap of progress, which may be taken to bear the same relation to the development of the mind as the act of birth does to that of the body. . . . Midway between the slowly evolving phases

See "On Truth," pp. 198, 219.　　† p. 208.

P

in utero, and the slowly evolving phases of after-growth, there is in the case of the human body a great and sudden change at the moment when it first becomes separated from that of its parent. And so, there is some reason to believe, it is in the case of the human mind."

We by no means accept the analogy as here given, but we deem it well to note this admission of a sudden leap in psychical human development. In *principle* it admits all we demand, and may be regarded as a case resembling that other sudden leap of evolution, before referred to *—the junction of the spermatozoon and the ovum, etc. † The existence of some real changes of kind in nature can hardly be denied by the consistent biologist, and we have seen ‡ how strongly even Mr. Wallace has quite recently affirmed their existence. But a change of kind must be sudden. An essential nature is, or it is not. It can never partly be and partly not be.

Mr. Romanes employs here, as in his former work, the uncouth and somewhat repulsive term "ejects," to denote the feelings accompanying a creature's spontaneous activities, and readily appreciated by other creatures seeing them. He says § he desires to "lay particular stress upon the point, which I do not think has been sufficiently noticed by previous writers—namely, the ejective origin of subjective knowledge." He regards such appreciation as hereditary, as shown by "the smile of an infant in answer to a caressing tone,

* See above, p. 12.

† As to these sudden psychical changes occurring in nature, see " On Truth," pp. 458, 439, 507, 508.

‡ See above, pp. 10, 27.   § p. 209.

and its cry in answer to a scolding one." It is this, he thinks, which leads savages to endow inanimate objects and the forces of nature with psychical attributes, and he finds further evidence of it "in the fact of psychological analysis revealing that our idea of cause is derived from our idea of muscular effort." *

This tendency, he adds, † leads man "in his early days" to regard the Ego as an ejection, resembling the others of his kind by whom he is surrounded, and he regards Max Müller's generalization that "I" is traceable to the expression, "This one," as "additional and more particular evidence of the originally ejective character of the idea of self." This we must reluctantly declare to be, to our judgment, simply nonsense. That men should be apt to attribute life to what is inanimate is but an instance of the law that we judge by experience, and that motion is commonly a sign of vitality. It is the same law which leads us spontaneously to judge other persons and things by ourselves. That animals instinctively apprehend in their way the dispositions of others, is surely a very simple form of Instinct. But to regard the "idea of self" as really made up of an assemblage of "ideas of other people," is like saying that a straight line is made up of a number of crooked ones, or that a collection of a number of musical instruments, all silent, could produce sound.

---

* Would Mr. Romanes, then, say that from such analogies he has good cause to disbelieve in Cause? For what we believe to be the true relation of our feelings of effort, etc., to our apprehension of causation, see "On Truth," pp. 48–52.

† p. 211.

Wundt says, "It is only after the child has distinguished by definite characteristics its own being from that of other people, that it makes the further advance of perceiving that these other people are also beings in and for themselves." This Mr. Romanes quotes, adding, very remarkably, "Now, this I do not question, although I do not think there can be much before or after in these two concepts." This sentence is indeed remarkable, since Wundt's position is simply fatal to that of Mr. Romanes. However quickly the idea of other people may come after the idea of self, the fact of such ideas coming *after* at all is absolutely fatal to the idea that what precedes them can be due to them and composed of them. Whether or not Wundt is justified in saying that a child must first distinguish its own being by definite characteristics, we regard it as absolutely certain that it could not have a conception of other people without also having a conception of itself also.

Nothing in Mr. Romanes's chapter on self-consciousness, even tends to show us how the gulf between mere sensitivity and intellect can be bridged over; or how consciousness can have arisen by any natural process whatever. We have, of course, long known that there are certain conditions antecedently necessary for its manifestation in man—such as mechanical forces, chemical energies, life, and sensitivity—but none or all of these suffice to explain consciousness, the origin of which remains shrouded in mystery as inscrutable to mere physical science as the origin of sensitivity, life, or physical energy itself. We see it there, where it shows itself in our fellow-men, and we note its increasingly clear manifestation in infancy. We can, indeed, make rational, and (we are convinced) perfectly valid, inferences as to its origin, just as our own mind can reveal to us its nature ; but its origin is entirely removed from that field of observation which is furnished to us by a study of the physical and psychical powers of merely animal life.

CHAPTER V.

REASON AND THE INFANT.

IN his eleventh chapter Mr. Romanes applies himself directly to the task of endeavouring to show how intellect is developed in the infant, from a state in which that faculty is non-existent. This he calls "the transition in the individual." We have already had to consider briefly and by anticipation, some statements made and anecdotes given by our author in support of his view; but here we have to consider its full and complete enunciation. From our position, as stated in our introductory chapter,* it follows that we have no difficulty in understanding the fact which is patent to every one; namely, that intellect becomes gradually manifest, in what seems at first but a mass of living, sentient matter—the new-born infant. We, of course, affirm that it is thus evolved, simply because it was *potentially* there from the first. Mr. Romanes would probably reply that he also regards it as potentially present in the infant, adding that it is potentially present in the brute also. He might possibly make a further distinction, and say that intellect is so potentially present in the child that but little is wanted to make it active and manifest, but that

* See above, p. 8.

it could only be developed into active manifestation in the remote descendants of any existing brute—descendants which should be submitted to a series of influences and conditions more or less similar to those which evolved it in the earliest intellectual ancestors of man. This would be the old scholastic distinction between *in potentia ad actum* and *in potentia ad esse*. Our position is that intellect is really *in esse* in the infant, though it is but *in potentia ad actum*, while in the brute we deny that there are grounds for asserting it to be potentially present in either sense of the term "*in potentia*." We would not venture dogmatically to affirm that God cannot have given to brutes a truly intellectual nature ; but there is no evidence that they do possess it—even the highest of them in their adult condition. All evidence, as far as it goes, is also against the possibility of such a thing having been brought about even by Omnipotence, since it would seem to involve an objective contradiction.*

Mr. Romanes's view is a very different one. He says at the outset † of this chapter, "Is it conceivable that the human mind can have arisen by way of a natural genesis from the minds of the higher quadrumana ? I maintain that the material now before us is sufficient to show, not only that this is conceivable, but inevitable."

It would be enough, then, to refute Mr. Romanes, to show, not that his conclusions are false, but merely that they are not necessary ones—that the facts are

* See "On Truth," pp. 385, 468.
† p. 213.

susceptible of another interpretation. We hope to do more than this.

Mr. Romanes begins his task by reiterating what no one dreams of denying, namely, that we share with animals our lower mental powers, and that differences between various conditions of the human intellect are but differences of degree. "The only question, then, that obtains is," he tells us, "as to the relation between the highest recept of a brute and the lowest concept of a man."

He then proceeds to recall to his reader's recollection his preceding exaggeration about the counting crow and the ape which discovered the "mechanical principle" of the screw,* statements which we have already criticized.† These "intelligent" animals he compares with the picture his imagination draws of palæolithic man, who, he tells us,‡ for "untold thou-

---

* Mr. Romanes says (p. 214), "Even here there is nothing to show that the monkey ever *thought* about the principle *as* a principle; indeed, we may rest well assured that he cannot possibly have done so, seeing that he was not in possession of the intellectual instruments—and, therefore, of the *antecedent conditions*—requisite for the purpose. All that the monkey did was to perceive receptually certain analogies : but he did not *conceive* them, or constitute them objects of thought *as* analogies. He was, therefore, unable to *predicate* the discovery he had made, or to set before his own mind as knowledge the knowledge which he had gained." We quote this passage in our desire to do full justice to Mr. Romanes ; but when we recollect that he denies conceptual power to any being which cannot speak of itself in the first person, his admission as to the limited powers of the monkey becomes valueless. Moreover, at p. 60, he has said (referring to this very same ape) that the "logic of recepts" is "able to reach generic ideas of *principles*, as well as of objects, qualities, and actions."

† See above, pp. 79, 86.   ‡ p. 214.

sands of years made no advance upon the chipping of flints." We would by no means be understood as denying the truth of this assertion,* but we regard it as one made somewhat too hastily. We have not yet met with evidence sufficiently decisive as to so prolonged a residence of palæolithic man in one region, nor do we see why palæolithic and neolithic man may not have existed simultaneously in different regions, just as "bronze" men and "iron" men, or even "bronze" men and "gunpowder" men did, ages afterwards.

After some pleasantry concerning our supposed "slovenly error" (elsewhere called "inexcusable") about "the simplest element of thought," † and after recapitulating assertions about animal language, Mr. Romanes proceeds to address himself to what he declares is, in his apprehension, "the central core of the question," and to give additional instances of what he calls "receptual and preconceptual ideation" on the part of infants. He tells us ‡ a daughter of his, aged eighteen months, gave the proper baby names to sheep, cows, pigs, etc., whether seen in unfamiliar picture-books, or on wall-papers or chair-covers in strange houses. In doing this we consider her to have made deliberate conscious affirmations concerning things whereof she had formed true concepts. Somewhat later, having called first her brother and then other children "Ilda," "whenever she

* See above, p. 33.

† The assertion that "an explicit judgment" was "the simplest element of thought" would have been much worse than "slovenly," had it ever been made. We have already explained ourselves upon this point. See above, p. 175, and below, p. 242.

‡ p. 218. See also above, p. 206.

came upon a representation of a sheep with lambs, she would point to the sheep and say, *Mama-Ba*, while to the lambs she would say, *Ilda-Ba*." Yet he ventures to affirm that in her case "speech in the sense of formal predication" had not begun. For our part, we consider this most distinctly shows true intelligence and pre-dication. Essentially there is no difference between such an affirmation and the most abstruse mathematical statement ever written down by a senior wrangler. Prof. Preyer is quoted * as saying that it is "a very general error" to suppose "all children on first beginning to speak use substantives only, and later pass on to the use of adjectives." Mr. Romanes's daughter "almost contemporaneously" acquired the use of a few proper verbs and prepositions. Yet he does not scruple to say (as we have seen) that in her case "speech in the sense of formal predication" had not begun! Her earliest gestures were, of course, very simple, but by the time she had attained two and a half years, she had deve-loped them into regular pantomime. "Coming into the house, after having bathed in the sea for the first time," she narrated her novel experience "by first pointing to the shore, then pretending to take off her clothes, to walk into the sea, and to dip: next, passing her hands up her body to her head, she sig-nified that the water had reached as high as her hair, which she showed me was still wet. The whole story was told without the use of a single articulate sound." Mr. Romanes observes † that "in its earliest stages, and onwards through a considerable part of its history," this

* p. 219.   † p. 221.

sign-making "is precisely identical with the corresponding phases of indicative sign-making in the lower animals"!   As if similar external movements may not be
due to very different internal causes, as in this case
the diverse results of the outcome of gesture-develop-
ment proves them to have been.   A man, a monkey,
and a toy automaton may take off the hat; but that
material sign of salutation is fundamentally different
in each case.   Dogs beg for water, and pull dresses
to open doors, and so far the movements of some young
children, of course, do to a certain extent resemble them;
but no one who will look into the eyes of such a child
can well fail to note therein an expression of meaning
and intelligence which not the keenest desires or emotions of a brute will impart to its organs of sight.*   But
even if this difference did not exist, the diverse outcome
is enough to make known an original difference of
nature.

Strongly, then, do we deny Mr. Romanes's assertion †
that "so far as the earliest phase of language is concerned, no difference even of degree can be alleged
between the infant and the animal."   It is wonderful
how he misunderstands the system of his opponents.
He asks,‡ "Will it be suggested that my daughter
had attained to self-consciousness . . . before she had
attained to the faculty of speech, and therefore to the
very *condition* to the naming of her ideas?   If so, it
would follow that there may be concepts without names,

---

* This has been repeatedly observed by me.   My attention was
first called to the fact by the late Dr. Noble, of Manchester,
author of "Mind and Brain," Churchill.

† p. 222.   ‡ p. 223, note.

and thus the whole fortress of my opponents would crumble away." Why, of *course*, we say there can be concepts without names. We have always strenuously affirmed it, and its affirmation, instead of being destructive to our "fortress," is the very rock on which it is built. Mr. Romanes says * that if his opponents do not "commit argumentative suicide" they must concede that the speechless infant is "confined to the receptual sphere of ideation." But instead of conceding this we have strenuously affirmed the very reverse.†

Having, then, so mistakenly assumed that self-consciousness must be reflex, and having attributed to the logical and conceptual gesture-language of children no more value than to the emotional manifestations of brutes, he says ‡: "The named recepts of a parrot cannot be held by my opponents to be true concepts, any more than the indicative gestures of an infant can be held by them to differ in kind from those of a dog."

Certainly, we are far indeed from regarding "the named recepts of a parrot" as concepts, but we none the less affirm that "the indicative gestures of an infant" are "different in kind from those of a dog"— just as "the indicative gestures" of the arms of a dog are different in kind from those of a telegraph post. External resemblance in action does not prove similarity of kind, if there is reason for thinking that the actions are respectively the result of influences which themselves are radically different in kind. The actions as external motions may be similar in appear-

* p. 225.   † See "On Truth," p. 234.
‡ p. 226.

ance, but as regards their real nature they may be fundamentally contrasted.

Mr. Romanes goes on * to consider that stage in the life of a child which he regards as anterior to the formation of true mental concepts, though a stage superior to the highest of those which mere animals can attain to. "Let us," he says, "consider the case of a child about two years old, who is able to frame such a proposition as *Dit ki* (Sister is crying)." This he affirms to be no truly intellectual act, but merely the bringing "*into apposition*" of two recepts (perceptions of its senses) which it has experienced simultaneously.

"The apposition in consciousness of these two recepts," he tells us, "is effected *for* the child by what may be termed *the logic of events:* it is not effected *by* the child in the way of any intentional or self-conscious grouping of its ideas."

Now, of course, Mr. Romanes does not here mean to deny that the child reflects on its mental act. Even adults very rarely do that. Such a denial, then, would be too absurdly superfluous. All he can mean to deny of the child, then, must be that direct, ordinary consciousness which attends all our everyday actions. Such a denial is, however, quite unwarranted. In saying *Dit ki*, the child gives expression (as we before said) to a true judgment. It is a judgment composed of two named concepts and an implied copula affirming through one concept, "ki," the existence of an action performed by an object, to which the other concept, "Dit," relates.

* p. 227.

The absolute enunciation of the copula "is" cannot be needed if we can see that it is meant; for, as Mr. Romanes has so well said,* so that any one *means*, the mode of expressing that meaning is unimportant. In such childish sentences as that quoted, the copula is evidently present in intention, though it may not be uttered, and as Mr. Romanes further on truly observes,† the greatest of all distinctions in biology is "potentiality." That is just it. It is the distinction between a nature which *can* and a nature which *cannot* form intellectual conceptions, which is the distinction between man and brute. But this latent power or "potentiality" can only be made known by the outcome. It is this which gives us such abundant reason for regarding new-born infants and defectively organized persons as potentially rational, and which justifies our denying rationality to animals, since they never show us they possess it—while we cannot doubt but that if they did possess it they would soon convince us all of that fact. We thus avoid both horns of our author's dilemma.‡

We conclude that the brute does not "judge," because it does not give the evidence of judgment which a child who says "Dit ki" does give. The child who uses that expression not only makes a judgment, but the things it affirms exist in its mind beside the judg-

---

* p. 164.   † p. 233.

‡ He says (p. 227), "I put to my opponents the following dilemma. Either you here have judgment, or else you have not. If you hold that this is judgment, you must also hold that animals judge. . . . If, on the other hand, you answer that here you have not judgment, I will ask you at what stage in the subsequent development of the child's intelligence you would consider judgment to arise?"

ment as well as in it. If they did not so exist, *i.e.* if the child did not consciously perceive both his sister and her crying condition, the statement would be mere meaningless babble. But, of course, the child does not advert to such psychical facts, and recognize what it says with reflex consciousness.

Mr. Romanes then attempts * to prove that there is no distinction of kind between what he calls preconceptual acts and true mental conception. But this is, of course, an utterly vain attempt, because every one who understands the position of Mr. Romanes's opponents knows that they affirm not only what he calls "preconception," but also what he calls "higher reception," to be truly conceptual. He distinguishes "ideation which is capable" of itself becoming an object of thought, from "ideation which is not" so capable—that which is denoted by speech being supposed by him to be alone so capable. But why cannot a statement made in gesture by a dumb man be thought of by him as being a statement? Mr. Romanes has himself declared that a deaf-mute had told him that he always thought by means of mental images of hand and feature movements, and therefore that deaf mutes *must* have thought of his statements as statements, *i.e.* must have reflected about them.

Finally, he deals with two supplementary considerations: (A) the first concerns † the great progress which can be made between childhood and maturity, and he concludes ‡ that "self-consciousness marks a comparatively low level in the evolution of the human mind." To show this he cites the case of his little girl

* p. 230. † p. 232. ‡ p. 233.

when four and a half years old, who when asked to say
what room was beneath the drawing-room of her home,
"first suggested the bath-room, which was not only
above the drawing-room, but also on the opposite side
of the house; next she suggested the dining-room,
which, although below the drawing-room, was also on
the other side of the house; and so on, the child clearly
having no power to think out so simple a problem,"
although she herself had wished to know what was
under the drawing-room. But this, in our eyes, did not
indicate a low level of intellect, but only a certain
incapacity for one kind of imagination. Such partial
incapacities are by no means rare. There are very good
classical scholars who seem unable to form for themselves the phantasmata they need in order to become
good mathematicians, and there are excellent mathematicians who have but a very feeble power of retaining
those sensuous distinctions which underlie, and are
needful for, classical proficiency.

Mr. Romanes continues,* "There is thus shown to be
even less reason to regard the advent of self-consciousness as marking a psychological difference of kind, than
there would be so to regard the advent of those higher
powers of conceptual ideation which subsequently—
though so gradually—supervene between early childhood
and youth. . . . Or, otherwise stated, the psychological
interval between my cebus and my child (when the
former successfully investigated the mechanical principle
of the screw by means of his highly developed receptual
faculties, while the latter unsuccessfully attempted to solve

* p. 233.

a most simple topographical problem by means of her lowly developed conceptual faculties) was assuredly much less than that which afterwards separated the intelligence of my child from this level of its own previous self."

Now, as to the cebus, etc., we have already made our criticism. But the answer to all this is given by Mr. Romanes himself a few lines later on, where he says (in words already quoted by us), "The greatest of all distinctions in biology, when it first arises, is thus seen to lie in its *potentiality.*" Once more, that is just it. It is, as we just said, the distinction between a nature which can, and a nature which cannot, possess conceptual power. Mr. Romanes completes his sentence by adding the words, "rather than in *origin.*" The meaning of these words is not clear. By this "potentiality" in which he declares lies the greatness of a distinction, he must mean the nature thus distinguished; for the "*potentiality*" cannot lie in "*the distinction itself.*" With this we fully agree. We have no objection to say also that such distinction lies more in the nature of an organism than in its origin. The distinction between a living man and a brute does, perhaps, lie rather in the distinctness of his nature from theirs than in his origin. For it is conceivable that the immaterial, psychical principle of any brute might have been formed by a distinct kind of action, as has been that of man ; but this similarity of origin would be of small account compared to the difference between these principles as regards their potentiality. On the other hand, had the human body been formed separately, but not endowed with a rational, but merely with a sentient nature, such a diversity of

Q

origin from the mode of origin of a brute would be of no account compared with the diversity between their innermost natures as revealed by their divergent capacities. This, however, cannot have been Mr. Romanes's meaning in the sentence quoted, which is certainly a very obscure one.

(B) His second supplementary consideration refers * to the fact "that even in the case of a fully developed self-conscious intelligence, both receptual and preconceptual ideation continue to play an important part." But this is what his opponents have ever distinctly affirmed, and we have reaffirmed it in our introductory chapter. Man is a sensitive organism ; an organism possessing vegetative powers ; a theatre of chemical changes, and a material substance manifesting physical properties—man is all this—as well as an intellectual being. Moreover, as we have also pointed out again and again, we have both consentience and simple, or direct, consciousness, as well as reflex consciousness. Mr. Romanes says,† "When I say, 'A negro is black,' I do not require to think all the formidable array of things that Mr. Mivart says I affirm." Certainly not! Nevertheless, whoever so affirms, affirms these things implicitly, and a very little examination suffices to show they were, and must have been latent, and to make their existence patent.‡

Certainly there is no need that we should "examine our own ideas" whenever we use rational language —direct knowledge, or consciousness, is enough to

---

* p. 234.   † p. 235.
‡ See "On Truth," p. 103, for implications contained in the assertion, "That is a horse."

constitute it such. It is also true that what we have learned with many an effort, may come afterwards to be done automatically, and it is lucky indeed for us that such is the case.* Were it not so, our time and labour would be incessantly occupied with the lowest stages of mental growth. Fortunately for us, after acquiring habitual *images* of objects, we acquire habitual *recognitions* of past mental acts, and so on, and thus the intellect is left free for higher activity, as we become able to do automatically, that which at first could only be done with much effort and great attention.

Here Mr. Romanes's psychological examination "comes to an end." † We think he has conspicuously failed to show that intellectual action (conceptual, pre-conceptual, or higher receptual) is "but a higher development" of the language of brutes. *À fortiori*, then, has he failed to show that such a development is, as he has said, ‡ "inevitable." But he has also failed to put before us any rational system of psychology, because he does not address himself to the real problem, having mistaken the true indication of self-consciousness. He has also failed because he does not distinguish between direct and reflex consciousness; because he attributes to brutes "ideas," and deems that perceptions generate recepts [!] (sensuous universals)—instead of being themselves intellectual acts of an intelligence which, with the aid of sense-impressions, perceives the actual presence of objects conceptually apprehended. He fails also, finally, because he ever greatly exaggerates the psychical faculties of brutes.

* See "On Truth," pp. 363, 364.   † p. 237.   ‡ p. 213.

CHAPTER VI.

REASON AND DIVERS TONGUES.

HAVING considered the infant mind, Mr. Romanes next turns to the very interesting study of divers tongues which various races of men speak or have spoken. He initiates his twelfth chapter very confidently. After asserting that he has refuted a position (our own) which he has entirely misunderstood, he adds * that the time has come when he "can afford to take a new point of departure. It is to Language that my opponents appeal: to Language they shall go." But the language to which they appeal is not that mere verbal predication which Mr. Romanes assumes it to be, but the external expression, whether by articulate or inarticulate sounds or by gesture, of internal intellectual apprehension. It is the *verbum mentale* which is alone important.

Our author here makes an observation which is not a little surprising. He tells us that "the new science of Comparative Philology has revealed the important fact that, if on the one hand speech gives *ex*pression to ideas, on the other hand it receives *im*pression from them." A "*new* science" was hardly needed to make this

* p. 238.

known: a fact which the whole school of Mr. Romanes's opponents have ever taught, and which we have
again and again insisted upon to ears and minds
evidently somewhat slow of apprehension.

In commencing his exposition of doctrines of
comparative philology, Mr. Romanes modestly dis-
claims any right to speak as an expert in that science.
We desire to make even less claim to any special knowledge on the subject. The criticisms we shall make,
however, do not require or depend upon any special
knowledge of that kind. We all admit that speech
changes and grows, and every assertion (not a repetition
of already noted errors) made about philosophy by Mr.
Romanes might be freely conceded without weakening
our own position. Still we think it expedient to
examine what follows, for although it is relatively
unimportant, the matter it deals with is valuable as
throwing some useful side-lights on the main question.
This is especially the case with some statements of Mr.
Romanes which we deem more or less interestingly
erroneous.

He says,* " Let it be noted that we are in the
presence of exactly the same distinction with regard to
the origin of language, as we were at the beginning of this
treatise with regard to the origin of man. For we then
saw that while we have the most cogent historical
evidence in proof of the principles of evolution having
governed the progress of civilization, we have no such
direct evidence of the descent of man from a brutal
ancestry. And here also we find that, as long as the

* p. 242.

light of history is able to guide us, there can be no
doubt that the principles of evolution have determined
the gradual development of languages, in a manner
strictly analogous to that in which they have determined
the ever-increasing refinement and complexity of social
organization.   Now, in the latter case we saw that
such direct evidence of evolution from lower to higher
levels of culture, renders it well-nigh certain that the
method must have extended backwards beyond the
historical period ; and hence, that such direct evidence
of evolution uniformly pervading the historical period,
in itself furnishes a strong *prima facie* presumption that
this period was itself reached by means of a similarly
gradual development of human faculty.   And thus,
also, it is in the case of language.   If philology is able
to prove the fact of evolution in all known languages as
far back as the primitive roots out of which they have
severally grown, the presumption becomes exceedingly
strong that these earliest and simplest elements, like
their later and more complex products, were the result
of a natural growth."

There is, of course, a parallelism between the course
of human speech and human intellectual conditions
generally, because the former is the explicit expression
of the latter.   But since, as Mr. Romanes most truly
says, we have no evidence (beyond inferential evidence)
as to the actual origin of man or of speech, it by no
means follows either that they arose by evolution, or
that their earliest condition was inferior to that of which
we have the earliest indication.   We have as much
evidence of decay and retrogression as of progression,

and even Mr. Herbert Spencer considers that all existing savages are degraded beings. It is hardly less improbable that primitive man was like one of the more degraded existing savages, than that he was what we should call highly civilized.

We are convinced we have certain evidence that man differs from every brute by a difference of kind, and if his nature is *essentially* different, his origin must also have been different, and there is an *à priori* probability that the difference as to the mode of his origin must run parallel with the difference of his nature. It may be that the earliest men in whose minds spontaneously arose the intellectual conceptions evolved by the aspects of nature, had clearer intuitions as to the real nature of things, and of the relations between them, than had later men, whose minds had become burthened with a multitude of conflicting impressions and opinions. That such is the case seems probable when we compare the clear, simple, yet profound conceptions of the Greek intellect, as exemplified by Aristotle, with the relatively obscure, involved, yet unsatisfactory philosophic speculations of our own day.

Mr. Romanes describes,* in an interesting manner, the Isolating, Polysynthetic, Agglutinative, Inflectional, and Analytic forms of language, and puts before us views as to their relative antiquity and inter-relations. He adopts Dr. Hales's suggestion † that new languages may have independently arisen from children who were isolated having accidentally lost their parents, and he supports his view by the assertion that languages

* p. 250.   † p. 260.

are most numerous in those most favoured regions—California and Brazil—where life might be most easily maintained by children thus circumstanced. We note this view without adopting it, but without any wish to contend against it. The facts * that "neglected children in some of the Canadian and Indian villages, and in South Africa, who are left alone for days, can and do invent for themselves a sort of *lingua franca,* partially or wholly unintelligible to all except themselves," and that "deaf-mutes have an instinctive power to develop for themselves a language of signs " (as we have before seen), well accords with the fact that man has ever an innate faculty for the external expression of internal conceptions.

In his thirteenth chaper, on roots of language, he quotes the one hundred and twenty-one given by Prof. Max Müller from Sanskrit. As to these he says,† "Scarcely any of them present us with evidence of reflective thought, as distinguished from the naming of objects of sense-perception." But they are, as he allows,‡ "concepts," always expressive of abstract or general ideas.

In a note§ he justly stigmatizes as "absurd " Prof. Max Müller's doctrine that "the formation of thought is the first and natural purpose of language, while its communication is accidental only." He very properly adds, "Such a 'purpose' would imply 'thought' as already formed." This may be quoted against Mr. Romanes himself, where he represents ‖ that

* p. 263.   † p. 273.   ‡ p. 269.
§ p. 274.   ‖ p. 83.

thought or reason is as much, or more, due to speech as speech to it.

Mr. Romanes remarks, after Prof. Max Müller, that the list of Sanskrit roots is composed exclusively of verbs. This is just what we should expect. For that of which all men are most immediately, constantly, and unreflectingly conscious, is their own activity or passivity.* We do not refer to feelings related to such states, but to direct, intellectual cognizance of them. This we think a noteworthy fact, however far these Sanskrit roots may be from being really primitive. Whatever may be their true date, they are, at any rate, the oldest we can, as yet, get at in language, and it is fair in the first instance to presume that the sort of words which are primitive in one or two languages are the sort of words which are primitive in all languages.

Mr. Romanes says,† "Words which were expressive of actions, would have stood a better chance of surviving as roots . . . because . . . more frequently employed, and because many of them must have lent themselves more readily to metaphorical extension—*especially under a system of animistic thought.*" "Metaphorical extension"! But what *is metaphor*, and what sort of being must have first employed it?

Had not the intellect the power of apprehending through sense, and expressing by sensible signs, what is *beyond* sense, metaphor would not exist. Neither would it exist if thought arose from language and followed it, instead of the opposite. It is precisely because speech is too narrow for thought, that words

* See "On Truth," pp. 16–27.   † p. 275.

are far too few to convey the ideas of the mind, that metaphor exists. It is interesting also to note that figurative, metaphorical language is natural and especially abundant amongst various uncultured tribes. We may conceive of primitive man, as it were, bursting with mental conceptions for which he had not adequate expression; he would have been spontaneously impelled into metaphor to a much greater extent and more universally than are the most metaphorical races of our own day.

Nothing could well be more unwise than to take the plainest and most material meanings of primitive words as being necessarily their only meanings. Figure, or metaphor, has been occasioned by poverty and sterility of visible or audible signs, but their *cause* is the wealth and fruitfulness of thought. Many primitive terms had thus, no doubt, double meanings from the first, and the mental and moral applications of hard, sharp, low, and high, were probably double accordingly. To this question, however, we shall return.*

As to "animistic thought," Mr. Romanes quotes,† in a note, as follows: "'It must be borne in mind that primitive man did not distinguish between phenomena and volitions, but included everything under the head of actions, not only the involuntary actions of human beings, such as breathing, but also the movements of inanimate things, the rising and setting of the sun, the wind, the flowing of water, and even such purely inanimate phenomena as fire, electricity, etc.; in short, all the changing attributes of things were conceived as

* See below, pp. 271–273.   † p. 275.

voluntary actions' (Sweet, *Words, Logic, and Grammar*)."

But this implies no defect of intelligence on the part of primitive man, who probably was far wiser in this matter than are many moderns. In ultimate analysis, all the phenomena of nature are to be recognized as really voluntary, being the result either of Divine volition or the permitted free-will of creatures. That the modes of expressing such a clear early intuition were defective, so as to have led to misinterpretation, is likely enough. To fancy, however, that primitive man, in attributing "volition" to fire, must have had a merely absurd meaning, such as ours would be were we to attribute volition to fire, may well be a mistaken fancy, seeing later differentiations of thought and expression had not yet taken place. In another note Mr. Romanes further says,* "There is an immense body of purely philological evidence to show that verbs are really a much later product of linguistic growth than either nouns or pronouns." But he, following Archdeacon Farrar, represents it as being "the correct view, that at first 'roots' stood for any and every part of speech, just as the monosyllabic expressions of children do." But if this was the case, such roots did practically include verbs. A *very* young child is conscious in acting and when being acted on, but predicates by monosyllables.

Concerning Prof. Max Müller's view that speech from its earliest origin must have been expressive of general ideas or concepts, Mr. Romanes remarks,†

* p. 275.   † p. 276.

" Now, of course, if any vestige of real evidence could be adduced to show that this 'must have been' the case, most of the foregoing chapters of the present work would not have been written.　For the whole object of these chapters has been to show, that on psychological grounds it is abundantly intelligible how the conceptual stage of ideation may have been gradually evolved from the receptual—the power of forming general, or truly conceptual ideas, from the power of forming particular and generic ideas.　But if it could be shown — or even rendered in any degree presumable—that this distinctly human power of forming truly general ideas arose *de novo* with the first birth of articulate speech,* assuredly my whole analysis would be destroyed: the human mind would be shown to present a quality different in origin—and, therefore, in kind—from all the lower orders of intelligence : the law of continuity would be interrupted at the terminal phase : an impassable gulf would be fixed between the brute and the man."

This is most true, but of course Mr. Romanes regards it as being so much evidence on his side.

He tries to weaken Prof. Max Müller's position by affirming † that the 121 Sanskrit roots are not "the aboriginal elements of language as first spoken by man."　But there is not the least need for us to suppose they were.　He is, however, unwarranted in making the assertion : "The 121 concepts themselves yield overwhelming evidence of belonging to a time

* We do not say this.　What we affirm is that with the origin of the intellectual faculty, external expression by sound or gesture, or both, arose also.

† p. 277.

immeasurably remote from that of any speechless progenitor of *homo sapiens ;* and in the enormous interval
(whatever it may have been) many successive generations
of words must *certainly* have flourished and died." Why
so ? we may ask. The assertion that such time must
have been "immeasurably remote" is a purely gratuitous
assertion ; as also is the affirmation that many generations of words " must *certainly* have flourished and died."
Supposing that speechless men did exist before speaking
ones, there is nothing to show they might not have
performed all the actions referred to in the list, and if
articulate speech began afterwards, then the 121 roots
might have easily been evolved in the "immeasurable"
period of (we should say) some twelve months at the
most !

He incidentally mentions * that Archdeacon Farrar
" has observed that the whole conversational vocabulary
of certain English labourers does not exceed a hundred
words," and adds, "Probably further observation would
have shown that the great majority of these were employed without conceptual significance. Therefore, if
these labourers had had to coin their own words, it is
probable that, without exception, their language would
have been destitute of any terms betokening more than
a pre-conceptual order of ideation. Nevertheless, these
men must have been capable, in however undeveloped
a degree, of truly conceptual ideation : and this proves
how unsafe it would be to argue from the absence of
distinctively conceptual terms to the poverty of conceptual faculty among any people whose root-words

* p. 280.

may have come down to us." This is *most true.* But to show what even an uneducated Sussex labourer (a mere cowherd) may be capable of, I will give the results of my questioning one, to elicit latent philosophical convictions of his, bearing on Idealism :

Myself. Lacey ! You often hear Sir Spencer Wilson's clock strike ?

Lacey. Bless you, sir, very often.

M. What do you think that sound is—something in the bell, something in the air, or something in your head ?

L. Why, something in the bell, sir, of course ; but the air has got something to do with it too, I think.

M. But when the clapper hits the bell it sets the bell shaking, that sets the air next it shaking, and so on to your ear, where it sets a very thin bit of skin shaking, and so you hear the sound.

L. Yes, sir.

M. Is there anything, then, in the bell altogether the same as your feeling of sound ?

L. Of course not, sir. Can't be.

M. And yet you say the sound is in the bell ?

L. Yes, sir.

M. Suppose every man and animal were dead, and the wind set the bell shaking, with no one to hear it ; would there be any sound ?

L. I can't answer that directly, sir ; that wants thinking about.

M. What was in the bell when it struck before would be in the bell when it struck now, wouldn't it ?

L. Of course it would, sir.

M. You say, then, that the sound is in the bell, yet nothing is there altogether the same as your feeling of sound?

L. That's what I say, sir.

M. You must mean, then, that the cause of the sound is in the bell, and that that cause is like, but not altogether the same as, your feeling of sound?

L. Yes, sir, that's just it; but the air has something to do with it too.

It seems to us that this rustic would be recognized by Aristotle as perfectly right in his philosophy of sound, and we consider that he is far ahead of Berkeley, Kant, or any other Idealist,* who has learnt *s'egarer avec méthode.*

As to the use of onomatopœia, Mr. Romanes very reasonably says that such words may easily become so disguised as to lose all trace of their mode of origin.

Noting facts as to a grandchild of the late Mr. Darwin, he tells us,† "The child, who was just beginning to speak, called a duck 'quack,' and by special association it also called water 'quack.'" It next extended the term to birds, insects, and fluids, and ultimately to coins, because it had seen an eagle on a French sou. These latter applications would truly show no trace of onomatopœia, but another remark is also to be noted. If this word "quack" was found amongst roots, how its real meaning would probably be underestimated!

The different onomatopoetic words which are used in different languages to denote the same thing, show

* As to Idealism, see "On Truth," Section II., and as to Sound and Idealism, see the same, pp. 114–118.

† p. 283.

clearly, as Archdeacon Farrar says,* "words are not mere imitations, but subjective echoes and reproductions."

M. Noiré's theory as to the origin of speech, so favoured by Prof. Max Müller, is designated † by Mr. Romanes the "'Yeo-he-ho' theory;" but he is ready to accept it as one form of onomatopœia. Yet he by no means assigns the origin of speech to any or all forms of onomatopœia. "If even," he says,‡ "civilized children ...will coin a language of their own in which the element of onomatopœia is barely traceable; and if uneducated deaf-mutes will spontaneously devise articulate sounds which are necessarily destitute of any imitative origin," why, he asks, should primitive man be supposed to have been only capable of mimicry? Why, indeed!

As to children of our own day, he truly says,§ "Even after the child has begun to learn the use of actual words, arbitrary additions are frequently made to its vocabulary which defy any explanation at the hands of onomatopœia—not only in cases where they are left to themselves, but even where they are in the closest contact with language as spoken by their elders." || When not controlled by their elders, children left much together may develop a newly-devised language, "unintelligible to all but its inventors."

He declares that, in any case, words were originally due to *psychogenesis*,¶ which we not only allow but assert.

In his next two chapters Mr. Romanes occupies

---

* p. 286.   † p. 290.   ‡ p. 291.   § p. 292.
|| He refers to his foot-note on his page 144.
¶ This term was, we believe, originally introduced by ourselves. See "On Truth," pp. 440, 509, 510, 521; also "The Cat" (John Murray), p. 526.

himself with what he calls "The Witness of Philology." *
Premising that his opponents place the psychological
distinction between man and brute in the faculty of
judgment possessed only by the former, he adds,† "I have
shown that, *by universal consent*,‡ this faculty is identical
with predication." With good reason we may object
to this statement, since he has actually quoted § from
us, amongst his categories of language, " Sounds which
are rational but not articulate, ejaculations by which we
sometimes express assent to or dissent from given propositions ; " also "Gestures which answer to rational
conceptions, and are therefore 'external' but not oral
manifestations of the *verbum mentale*."

He also says ‖ that he has been meeting his
" opponents on their own assumptions, and one of these
assumptions has been that language must always have
existed as we now know it—at least to the extent of
comprising words which admit of being built up into
propositions to express the semiotic intention of the
speaker." But certainly we have never made any
assumption of the kind.

" As a matter of fact," our author dogmatically informs us, " language did not begin with any of our
later-day distinctions between nouns, verbs, adjectives,
prepositions, and the rest : it began as the undifferentiated protoplasm of speech, out of which all these ' parts
of speech ' had afterwards to be developed by a prolonged course of gradual evolution."

* Chapters xiv. and xv.   † p. 294.
‡ The italics are ours.
§ p. 86.   See also " On Truth," p. 235.   ‖ p. 295.

He quotes Schelling as saying, "Die Sprache ist nicht stückweis oder atomistisch; sie ist gleich in allen ihren Theilen als Ganzes und demnach organisch entstanden," adding, "This highly general and most important fact is usually stated as it was, I believe, first stated by the anthropologist Waitz, namely, that 'the unit of language is not the word, but the sentence ;' and, therefore, that historically the sentence preceded the word. Or, otherwise and less ambiguously expressed, every word was originally itself a proposition, in the sense that of and by itself it conveyed a statement."

Now, here, in the first place, we would remark that on Mr. Romanes's Nominalist principles, if a thought is nothing but a word, and if the earliest and "simplest element of language" is a statement or judgment, then obviously the simplest element of thought must be a judgment. It is surely, then, somewhat unreasonable to reproach us with having been guilty of gross and "unpardonable" negligence, for asserting what Mr. Romanes himself not only asserts, but so places it at the root and foundation of his whole system, that to remove it necessarily brings down his own unstable intellectual edifice in utter ruin!

Our position is as follows :—

(1) Thought is the root of and primary to language, oral or other.

(2) Language is the external expression of the *verbum mentale.*

(3) The simplest element of thought is an implicit judgment.

(4) The simplest element of language must, therefore, also be the external expression of an implicit
judgment, *i.e.* a term.

Thus, that in primitive speech every word should be
an implicit judgment, is most natural, and what might
be expected. But much more follows from these premisses.

If Mr. Romanes's assertion could be proved true, it
would but make yet more glaring the distinction between the intellect of man and the highest psychical
power possessed by any brute. All language and all
ratiocination are but consequences of the peculiarity of
our nature, which consists of an intellect coexisting
with a material organism in one essential unity. It is
the less perfect, material side of our dual being which
alone necessitates either language or ratiocination. An
intelligence of a higher order than ours, capable of
energizing *without* an organism—which, as we experience it, is thus an impediment—could dispense with
both signs and ratiocinations, and would see latent and
implicit truths at once. Therefore, the less of either
may be needed for the perception of truth or for the
making it known, by so much the more is a higher
intellectual condition approximated to. Thus it is that
specially gifted intellects can attain, at a glance, truths,
to reach which less gifted natures need a long course of
demonstration. Thus, also, it is that some exceptionally
endowed minds can, with a few pregnant words, bring
to the minds of others perceptions which could be conveyed by inferior natures only by long and laboured
discourses. Therefore the minimum of language and

of reasoning which can possibly coexist with the due expression of thoughts and inferences is the best. Therefore, again, since the quickest and easiest signs are articulate ones, in an ideal language, every sentence should be capable of expression by a monosyllabic word, and every inference by the utterance of three monosyllables.

It is not at all true, or a matter *of course* that " the more that a single word thus assumed the functions now discharged by several words when built into a proposition, the more generalized—that is to say, the less defined—must have been its meaning." Such may or may not have been the case, according to circumstances.

Mr. Romanes cites * various childish expressions to support his view ; but, in the first place, primitive man was not a child nor in the position of a child, and a *very* young child does not adequately pourtray the mental condition of an adult human ancestor, any more than its body shows us what any adult human ancestor's body was actually like. In the second place, supposing a child does use the words, " Ta, ta," or " Ba-ba," or " Bye-bye," in more senses than one, we may ask, why should it not? It can do so quite as rationally as when, being adult, it uses the one word "box" in several senses.

Much that Mr. Romanes here urges might be questioned ; but for our purpose it is *quite* unnecessary so to do. We have thus no objection, for argument's sake, to concede that † " the earliest indications of grammar are given by the simultaneous use of sentence-words and

* p. 296.   † p. 297.

gesture-signs," or "that predication is but the adult form" of the sign-making of many a speechless child.

It is also quite true, as Mr. Romanes quotes * Prof. Max Müller as saying, that "*Va*, weave, whether as a reminder or as a command, would have as much right to be called a sentence as when we say 'Work,' *i.e.*, 'Let us work.' . . . A master requiring his slaves to labour, and promising them their food in the evening, would have no more to say than 'Dig—Feed,' and this would be quite as intelligible as 'Dig, and you shall have food,' or, as we now say, 'If you dig, you shall have food.'"

It may also be quite true, as the Professor is further quoted † as saying, that "if we watch the language of a child, which is really Chinese spoken in English, we see that there is a form of thought, and of language, perfectly rational and intelligible to those who have studied it, in which, nevertheless, the distinction between noun and verb, nay, between subject and predicate, is not yet realized."

Mr. Romanes tells us ‡ (and we have no objection) "that one of the earliest parts of speech to become differentiated" were pronouns "originally indistinguishable from" adverbs, and "concerned with denoting relations of place. . . . '*Hic, iste, ille*, are notoriously a sort of correlatives to *ego, tu, sui*. . . .' There is very good reason to conclude that these . . . were in the first instance . . . articulate translations of gesture-signs—*i.e.*, of a pointing to place-relations. *I* being equivalent to *this one, he* or *she* or *it* to *that one*, etc."

* p. 299.   † p. 300.   ‡ Ibid.

He affirms, and quotes others who agree with him in deeming, that man originally spoke of himself in the third person, Sayce telling us that "the Malay *ulun*, 'I,' is still 'a man' in Lampong, and the Kawi *ugwang*, 'I,' cannot be separated from *nwang*, 'a man.'" But it would not be of the slightest consequence to our argument if we Englishmen, here and now, never spoke of ourselves but as "this man," or "this one here." By such expressions we should mean "I" not a bit the less, and, as Mr. Romanes has truly said, the only really important thing in the question is what a man *means*.

If, again, what Prof. Max Müller is represented * as saying about the Aryans is true, it does not matter to us. Prof. Max Müller says, "It was one of the characteristic features of Sanskrit, and the other Aryan languages, that they tried to distinguish the various applications of a root by means of what I have called demonstrative roots or elements. If they wished to distinguish the mat as the product of their handiwork, from the handiwork itself, they would say, 'Platting— there;' if they wished to encourage the work they would say, 'Platting—they, or you, or we.' We found that what we call demonstrative roots or elements must be considered as remnants of the earliest and almost pantomimic phase of language."

This may be very true, and we have no objection ; but, to show how uncertain it all really is, we have but to quote the next paragraph of Mr. Romanes. He there says:† "It is the opinion of some philologists,

* p. 302.   † Ibid.

however, that these demonstrative elements were probably 'once full or predicative words,'" and he quotes Prof. Sayce as saying, "It is difficult to conceive how a word could ever have gained a footing if it did not from the first present some independent predicative meaning." To this Mr. Romanes again replies that we should "remember the sounds which are arbitrarily invented by young children and uneducated deaf-mutes, not to mention the inarticulate clicks of the Bushmen." But why are we to suppose that such clicks and arbitrarily invented sounds never had any "independent predicative meaning"? Certainly the arbitrarily invented sounds of many children and deaf-mutes must indisputably *have* such meaning.

Prof. Sayce is quoted * as saying that "an inflectional language does not permit us to watch the word-making process so clearly as do those savage jargons, in which a couple of sounds, like the Grebo *ni ne*, signify 'I do it,' or 'You do not,' according to the context and the gestures of the speaker. Here by degrees, with the growth of consciousness and the analysis of thought, the external gesture is replaced by some" uttered sounds. Now, if the Professor means by "the growth of consciousness," its evolution from a state of mind devoid of consciousness, he errs greatly. For the sounds *ni ne* could never be uttered with *meaning* by any unconscious being. We take it he only means the greater diversity of direction of consciousness, and we are supported in this belief by his expression—"and the *analysis* of thought." But, how-

* p. 303.

ever this may be, the quotation affords an admirable example of the cheap and easy way in which the intellectual processes of different races of mankind are disposed of as may happen to suit the purpose of the disposers. The utterer of *ni ne* is just as rational essentially as Prof. Sayce or the present writer. We have in our own language precisely similar phenomena. The expression, " My work," may signify either " I do it," or " You do *not*," according to the context and the gestures or tones of the speaker. A man may say, " My *work*," pointing to the product with a look showing lively satisfaction at being able to boast himself as the performer of so remarkable a feat. He may say, " *My* work " while pointing to his own body, with a look showing strong disapprobation at the idea of another person pretending to have been the doer of it.

We have no desire to affirm the existence of any original distinction between adjectives and substantives as regards *words*, though we are quite sure it existed as to *meanings* as it does to-day in a multitude of instances—such, *e.g.*, as " cannon-ball " and " pocket-book," in which a word is not only, as Mr. Romanes says,* an adjective " in virtue of " " position," but in virtue of the intention of the utterer of it. As Prof. Max Müller very truly observes,† adjectives are outwardly like substantives, but " are conceived as different from substantives the moment they are used in a sentence for the purpose of predicating or of qualifying a substantive."

Such terms ‡ as " digging-he " to express a labourer,

* p. 305.   † p. 306.   ‡ See p. 307.

or "digging-it" to denote a spade, or "digging-here" for labour itself, answer fully to express really intellectual conceptions.

We have now to advert to, and animadvert upon, the censures expressed by Mr. Romanes on his psychological opponents, concerning their statements with reference to the "idea of being." Our author says,* " Seeing that my psychological opponents have laid so much stress upon the substantive verb as this is used by the Romance languages in formal predication, I will here devote a paragraph to its special consideration from a philological point of view. It will be remembered that I have already pointed out the fallacy which these opponents have followed in confounding the substantive verb, as thus used, with the copula—it being a mere accident of the Romance languages that the two are phonetically identified." It will also be remembered that we have already replied † to this, but we may again remark that in the word "is," used as a copula, existence (real or ideal) *is* implicitly contained. Mr. Romanes goes on, "Nevertheless, even after this fallacy has been pointed out to them, my opponents may seek to take refuge in the substantive verb itself : forced to acknowledge that it has nothing especially to do with predication, they may still endeavour to represent that, elsewhere, or in itself, it represents a high order of conceptual thought. This, of course, I allow ; and if, as my opponents assume, the substantive verb belonged to early, not to say primitive modes of speech, I should further allow that it raises a formid-

able difficulty in the otherwise even path of evolutionary explanation.   But, as a matter of fact, these
writers are no less mistaken about the primitive nature
of the substantive verb itself, than they are upon the
function which it accidentally discharges in copulation."

He then refers to the following assertion of ours—
before quoted * by Mr. Romanes : "If a brute could
think 'is,' brute and man would be brothers. 'Is,' as
the copula of a judgment, implies the mental separation,
and recombination of two terms that only exist united
in nature, and can therefore never have impressed the
sense except as one thing.   And 'is,' considered as a
substantive verb, as in the example, 'This man is,'
contains in itself the application of the copula of judgment to the most elementary of all abstractions—
'thing,' or 'something.'   Yet if a being has the power
of thinking—'thing,' or 'something,' it has the power of
transcending space and time by dividing or decomposing
the phenomenally one.   Here is the point where instinct
ends and reason begins."

To this statement of ours† we most thoroughly
adhere, and are unable to find that Mr. Romanes can
bring one valid argument against it.   But he seems
to think that people who have no distinct vocables
answering to our words "exists," or "existence," cannot
have the conceptions thereto answering.   His whole
contention rests on this, and on the absurd notion that
a child who only speaks of himself as "Charley," is not
a self-conscious being.   Nevertheless we shall see that,

* p. 167.

† Originally made in "Lessons from Nature," pp. 226, 227.

only four pages further on,* he declares unequivocally that existence can be signified and made plain by expressions which nevertheless do not denote it by a separate term.

Then he goes on,† "In order to prove that the substantive verb is really very far from primitive, I will furnish a few extracts from the writings of philological authorities upon the subject." He then tells us that the Hebrew word *Kama* means primitively "to stand out," and that the verb *Koum*, "to stand," *passes into* the sense of "being." But what more could we require? Does Mr. Romanes think we suppose that primitive man started a word to denote abstract existence without any other meaning accompanying it? We are far indeed from entertaining such a notion. Again, the Sanskrit *As-mi* (the foundation of all the Indo-European words denoting "to be") is declared to be "but a formation on the demonstrative pronoun *sa*, the idea meant to be conveyed being simply that of local presence." But what then? How does the use of the term to denote "local presence" deprive it of the power of denoting "existence"? Is "existence" inconsistent with "local presence"? In order that a thing may be present anywhere, is it absolutely needful that it *should not exist at all?*

"May we not then," says Mr. Romanes, "ask with Bunsen, 'What is *to be* in all languages but the spiritualization of *walking* or *standing* or *eating?*'" To this we reply, Certainly you may so ask, and a rational man will probably give some such answer as the follow-

---

* p. 312.   † p. 309.

ing one : " What are we to understand by your use of the term 'spiritualization'? Is it a hocus pocus, by which you would slip in an intellectual signification into what is merely sensuous?" We think it better to use a less equivocal term. We say, first, that actual real material "walking, standing, and eating" necessarily imply existence in whatever walks, stands, or eats. Secondly, we say that the ideas of "walking, standing, and eating" necessarily carry with them the idea of existence as therein implicitly contained. Thirdly, we say that " to be " in all languages is much more than an implicit signification contained in " walking, standing, or eating ; " for it is contained really in every other *real* action and object, and ideally and implicitly in every other *ideal* action or object, as in the three actions which Bunsen selected. If it be rejoined, what was meant was simply that in most or all languages which have not the substantive verb itself, its place is supplied by an extension or specialization of meaning applied to the three terms given, we further reply that we are very happy it should be so. We have not the philological knowledge requisite to affirm or deny the assertion, which is an interesting one from a philological point of view, but has no special interest for us, being utterly beside the question under consideration.

Mr. Romanes then quotes from Mr. Garnett ("On the Nature and Analysis of the Verb "), very much to our satisfaction, as that writer quite expresses our own view. The only important matter, as Mr. Romanes has said,* is what a *man means*, and if he means to predi-

* p. 164.

cate existence, and succeeds in doing what he wants, that is all that he or we could require. Mr. Garnett tells us * that the Coptic is defective as regards the substantive verb, but he significantly adds that the Egyptians "had at least half a dozen methods of rendering the Greek verb-substantive when they wished to do so. . . . If a given subject be 'I,' 'thou,' 'he,' 'this,' 'that,' 'one ;' if it be 'here,' 'there,' 'yonder,' 'thus,' 'in,' 'on,' 'at,' 'by ;' if it be 'sits,' 'stands,' 'remains,' or 'appears,' we need no ghost to tell us that it *is*."

Mr. Romanes next depicts what he regards as the gradual impoverishment of language as we go backwards in time through progressive simplifications, as to all which, though we do not profess agreement, we have, for our purpose, no occasion whatever to contest his assertions. " In view of these facts," he tells us,† "it is impossible to withhold assent from the now universal doctrine of philologists—' language diminishes the farther we look back, in such a way that we cannot forbear concluding it must once have had no existence at all.' " This " universal doctrine " is a quotation from Geiger, whose ignorant prejudice is apparent to every qualified observer. But we fully allow there *was* a time when no rational language existed, and it was a time which existed before man's appearance on the surface of this planet. With the advent of man, the advent of language simultaneously occurred.

Mr. Romanes, in his effort to show the evolution of language (which evolution he deems, so mistakenly,

* p. 310. † p. 314.

to be fatal to his opponents), calls in the aid of other writers, and, amongst them, he once more quotes from Mr. Sweet * as to Primitive Man not having used the copula, but only placed words in apposition. Thus, he tells us, " the verb gradually came to assume the purely formal function of predication." He continues, " The use of verbs denoting action necessitated the formation of verbs to denote 'rest,' 'continuance in state,' and when, in course of time, it became necessary in certain cases to predicate permanent as well as changing attributes, these words were naturally employed for the purpose, and such a sentence as 'The sun continues bright' was simply 'The bright sun' in another form." But this is what we meant by saying the simplest element of thought is a judgment. The concept " bright sun " is implicitly the judgment " the sun is bright." But what is meant by the expression, "*when it became necessary*"? Necessary: why, and for whom? There could be no necessity save for man, " the meaner," when he felt a need to give expression to his " meaning." But to feel the necessity of expressing his meaning, he must first *have* it. Therefore it is manifest that the thought must have preceded the expression. It was not and could not have been formed by a word ; but it existed, and so formed the word. The same writer goes on to say that not only the order but " the very idea of the distinction between subject and predicate is purely linguistic, and has no foundation in the mind itself. In the first place, there is no necessity for a subject at all : in such a sentence as 'It rains'

* p. 315.

there is no subject whatever, the *it* and the terminal *s* being merely formal signs of predication." This is a great mistake : not only in " it rains," but also in the mere concept " rain," subject, predicate, and copula may truly and implicitly exist. What is meant by the word "rain," and still more by " it rains," uttered in the sense meant, is really this : (1) The conception of the falling of rain ; (2) the conception of time present ; and (3) the conception of the existence of the falling action during present time. " Falling rain is present now " is the full explicit statement of the implicit predication contained in the words " rain " and "it rains." He goes on, "' It rains : therefore I will take my umbrella,' is a perfectly legitimate train of reasoning, but it would puzzle the cleverest logician to reduce it to any of his figures." But this is not true. It is most easily so reduced as follows :—

A time of falling rain is the time to take an umbrella. The present time is a time of falling rain ; therefore the present time is the time to take an umbrella.

But of course we do not, for we have no need to, consciously go through any such explicit process, on account of the lightning-like rapidity of thought.

He continues,* " Again, the mental proposition is not formed by thinking first of the subject, then of the copula, and then of the predicate ; it is formed by thinking of the three simultaneously." Of course it is : they are evolved simultaneously into explicit recognition from their implicit coexistence in a concept. Again, he says, " When we formulate in our minds the proposition, ' All

* p. 316.

men are bipeds,' we have two ideas, 'all men' and 'an equal number of bipeds,' or, more tersely, 'as many men, as many bipeds,' and we think of the two ideas simultaneously (*i.e.*, in *apposition*), not one after the other, as we are forced to express them in speech." But who supposes that our thoughts are bound to follow the order which may be necessary for expression? Only a Nominalist would be guilty of such an absurdity. Besides this, the statement is doubly erroneous: it errs both by excess and defect. We have no need of the conception of equality of numbers, or of any numerical relation at all, in thinking "all men are bipeds." On the other hand, the ideas of coexistence and identity are absolutely essential. In the form which Mr. Romanes gives, however, these ideas of coexistence and identity have no place. The words "as many men, as many bipeds" are quite insufficient to express the notion "all men are bipeds." "As many X, as many Y" might mean things existing in succession, or coexisting, but distinct in kind. Thus, in speaking of trains of railway carriages, we may say, "As many foremost vehicles, so many hindmost vehicles," or we may say, of sheep in a flock, "As many sheeps' heads, as many sheeps' tails." But in saying, "All men are bipeds," we mean that the men actually are identical with the bipeds supposed, and that they all were, are, and will be bipeds, twofootedness and humanity being recognized as coexisting. Therefore the idea of "existence" forms a necessary part of the notion, and, however its expression may be suppressed, must be present in the conception if it is not to be meaningless. Therefore the author cited is utterly wrong in saying, "When we formulate in our minds the proposition, 'All men are bipeds,' we have *two* ideas." We have *three* ideas: (1) men ; (2) twofootedness ; and (3) identity of existence.

Mr. Romanes next observes * that "we are not left to mere inference touching the aboriginal state of matters with regard to predication. For in many languages still existing we find the forms of predication in such low phases of development, that they bring us within easy distance of the time when there can have been no such form at all."

As an example, he tells us † that "in Dayak, if it is desired to say, 'Thy father is old,' 'Thy father looks old,' etc., in the absence of verbs it is needful to frame the predication by mere apposition, thus :—' Father-of-thee, age-of-him.' Or, to be more accurate, . . . 'His age, thy father.' Similarly, if it is required to make such a statement as that 'He is wearing a white jacket,' the form of the statement would be, ' He-with-white with-jacket,' or, as we might perhaps more tersely translate it, ' He jackety whitey.'" But how does this in the least tell against the presence of distinct intellectual meaning in the utterance of such phrases? They may strike the imagination of the unthinking, but, in sober truth, the assertion, "He jackety whitey," is essentially as good as the assertion, "That man's upper outmost vesture has the hue of snow."

Again, he tells us,‡ "In Feejee language the functions of a verb may be discharged by a noun in construction with an oblique pronominal suffix, *e.g.*,

* p. 316.　　† p. 317.　　‡ p. 318.

S

loma-qu = heart or will-of-me, = *I will.*" But why should
" will-of-me " be considered incapable of plainly making
known a voluntary assent ? In our English tongue an
emphatic assent may be given by an expression apparently much less close to the idea of volition. An
English youth asking another whether he is willing to
take part in some project would be sufficiently assured
of the assent of the latter if he replied, " I believe you."

We do not doubt that the parts of speech of Euro-
pean grammarians are, "as far as *external* form is
concerned," inapplicable to the Polynesian languages.
But the fact, however interesting, is not of the slightest
importance to our contention. "I will eat the rice,"
may require to be rendered, " The-eating-of-me-the-
rice = My eating will be of the rice." Such expressions
are as reasonable and logical as need be.

Recurring to his opponents' challenge * to " produce
the brute which ' can furnish the blank form of a judgment '—the ' is ' in A is B," he observes,† " Now, I
cannot, indeed, produce a brute that is able to supply
such a form ; but I have done what is very much more
to the purpose—I have produced many nations of still
existing men, in multitudes that cannot be numbered,
who are as incapable as any brute of supplying the
blank form that is required. Where is the ' is,' in ' Age-
of-him Father-of-thee ' = ' His-age-thy-father ' = ' Thy-
father-is-old '? Or, in still more primitive stages of
human utterance, how shall we extract the blank form
of predication from a ' sentence-word,' where there is
not only an absence of any copula, but also an absence

* See " Lessons from Nature," pp. 226, 227.   † p. 312.

of any differentiation between the subject and the predicate?" To this we can reply in the lately cited words,* "If a given subject be 'here,' 'there,'" etc., "we need no ghost to tell us that it *is*." Here Mr. Romanes's whole contention shows the absurdity of Nominalism. "Is" the concept, is there plainly enough, though "is" the "spoke word" be absent.

He continues,† "Of course all this futile argument on the part of my opponents, rests upon the analysis of the proposition as this was given by Aristotle." To this we reply, it does not rest one bit on any such analysis, but on the perception of the thought underlying propositions, whether expressed in Greek, Dayak, Chinese, or Polynesian phraseology.

This answer Mr. Romanes anticipates as a possibility, ‡ saying, that in order to meet it, he must refer to points which he considers were established by him in previous chapters, and which we have already, we think, sufficiently refuted.

He then refers to propositions made by children, anteriorly to what he deems the advent of self-consciousness, "*prior to the very condition which is required for any process of conceptual thought.*" But, as we have shown, consciousness is plainly present long before the period which Mr. Romanes arbitrarily assigns for its advent. Again, he says § that such propositions are "due to merely sensuous associations and the external logic of events"—a thing we utterly deny. "Will any opponent venture to affirm," he asks, "that preconceptual ideation is indicative of judgment?" We reply, *of*

* From p. 312.   † p. 320.   ‡ p. 321.   § p. 323.

course it is, and we affirm that this is manifestly an utterly different thing from confounding recepts and concepts.

Again, he asks, will we affirm that "even in the earlier and hitherto undifferentiated sentence-word we have that faculty of predication on which is founded the distinction between man and brute"? and we reply most certainly we do. He next declares,* that if we answer as we have just answered, "the following brief considerations will be sufficient to dislodge" us. "If," he says, "the term 'predication' is extended from a conceptual proposition to a sentence-word, it thereby becomes deprived of that distinctive meaning upon which alone [as he supposes] the whole argument of my opponents is reared. For, when used by a young child (or primitive man), sentence-words require to be supplemented by gesture-signs in order to particularize their meaning, or to complete the 'predication.' But, where such is the case, there is no longer any psychological distinction between *speaking* and *pointing :* if this is called predication, then the predicative 'category of language' has become identified with the indicative : man and brute are conceded to be 'brothers.'"

This is an entire mistake. The use or need of gesture does not make language a bit less truly conceptual and abstract. There is no psychological distinction between speaking and pointing, or we could have no expression of abstract ideas by pantomime as in ballets. Mr. Romanes, as an example in point, tells us† of an infant of his still unable to articulate a word, but who, having

* p. 324.   † p. 324.

knocked his head, ran to his father. On being asked where he was hurt, "he immediately touched the part of his head in question." "Now, will it be said," he asks, "that in doing this the child was predicating the seat of injury?" We reply, most unquestionably it was. The predication was of a rudimentary kind; but our knowledge of the nature of children from their growth and development, makes us perfectly clear that it really was a predication. Then, says Mr. Romanes, there is no essential difference between men and brutes, for "the gesture-signs which are so abundantly employed by the lower animals would then also require to be regarded as predicatory, seeing that . . . they differ in no respect from those of the speechless infant." This assertion we hold to be untenable, for our knowledge of the growth and development of animals makes it clear that apparently significant movements * made by them (as when a cat has a bone fixed between its back teeth) are not really a predication. No gestures of brutes need be taken as being assertions about facts, since they are all otherwise explicable. Could they, once more, make gestures due to a real, conscious memory and intention similar to that of Mr. Romanes's child, they would soon make us quite certain of their power in this respect. If they could do it at all they would do it repeatedly and whenever they had need to make their meaning known to other conscious intelligences. Thus Mr. Romanes's opponents, in allowing the quality of predication not only to sentence-words, but to mere manual signs also, in no way thereby impair the full force of the essential

* See "On Truth," p. 355.

distinction they assert.   They can thus maintain as firmly as ever that intellectual language is "the Rubicon of Mind."   Between the mere language of feeling and the sensuous cognition of brutes, on the one hand, and intellectual language and perception on the other, there remains an essential distinction of kind—that is, of origin.   Whether we look to the psychogenesis of the individual or to that of the race, we alike see the full force of the distinction, and recognize, in harmony therewith, the entire absence of any evidence of transition from the emotional sign-making power of the brute to the faculty of conceptual expression possessed by man.

Mr. Romanes passes next * (in Chapter XV.) to a consideration of what he calls "the passage of receptual denotation into conceptual denomination, as this is shown to have occurred in the prehistoric evolution of the race."   He means by this, the origin of words expressing concepts.   He every now and again makes use of assertions which much too strongly affirm as true that of which he has got to prove the truth.   Thus he speaks † of "what is *undoubtedly* the earliest phase of articulate sign-making," as if he had witnessed primitive man at work, and this though (to show how uncertain even less disputable matters may be) he has himself told us ‡ that while some authorities consider polysynthesis to be a survival of what was once the universal form of languages, yet, "on the other hand, it is with equal certainty affirmed that 'polysynthesis' is not a primitive feature, but an expansion of agglutination."   Again, speaking § of the child's "ultimate germ of

* p 326.   † p. 327.   ‡ p. 255.   § p. 327.

articulate sign-making," he tells us that in it this phase "does not appear to be either so marked, or important, or, comparatively speaking, of such prolonged duration as it was [!] in the development of speech in the race." Yet he is really sustained by nothing but an *à priori* prejudice as to what he thus dogmatically says "*was.*" His feeling is based on the notion that the ontogeny of the individual in zoology is a guide to the phylogeny of the race which it represents in a much shortened form. This zoological fact, however, if certainly a fact, is not at all a constant one.   Often, *e.g.*, in the metamorphoses of some insects, special adaptations are interposed, and often, *e.g.*, in spiders, the process is an exceedingly direct one.   We cannot, therefore, be sure that the development of the child is a contraction of that of the race.   Mr. Romanes contends with much reason that infants who do not seem to use distinct parts of speech nevertheless mean them, and in their own way do virtually use them. He takes as instances * the before-cited childish expressions, " Ot "=" This milk is hot ; " " Dow " = "My plaything is down ; " " Dit ki " = " Sister is crying ; " "Dit dow ga "=" Sister is down on the grass."   He says, " In all these cases it is evident that the child is displaying a true perception of the different functions which severally belong to the different parts of speech " Of course Mr. Romanes means a practical perception, *i.e.* that the child consciously, but without reflex consciousness, tries to express meanings, the perfect expression of which would require parts of speech, and so instinctively and meaningly uses its imperfect terms as

* p. 328.

it does. Of course the child has no reflex perception of any function of any kind.

Our author continues,[*] "So far as psychological analysis alone could carry us, there would be nothing to show that the forcing of one part of speech into the office of another, which so frequently occurs at this age, is due to anything more than *the exigencies of expression* [†] where as yet there are scarcely any words for the conveyance of meaning of any kind. . . . What may be termed this grammatical abuse of words becomes an absolute necessity where the vocabulary is small, as we well know when trying to express ourselves in a foreign language with which we are but slightly acquainted. And, of course, the smaller the vocabulary, the greater is such necessity ; so that it is greatest of all when an infant is only just emerging from its infancy." He adds, " It is on account of the uncertainty which here obtains as between necessity and incapacity, that I reserved my consideration of ' sentence-words ' for the independent light which has been thrown upon them by the science of comparative philology."

The difference which he affirms between the infant of to-day and primitive man, as to the duration and importance of the use of terms not yet differentiated into parts of speech, he tries to explain as follows:[‡] " An infant of to-day is born into the medium of already-spoken language ; and long before it is itself able to imitate the words which it hears, it is well able to understand a large number of them. Consequently,

* pp. 328, 329.   † The italics are ours.
‡ pp. 329–331.

while still literally an *infant*, the use of grammatical forms is being constantly borne in upon its mind ; and, therefore, it is not at all surprising that, when it first begins to use articulate signs, it should already be in possession of some amount of knowledge of their distinctive meanings as names of objects, qualities, actions, states, or relations. Indeed, it is only as such that the infant has acquired its knowledge of these signs at all ; and hence, if there is any wonder in the matter, it is that the first-speaking child should exhibit so much vagueness as it does in the matter of grammatical distinction.

"But how vastly different must have been the case of primitive man! The infant, as a child of to-day, finds a grammar already made to its use, and one which it is bound to learn with the first learning of denotative names. But the infant, as an adult in primeval time, was under the necessity of slowly elaborating his grammar together with his denotative names; and this, as we have previously seen, he only could do by the aid of gesture and grimace. Therefore, while the acquisition of names and forms of speech by infantile man must have been thus in chief part dependent on gesture and grimace, the acquisition by the infantile child is now not only independent of gesture and grimace, but actively inimical to both. The already-constructed grammar of speech is the evolutionary substitute of gesture, from which it originally arose ; and, hence, so soon as a child of to-day begins to speak, gesture-signs begin at once to be starved out by grammatical forms. But in the history of the race gesture-signs were the nursing-mothers of grammatical forms; and the more that their progeny grew, the greater must have been the variety of functions which the parents were called upon to perform. In other words, during the infancy of our race the growth of articulate language must not only have depended, but also reacted upon that of gesture-signs—increasing their number, their intricacy, and their refinement, up to the time when grammatical forms were sufficiently far evolved to admit of the gesture-signs becoming gradually dispensed with. Then, of course, Saturn-like, gesticulation was devoured by its own offspring; * the relations between signs appealing to the eye and to the ear became gradually reversed; and, as is now the case with every growing child, the language of formal utterance sapped the life of its more informal progenitor."

We have thought it better to cite this passage entire, that Mr. Romanes's position and argument may be thoroughly well understood by our readers.

Now, we will put entirely on one side, for argument's sake, any notion of man having been created at once in the plenitude of his intellect, and bodily and mental activity. We will assume him to have had an origin, different indeed in kind from that of any other animal, but yet not such as to have placed him in a better position than the lowest we could assign to a mature rational being at all. Under such circumstances, need we assign to the earliest form of language the conditions which Mr. Romanes assign to it?

---

* It had hitherto been our impression that Saturn devoured his children himself, not that he was devoured by them.

Clearly we need not. Primitive man must have felt, as Mr. Romanes says * the child did, "the *exigencies of expression*," and if so, expressed himself as best he could, by combinations of bodily, facial, and oral movements. If he meant to express anything, that, as Mr. Romanes has allowed,† was the one thing necessary. A sign made up of an inarticulate sound accompanying motions of the hands and body and facial contortions, may be as truly the expression of conceptions (*essentially* intellectual language) as would be the utterance of a group of articulate sounds. No doubt such primitive men would have had difficulties to contend with which our children have not ; but how does such a circumstance even tend to show that their intellectual *nature* was different from that of our own senior wranglers and cabinet ministers ?

Mr. Romanes next addresses himself to the consideration of " sentence-words," and he asks ‡ the strange question, " Can anything in the shape of spoken language be more primitive than the very first words which are spoken by a child, or even by a parrot ? " He considers that sentence-words are more primitive still, because even a parrot may learn to use words by association, while primitive man could not have learned them thus, but must have invented them. But what a curious confusion is here ! Because one man makes a machine, his action may be called less perfect and more primitive than the act of another man who uses it after it is made ; but the intelligence of the man who acts in the latter case need be very small compared with

* p. 329.   † p. 164.   ‡ p. 331.

that of the first inventor of the machine. How infinitely less the intelligence of a brute who may happen to use a machine of the kind! Is the intelligence of a squirrel or white mouse which turns in its wheel-cage greater than that either of the child who purposely gets the wheel-cage to put its pet in, or that of the man who made the cage? Mr. Romanes must somehow see this, for he says,* "In order that he should assign names, primitive man must first have had occasion to make his preconceptual statements about the objects, qualities, etc., the names of which afterwards grew out of these statements, or sentence-words." That is to say, he must have been an essentially intellectual person.

Mr. Romanes next considers † the value of these supposed earlier sentence-words. After stating his hypothesis about the genesis of such early words with the help of gesture—the sound having no meaning apart from the gesture—he says, "From these now well-established *facts*, [!] we may gain some additional light on . . . the extent to which primitive words were 'abstract' or 'concrete,' 'particular' or 'general,' and therefore, 'receptual' or 'conceptual.'" Here he censures Prof. Max Müller for proclaiming the truth that language proceeded from the abstract to the concrete, or, as Mr. Romanes phrases it,‡ that human thought "sprang into being Minerva-like, already equipped with the divine inheritance of conceptual wisdom."

He blames § the Professor for adopting, as he says, "the assumption that there can be no order of words which do not, by the mere fact of their existence,

* p. 332.   † p. 334.   ‡ p. 335.   § p. 336.

imply concepts." He tells us that the Professor "does not sufficiently recognize that there may be a power of bestowing names as signs, without the power of thinking these signs as names." Mr. Romanes thus implies that a name cannot denote a concept unless he who employs it adverts to the fact of its being a name. But a name signifies a concept, without any advertence on the part of the utterer of it to its conceptual nature, or to the fact that it is a name; nor is it less conceptual in essence because the utterer of it is at the time of his utterance and for some time afterwards unable from circumstances to advert to and recognize the fact that it *is* a name. Mr. Romanes gives,* as his case in point, the instance of a child of his who "on first beginning to speak had a generalized idea of similarity between all kinds of brightly shining objects, and therefore called them all by the one denotative name of 'star.' The astronomer has a general idea answering to his denominative name of 'star;' but this has been arrived at after a prolonged course of mental evolution, wherein conceptual analysis has been engaged in conceptual classification in many and various directions: it therefore represents the psychological antithesis of the generalized idea, which was due to the merely sensuous associations of preconceptual thought. Ideas, then, as general and generic severally occupy the very antipodes of Mind." This is really nonsense. The child's term "star," was in its way as good and true a "universal" as the term "star" of the greatest astronomer who ever lived or shall live. But the

* p. 336.

two terms, though identical in sound and appearance, denote two very different concepts or universals—as truly as the term "trumpeter" respectively stands for the two very distinct concepts—a man and a pigeon.

"No one," he says,* "will maintain that the sentence-words of young children exhibit the highest elaborations of conceptual thought, on the ground that they present the highest degree of 'generality,' which it is possible for articulate sounds to express." Indeed! we reply. We ourselves will maintain it, and stoutly, too, if Mr. Romanes considers the word "thing," as used by young children, to be a "sentence-word." Naturally he denies to early man what he thus denies to the child. Just as naturally we affirm that primitive man in a sentence-word, even if thought out only by the aid of gesture, may, nay, must have, attained to concepts of the very highest generality, though, of course, neither the child, the ancient man, nor the modern peasant, recognizes its nature and generality by a reflex mental act. We altogether, then, deny the distinction which Mr. Romanes seeks to establish between generic and general ideas, other than the distinction (which is profound indeed) between (1) general ideas and (2) psychical states which are no ideas at all, but the mere unconscious, consentient energies named by us "Sensuous Universals."

The next point urged by Mr. Romanes is the resemblance which he affirms to exist between the syntax of gesture-language, that of baby-talk, and what he therefore assumes to have been the mode of speech of primitive man. This we do not in the least care to

* p. 338.

contest. It shows how perfectly logical gesture-language may be, and therefore, we may infer, always *was* as soon as it *existed at all.*

He then endeavours to show that language was at first essentially sensuous (what he calls receptual), and not intellectual. Here we must distinguish: As we have said again and again, being rational animals, we must use bodily signs to denote our thoughts, and require to have· our conceptions first aroused by the incidence of sense-impressions in groups and groups of groups. Every highest conception of ours depends on the recognition of preceding acts of conception, and these on the imagination of the sense-impressions which called them forth. Thus there is, and must be, a sensuous element accompanying every concept.* But this sensuous element is not the concept itself, since it exists beside, or rather, underlies the concept. Our earliest perceptions, though, of course, truly conceptual, contain concepts of a lowly order, called forth by sense cognitions. Nevertheless, the very highest universals, even that of " being," are latent in every one of them. Now, Mr. Romanes, believing as he does that the lower concepts are but sense cognitions with names to them, naturally declares † that the evolutionist would clearly "expect to find more or less well-marked traces, in the fundamental constitution of all languages, of what has been called 'fundamental metaphor '—by which is meant an intellectual extension of terms that originally were of no more than sensuous signification. And this," he adds, "is precisely what we

* See " On Truth," p. 88.   † p. 343.

do find." But "what we do find" is exactly what our combined intellectual and corporeal nature would lead us to expect, and is *absolutely fatal* to the doctrine of the common nature of man and brute. As we have before said, * the very existence of "metaphor" is proof positive of the intellectual nature and activity of the human mind. Had not the intellect the power of apprehending through sense, and expressing by sensible signs, things which are beyond sense, metaphor could not exist. Neither could it exist if thought arose from language and followed it, instead of the opposite.

It is precisely because speech is too narrow for thought, and because words are too few to convey the ideas of the mind, that metaphor exists. It is interesting to note that figurative, metaphorical language is natural to, and especially abundant amongst, various uncultured tribes. Mr. Romanes says,† "The whole history of language, down to our own day, is full of examples of the reduction of physical terms and phrases to the expression of non-physical conceptions and relations." We say, not the "*reduction,*" but the "*elevation*" of such terms ; and how could such elevations take place if "names" preceded "thoughts"?

With truth does Mr. Romanes say that metaphor is universal, and he quotes Carlyle as making the just remark, "An unmetaphorical style you shall seek in vain, for is not your very *attention* a *stretching to ?* " The sensuous element in language does not show that the earliest ideas were themselves sensuous, but rather the wonderful spontaneity of the human intellect,

---

* See above, p. 233.   † pp. 343, 344.

whence, by the help of the "beggarly elements" supplied by the senses, the loftiest concepts spring forth, Minerva-like, armed with the sharp spear of intellectual perception and swathed in the ample mantle of signs, woven of the warp of matter and the woof of thought.

It is this power of metaphor-making which most plainly displays to us the intellect actually at work, evolving ever new external expressions for freshly arising internal perceptions. Metaphor belongs to man alone. It is the especial privilege and sign of his nature. Not the highest brute—no elephant, no chimpanzee—could ever evolve a metaphor.

That a higher meaning must be latent in terms which Mr. Romanes would regard as exclusively sensuous, is made especially evident by ethical propositions. He tells us that such propositions are made up of terms no one of which is itself ethical. We would ask him then : What do you understand by an ethical proposition itself when fully evolved? Do you deny that you can understand by it any ethical conception at all ? If so, you deny that there is any distinction between right and wrong, and if you deny that you have any such perception now, no wonder you deny that early man had any perception of the kind. If, on the other hand, you affirm that you can understand such a fully evolved ethical proposition, whence did its meaning come? It must have been put into it by some irrational agency or by man himself. If the former, then we have a positive deification of unreason. If the latter, then clearly man must be different in nature and essence from any and every brute whatever.

T

Mr. Romanes concludes this chapter by some observations concerning the real or supposed deficiency of language-structure amongst savages.   In a note he tries to meet * the assertions of such writers as "Du Ponceau, Charlevoix, James, Appleyard, Threlkeld, Caldwell, etc., who have sought to represent that the languages of even the lowest savages are 'highly systematic and truly philosophical,'" as follows : He tells us that their opinion "rests on a radically false estimate of the criteria of system and philosophy in a language.   For the criteria chosen are exuberance of synonyms, intricacies or complications of forms, etc., which are really works of a low development."

However this may be, such languages are lofty indeed compared with any signs which are made by even the highest animals.   The tales we read about the mental defects of savages are hardly, if at all, more trustworthy than anecdotes about the psychical powers of animals. Love of the marvellous, credulity, exaggeration, and, above all, hasty and inconclusive inferences, abound in both—as Mr. Tylor has shown us again and again.

Mr. Romanes tells us, † as one example, that "the Society Islanders have separate words for dog's-tail, bird's-tail, sheep's-tail, etc., but no word for tail itself— *i.e.,* tail in general." This is no great loss. We have one, and ours is wrong and hopelessly misleading. ‡ To use the same term, as we do, for what we call the "tails" of a peacock, a monkey, and a lobster, is to be

---

* p. 349.   † p. 350.
‡ See our lecture on "Tails," reported in *Nature* of Sept. 25 and Oct. 2, 1879.

in far worse plight than a Society Islander thus seems
to be.   As to the Tasmanians, he tells us,* on the
authority of a vocabulary, that they had no word for
tree, hard, soft, warm, cold, long, short, and round.
We do not believe the vocabulary, and regard its representation as being as absurd and incredible one way as
the tales about the rational cockatoo and the pious bees
on the other.   Does Mr. Romanes really mean that no
one Tasmanian could make another understand that
anything was hot or cold, or that a weapon was too short
or too long ?   We are persuaded he does not mean
this ; but if he does not, then he does not really mean
to deny that Tasmanians could explain themselves " by
equivalent expressions " as to such matters.

Dr. Latham is quoted as telling us, " that a Kurd
of the Zara tribe, who presented Dr. Sandwith with a
list of native words, was not 'able to conceive a hand
or father except so far as they were related to himself
or something else.'"   Now, it is very likely that we
have here some misunderstanding on the part either of
Dr. Latham, Dr. Sandwith, or the Kurd.   It is simply
incredible that the Kurd could not think of a hand
(or a father), not *his*, nor that *of Dr. Sandwith*, nor that
of *some other given man*.   It is, however, very likely
that the Kurd understood his questioner as asking him
whether he could conceive of a father or a hand not
related to him or any one else ?   The natural and
proper reply to that would be that he could not, nor
could either Dr. Latham, Dr. Sandwith, or Mr. Romanes,
unless it was a merely ideal hand or father.   As to any

* p. 352.

further questions about savages, we are content to refer
our readers to what we have elsewhere * written on the
subject.

Mr. Romanes seems to imagine † that a Tasmanian,
having had no word for "tree," could only have been
surprised at seeing a tree "standing inverted with
its roots in the air and its branches in the ground,
in just the same way a dog is surprised when it first
sees a man walking on his hands : the dog," he tells
us, "will bark at such an object because it conflicts
with the generic image which has been automatically
formed by numberless perceptions of individual men
walking on their feet. But, in the absence of any
name for trees in general, there is nothing to show
that the savage has a concept answering to 'tree,'
any more than that the dog has a concept answering
to 'man.'" This is, indeed, a surprising assertion, since
Mr. Romanes allows that even the Tasmanians must
have had many concepts since they had true language ;
but to no dog would he concede the possession of any
concept at all. Surely, then, a being whose mind was
stored with many concepts, must be allowed to have
been affected by a sight of an inverted tree, in a very
different way from that in which a dog is affected by
the sight of an inverted man !

One of the most wonderful sentences in Mr.
Romanes's book, however, is that which comes next.
He says, ‡ "Indeed, unless my opponents vacate the
basis of Nominalism [!] on which their opposition is
founded, they must acknowledge that in the absence of

* See " On Truth," chap. xix.   † p. 353.   ‡ Ibid.

any *name* for tree there *can be no conception* of tree." But his opponents, as he ought to know, are most ardent opponents of Nominalism, which they regard as a most unreasonable philosophy.

Finally, we must traverse the conclusions with which Mr. Romanes ends this chapter, because, as we have more than once observed, the need of adding bodily and facial expression to voice, in no way destroys the conceptual character of language, while " sentence-words " are so far from being non-conceptual that, as we have said, an ideally perfect language would consist of nothing but monosyllabic sentence-words. Neither can we regard names, due to onomatopœia, as less truly conceptual than any of the terms which Mr. Romanes has freshly coined for this work, nor need metaphorical expressions, derived from such onomatopoetic terms, be less truly conceptual than metaphoric expression derived from other sources. We have also pointed out how the placing two terms in apposition, as in saying A B, may truly constitute an essential predication, and involve the presence of self-conscious intellect, as truly as saying A *is* B.

Mr. Romanes asks,* " Will it be maintained that the man-like being who was then [*i.e.*, before spoken language was used] unable to communicate with his fellows by means of any words at all was gifted with self-consciousness ? " To which we reply, supposing man did primitively exist in such a condition (which we regard as a mere groundless speculation), he certainly *was* " gifted with self-consciousness."

* p. 356.

Mr. Romanes founds his hypothesis upon Geiger's assertion that "language diminishes the farther we look back in such a way, that we cannot forbear concluding it must once have had no existence at all." * "Who will venture to doubt it?" Mr. Romanes asks. We reply, we not only doubt it, but we deny it, and say it is demonstrably absurd. All that we should be warranted in concluding from such a fact, if it were a fact, would be that language, at its origin, was in a very undeveloped condition. Suppose a tribe of animals or plants to have been found to have been smaller and smaller in size, by a regular and unvarying degree of diminution, as we proceeded downward through the successive geological strata : who from that would conclude that the earliest members of the group had *no dimensions at all?* There was, we are quite sure, a time when language was not, but that was the time when man himself was not.

Mr. Romanes continues,† "Should so absurd a statement be ventured [as that speechless man might be self-conscious], it would be fatal to the argument of my adversaries ; for the statement would imply, either that concepts may exist without names, or that self-consciousness may exist without concepts." But that concepts may exist without names is the very essence of our contention. The anecdote of his "talking bird," is next recurred to, as if there was any parity between the so-called "naming" of dogs by a parrot and the "naming" of bright things "star" by a child. There

* "Development of the Human Race," Eng. Trans., p. 22.
† p. 356.

is no proof whatever that the bird "names." The bird may, on seeing a dog, be thereby excited to emit the sound the emission of which it had previously associated with the feelings aroused by the dog's presence. Supposing the bird to have a consentient, unconscious craving* for the sight of the dog, the automatic emission of the sound would then be abundantly accounted for by such past association. It would be an unconscious employment of a means to an end sensuously craved after. The subsequent history, or outcome, in the case of the child, gives us reason to suppose that it really named at first, because it indubitably "names" afterwards. In the case of the parrot this kind of evidence tells the other way.

Reversing, then, Mr. Romanes's concluding observations,† we say : brief and imperfect as our criticism of Mr. Romanes's position has been, we are honestly unable to see how the testimony of consciousness and observation combined could have been more uniform, multifarious, consistent, complete, and overwhelming, than we have found it to be. In every single case the witness of philology has agreed with the teaching of psychology. The faculty of language being a power living in us, directly and circumstantially narrates to us the necessary conditions of its own origin and evolution. It has told us that even if we suppose there was once a time when men were altogether speechless, and able to communicate with one another only by means of gesticulation and grimace, that yet bodily and facial expression were the expressions of conceptual thought.

* See " On Truth," pp. 200, 350.   † pp. 357, 359.

Nor if sentence-words could not be understood without the accompaniment of gesture, did such gesture in the least deprive them of their intellectual, conceptual nature. Assuming, for argument's sake, that the grammatical structure of spoken-language was originally the offspring of gesture-signs, its intellectual character is in no way thereby destroyed. Nor was early man, any more than the child of to-day, a bit less truly self-conscious, if he spoke of himself exclusively in what we call the third person. We find in all languages (other than emotional), whether of word or of gesture, just that sensuous accompaniment which reason and observation combine to show us must be present in every external expression of the meanings of an intellectual animal like man, because it must be present *beside* his internal thought, since we can never think without phantasmata. On the one hand, every act of our intellect needs a sensuous accompaniment, which must have preceded it ; while, on the other hand, every perception of, and through our senses, contains what is altogether beyond sense. If, then, it is true in this sense to say, " *Nihil in intellectu quod non prius fuerit in sensu,*" it is no less true to say, " *Nihil in intellectu quod unquam fuerit in sensu.*" So also if in one sense we say, with Garnett, " *Nihil in oratione quod non prius in sensu,*" we must none the less also say in another sense, " *Nihil in oratione quod prius in sensu.*"

The impossibility of the evolution of intellect from speech having been recognized through the recognition of what "thought" really is, we see how only "the flippant and the ignorant" can deem such agencies as those allowed by Mr. Romanes, adequate "to produce such a result." It is true, as Herder says, that no abstract term in any tongue has been attained to without the aid of sensation and of tone, but the abstraction itself no more consists of the mere aids to its production, than the new-born child is identical with the accoucheur or the obstetric forceps which may have brought it into the world. To our mind it is simply inconceivable that any stronger proof of the utter impossibility of mental evolution could be furnished, than is furnished by the one great fact of the structure, the warp and woof, of the thousand dialects of every pattern which are now spread over the surface of the globe. We cannot speak to each other in any tongue without declaring the presence of an intellectual, conceptual element in every vocal term. Such elements are the most essential part of every utterance of speech now, and must therefore have coexisted with the sensuous elements at the origin of speech. We cannot so much as discuss the "origin of human faculty" itself, without announcing in the very medium of our discussion how necessarily distinct that origin has been. It is to Language that Mr. Romanes, following his opponents, has resolved to appeal : by Language he is hopelessly condemned.

CHAPTER VII.

REASON AND PRIMITIVE MAN.

THE next section of the subject—to the consideration of which Mr. Romanes addresses himself * in his sixteenth chapter—is what he regards as having been the most probable course of man's actual physical evolution from some non-human animal—a process he calls, "The transition in the race."

Almost at the beginning of the chapter he observes, with much justice, "Any remarks which I have to offer upon this subject must needs be of a wholly speculative or unverifiable character. . . . I will devote the present chapter to a consideration of three alter- native—and equally hypothetical — histories of the transition. But, from what I have just said, I hope it will be understood that I attach no argumentative importance to any of these hypotheses."

Such being the case, we might almost dispense ourselves from the task of following him over ground which is thus avowedly not solid enough to really serve the purpose of a happy hunting-ground, or to sustain Mr. Romanes in any struggle with an opponent. We think, nevertheless, that our readers might have some

* p. 360.

just cause to feel disappointed if we passed by this sixteenth chapter entirely in silence. Therefore we will very briefly refer to what appear to us to be the most noteworthy portions of its contents.

Our author first notices the hypothesis of sundry German philologists, to the effect that sounds (articulate and other) had first been emitted "in the way of instinctive cries, wholly destitute of any semiotic intention," which cries, "by repeated association," acquired, "as it were automatically, a semiotic value." Now, as we pointed out in our introductory chapter, we are far from contesting that there never could have been creatures more man-like than any existing ape, which creatures gave forth articulate, *instinctive* cries, having a practical, but no intentional, significance. Such creatures, however, obviously were not men. Nevertheless, Mr. Romanes himself very rationally rejects * this German hypothesis as "ignoring the whole problem which stands to be solved—namely, the genesis of those powers of ideation which first put a soul of meaning into the previously insignificant sounds." The hypothesis is, we think, none the less distinctly worthy of note, as showing the absurd lengths to which theorists in difficulties will go.

Mr. Romanes, however, only rejects the theory because it assumes that men began to speak without having first acquired a sign-making faculty of gesture sign-making. But the very same fundamental *ignoratio elenchi* tells as much against him, as it does against the hypothesis he thus criticizes. For his view really "ignores

* p. 362.

the genesis of those powers of ideation which first put a soul of meaning into the " gesture signs, as much as the hypothesis he objects to ignores the process of putting meaning into vocal signs. Not, of course, that Mr. Romanes thinks so. He fancies that he finds "even in the lower animals, the signmaking faculty in no mean degree of development." But this we deny, for the reasons before stated.* Animals, of course, make instinctive movements, which are responded to by their fellows, and so might the " Urmenschen " of these German theorists ; but real signs such movements would not be, unless they were *meant* to be signs, and consciously depicted something a knowledge of which they were intended to convey.

The second hypothesis of the origin of language he adverts to, is the well-known one of Mr. Darwin—the spontaneous vocal imitation by a monkey of some other animal's voice as a sign to denote its presence. In this connection Mr. Romanes says,† speaking of the chimpanzee " Sally " at the Zoological Gardens, " It does not seem to me difficult to imagine that such an animal should extend the vocal signs which it habitually employs in the expression of its emotions and the logic of its recepts, to an association with gesture-signs, so as to constitute sentence-words indicative of such simple and often-repeated ideas as the presence of danger, discovery of food, etc." There is, of course, not the least *difficulty in imagining* this ; but, as a fact, the animal does not do it, though, if it did do so, such a fact would not constitute any difficulty for

* See above pp. 7, 65, 128.   † p. 368.

us, since we have already observed, here and else-where,* and Mr. Romanes himself has declared, that animals make practical signs of the kind, though not articulate ones, and the presence of such mere practical means to a practical end, gives no clue to the intro-duction of a "soul of *meaning*" into them. Mr. Darwin is quoted as asking, "May not some unusually wise ape-like animal have imitated the growl of a beast of prey, and thus told his fellow-monkeys the nature of the expected danger?" and Prof. Whitney as saying of some hypothetical pithecoid men, "There is *no difficulty in supposing* them to have possessed forms of speech, more rudimentary and imperfect than ours." We say again, of course not; there is no difficulty in supposing anything we want to suppose; but no intensity or reiteration of idle "suppositions" will afford a fragment of evidence in support of what is so "supposed." It is always the same kind of fallacy which besets these speculators: sensitive phenomena are supposed to be divided and subdivided till they are imagined to be subdivided enough for the entrance of a grain of conceptual power into them. Such a grain having once been smuggled in unnoticed, there is then really no difficulty in seeing how it may augment till it attains the level of the intellect of a Scotus. But phenomena are not really to be explained by merely being sub-divided or even pulverized. Of course Mr. Romanes him-self thus slips in intellect, without saying so, although not with any personal disingenuousness, but with an entirely innocent unconsciousness of what he is doing.

* See "On Truth," p. 352.

His own (the third) hypothesis is substantially like Darwin's, save that he imagines the spontaneous evolution not of significant *sounds*, but of significant *gestures*, which subsequently serve to guide and develop subsequently arising vocal sounds, articulate and inarticulate.

"Let us try to imagine," he says,* a community of beings "considerably more intelligent than the existing anthropoid apes, although still considerably below the intellectual level of existing savages. It is certain [!] that in such a community natural signs of voice, gesture, and grimace, would be in vogue to a greater or less extent. As their numbers increased . . . such signs would [through natural selection] require to become more and more conventional, or acquire more and more the character of sentence-words." Here, indeed, we have the intellect slipped in surreptitiously. "The first articulation," he subsequently tells us,† "probably consisted in nothing further than a semiotic breaking of vocal tones, in a manner resembling that which still occurs in the so-called 'chattering' of monkeys. . . . The great difference would be that . . . it must have partaken less of the nature of cries, and more of the nature of names." "More!" But things are "names" or "not-names"; there can be no "more" or "less" in the matter. It is by such gross philosophical mistakes and consequent verbal slovenliness that we have "intellect" unwarrantably introduced where it has no legitimate place.

A great deal is said about the "clicks" of Hot-

* p. 371.   † p. 372.

tentots, which Prof. Sayce is quoted * as observing " still survive to show us how the utterances of speechless man could be made to embody and convey thought." It could, of course, convey it fast enough if thought was there to be conveyed ; but no "clicking" could ever originate and introduce it. The Hottentot word for the moon is said to be "clicks," followed by the monosyllable "*Khāp.*" But why is this not as truly conceptual a name for the moon as either Luna or Σελήνη ?

Mr. Romanes makes use of Time as a very potent magician to effect the transformations his hypothesis needs. Speaking of his hypothetical speechless-man, he says,† "I believe this most interesting creature probably lived for an inconceivably [!] long time before his faculty of articulate sign-making had developed sufficiently far to begin to starve out the more primitive and more natural systems ; and I believe that even after this starving-out process did begin, another inconceivable [!] lapse of time must have been required for such progress to have eventually transformed *Homo alalus* into *Homo sapiens.*" Again, he tells us ‡ that the epoch during which sentence - words prevailed was probably immense ; and, again, § "The probability certainly is that immense [!] intervals of time would have been consumed in the passage through these various grades of mental evolution ;" and yet again, ‖ "It was not until. after æons of ages [!] had elapsed that any pronouns arose as specially indicative of the first person." In fact, however, Time could do absolutely

* p. 374. † p. 379. ‡ p. 385.
§ p. 386. ‖ p. 387.

nothing in bringing about any change of the kind ; whereas, if intellect could be thus introduced at all, it might have made its subsequent progress at a relatively very rapid rate.

But we must let Mr. Romanes describe in his own words the stages by which he is disposed to think the progress of mental evolution from the brute to man most probably took place.   His words are * :—

" Starting from the highly intelligent and social species of anthropoid ape, as pictured by Darwin, we can imagine that this animal was accustomed to use its voice freely for the expression of its emotions, uttering of danger-signals, and singing.   Possibly enough, also, it may have been sufficiently intelligent to use a few imitative sounds in the arbitrary way that Mr. Darwin suggests ; and certainly sooner or later the receptual life of this social animal must have advanced far enough to have become comparable with that of an infant at about two years of age.   That is to say, this animal, although not yet having begun to use articulate signs, must have advanced far enough in the conventional use of natural signs (or signs with a natural origin in tone and gesture, whether spontaneous only or intentionally imitative), to have admitted of a tolerably free exchange of receptual ideas, such as would be concerned in animal wants, and even, perhaps, in the simplest forms of co-operative action.   Next, I think it probable that the advance of receptual intelligence which would have been occasioned by this advance in sign-making, would in turn have led to a further development of the latter—

* p. 377.

the two thus acting and re-acting on one another, until the language of tone and gesture became gradually raised to the level of imperfect pantomime, as in children before they begin to use words. At this stage, however, or even before it, I think very probably vowel-sounds must have been employed in tone-language, if not also a few of the consonants. And I think this not only on account of the analogy furnished by an infant already alluded to, but also because in the case of a 'singing' animal, intelligent enough to be constantly using its voice for semiotic purposes, and therefore employing a variety of more or less conventional tones, including clicks, it seems almost necessary that some of the vowel sounds—and possibly also some of the consonants—should have been brought into use. But, be this as it may, eventually the action and re-action of receptual intelligence and conventional sign-making must have ended in so far developing the former as to have admitted of the breaking up (or articulation) of vocal sounds, as the only direction in which any further improvement of vocal sign-making was possible. I think it not improbable that this important stage in the development of speech was greatly assisted by the already existing habit of articulating musical notes, supposing our progenitors to have resembled the gibbons or the chimpanzees in this respect. But long after this first rude beginning of articulate speech, the language of tone and gesture would have continued as much the most important machinery of communication : the half-human creature now before our imagination would probably have struck us as a wonderful adept at making

U

significant sounds and movements, both as to number and variety; but in all probability we should scarcely have been able to notice the already developing germ of articulation. Nor do I believe that, if we were able to strike in again upon the history tens of thousands of years later, we should find that pantomime had been superseded by speech. On the contrary, I believe we should find that, although considerable progress had been made in the former, so that the object then before us might appear deserving of being classed as *Homo*, we should also feel that he must needs still be distinguished by the addition *alalus*."

He then continues, * "Lastly, I believe that this most interesting creature probably lived for a considerably long time," etc., as just before quoted by us.

As to this passage, we have, of course, to protest against the idea of the imaginary ape uttering any "danger-signals," still more against its using "imitative sounds in the arbitrary way that Mr. Darwin suggests," and instead of allowing that "it must have advanced," sooner or later, so as "to have become comparable with an infant about two years of age," we affirm it could never have done so, or attained to any "tolerably free exchange [!] of receptual ideas"—which are not "ideas" at all. What, also, can be more misleading or unreasonable than to say, "Next, I think it probable that the advance of receptual intelligence which would have been occasioned by the advance in sign-making, would in turn have led to a further development of the latter— the two thus acting and reacting on one another"? But

* p. 379.

no irrational bodily movements could generate intellect, nor could mere consentience cause "a further develop-ment" of signs, since, as we have seen,* in order that a sign should even exist, true intelligence must be already present. We have here presented to us the interaction of merely sensuous faculties under the misleading terms, "receptual intelligence" and "signs," with an implied supersensuous result. Thus is intellect again silently "slipped in," and when once it has been so smuggled in unnoticed, it is, of course, easy enough to explain any subsequent progress by it. If once an ape in some mysterious way became (like a child) potentially a man, any one can see how human characteristics would thereafter become manifest in it. Only thus can we rationally say (as Mr. Romanes says) that the animal's intelligence "*must* have advanced."

As to Noiré's hypothesis, we think, with Mr. Romanes,† that it can at best be considered but a branch of the onomatopoetic theory ; but we think it most improbable that it contains any measure of truth, or that it was "one among many other ways in which, during many ages, many communities of vociferous though hitherto speechless men may have slowly evolved the act of making articulate signs."

Mr. Romanes says that his hypothesis will probably be objected to on the ground that it amounts to a *petitio principii*—as, in fact, it does ; and this, we hope, has been made sufficiently clear. He further observes : "The question has been raised expressly and exclusively on the faculty of conceptual speech, and it is conceded that

* See above, pp. 65, 122, 128.   † p. 381.

of this faculty there can have been no earlier stage than that of articulation." But, as we have pointed out again and again, the question does *not* concern conceptual speech, but *mental* conception ; and it has been also expressly pointed out that mental conception by no means depends on the power of articulation, but may exist for a long time, or always, without it.

Mr. Romanes accuses his opponents of begging the question if they assume "that prior to the appearance of the earliest phase of articulation, it is impossible that any hitherto speechless animal should have been erect in attitude, intelligent enough to chip flints, or greatly in advance of other animals in the matter of making indicative [non-conceptual] gestures, and probably vocal tones." But we assume nothing of the kind. It is possible, as we said in our first chapter, that so-called palæolithic man may not have been human at all. We have also no evidence as to the degree of development to which mere instinct can attain without being able to make one gesture indicative of the possession of a real idea of any kind. Mr. Romanes cites * an account of monkeys opening oysters with selected stones, which we can well credit. Nor would the shaping of a stone by an anthropoid ape greatly surprise us, any more than the skilful treatment of trees by the beavers which fell them.

As to Mr. Romanes's further observations concerning the possible or probable growth and development of articulation, as it is altogether beside our contention, nothing need now be added to what has already

* Note, p. 382.

been said.   But we may as well, perhaps, once more note
the absurd importance attached to the use of the first
person in speech, as to which Mr. Romanes says,* " Now,
this point I consider one of prime importance.   For," he
adds, " it furnishes us with direct evidence of the fact
that, long after mankind had begun to speak, and even
long after they had gained considerable proficiency in
the art of articulate language, the speakers still continued
to refer to themselves in that same kind of objective
phraseology as is employed by a child before the dawn
of self-consciousness. . . . The outward and visible sign
of this inward and spiritual grace is given in the subjective use of pronominal words."   All this we once
more utterly deny.   A man, pointing to himself, may,
by that alone, as truly say " I " mentally, as if he uttered
that vocable in every known language which possesses
such a term.

"But if these things," he argues,† "admit of no
question in the case of an individual human mind —
if in the case of the growing child the rise of self-
consciousness is demonstrably the condition to that of
conceptual thought,—by what feat of logic can it be
possible to insinuate that in the growing psychology of
the race there may have been conceptual thought before
there was any true self-consciousness?"   By what *il*logical feat, indeed, can such an absurdity as unconscious
conception be made to seem possible?   Mr. Romanes's
argument is valid but vain, because consciousness
exists in the child unable even to speak at all, and
therefore may well have existed in tribes of men (if such

* p. 388.   † Ibid.

there are, or ever were) with no way of speaking of themselves save in modes which correspond with our use of the third person.   We do not deny that what is valid for the child is valid for the race, though the parallel between "the race" and "a child" is by no means exact.   Mr. Romanes, however, affirms the resemblance, and since in the child the origin of self-consciousness is *not* " marked by the change from objective to subjective phraseology," neither need it be so in the race.

This penultimate chapter, though it is interesting as a record of speculative imaginings, and as indicating conspicuously the fallacies which traverse Mr. Romanes's work from cover to cover, is in itself valueless, since (as we have seen) its author, with commendable candour, has declared * that he attaches "no argumentative importance to any of these hypotheses."

The last chapter of Mr. Romanes's work, being merely a summary and brief restatement of what has gone before, does not, we think, need any detailed criticism from us.   Therein he speaks † of a great weight of "authority" on his side.   Did we so appeal, we, in our turn, might boast that we have supporting us a consensus of the deepest and acutest intellects which the world has ever seen.   But, as we said at the outset, we rest our case on no "authority," but on reason only ; and, with a simple appeal from Mr. Romanes, to that reason which he has so inadequately appreciated, we leave the arguments we have advanced to the calm and unprejudiced judgment of our readers.

* p. 361.   † p. 395.

CHAPTER VIII.

CONCLUDING REMARKS.

IN the foregoing chapters we have set forth and esti-
mated, to the best of our ability, the arguments of what
may be deemed the crowning effort of that school which
would deduce all the faculties of the human intellect
from the powers of the lower animals. The author of
the book we have criticized is a man in many ways exceptionally gifted. Earnest, versatile, active, and indus-
trious, and able to devote as much time as he pleases
to the prosecution of what is evidently a labour of love,
we think it unlikely that he can be succeeded by any
one better qualified personally for the task he has undertaken. When we further call to mind the fact that he
has had the advantage of intimacy with the late Mr.
Charles Darwin, and with the still surviving Mr. Herbert
Spencer, and that he also enjoys the friendship and
sympathy of most of the leading members of the party
of whose opinions he is the exponent, we deem it
extremely improbable that any one could come forth
from a more favourable environment than that from
which he issues, as a champion specially trained and
carefully armed, to do effective battle against the
asserters of the essential intellectuality of man.

For eighteen years we have looked in vain for a Darwinian ready and willing to address himself seriously to the arguments which seemed to us to demonstrate the impossibility of the evolution of intellect from sense. During the last half-dozen years or so we have, however, been more hopeful, for we thought we had some reason to believe that Mr. Romanes was industriously preparing himself to undertake that task. But what, after all, is the result of this long preparation, these arduous studies, the counsel and advice of predecessors and contemporary sympathizers? Do we meet in this book, in spite of the pains and labour which have been lavished upon it, with one really new argument in defence of the cause it would sustain?

We must confess to no small feeling of disappointment at finding we had no real novelty, no freshly discovered difficulty to contend with, but had mainly to occupy ourselves with the explanation of misunderstandings and the unravelling of curiously entangled conceptions. The real contention of the author is an old and familiar one, and may be thus briefly put: "The infant *shows* no intellectual nature, therefore it *has* none. Savages are intellectually inferior to us in varying degrees, therefore their ancestors had no intellect at all." The argument in favour of these assertions really reposes almost exclusively on a supposed *à priori* probability derived from that view of evolution which Mr. Romanes (following Mr. Darwin, Professor Haeckel, etc.) favours. But the author, as we have seen, seeks to sustain these two fundamental propositions by statements and representations which we have successively combated in the preceding pages. Such are (1) his representation that a child which can talk, but which does not speak of itself as "I," cannot be self-conscious; (2) his statement that concepts are but sense-perceptions named; (3) his representation of "percepts" as not being truly intellectual states at all; (4) his failure to distinguish between direct and reflex self-consciousness; (5) his serious relation of incredible tales about animals; (6) his confused representation of sign-making, wherein, from neglect to define what is and should be meant by "a sign," he is led to read into the so-called "sign-making" actions of animals, meanings which need not necessarily be attributed to them, and which other facts show us ought not to be attributed to them; and, lastly, (7) his curious statements about his opponents, which result from his inexplicable failure to comprehend their standpoint. This failure is so utter that, as we have seen, he actually takes for granted that his opponents are "Nominalists"—a mistake which, when we first met with it, seemed to us so impossible, that we thought we must ourselves have misunderstood the author we had undertaken to criticize.

Having most carefully considered every argument put forward by Mr. Romanes, and tried our best to weigh accurately every fact brought forward by him, we must confess ourselves more than ever confident of the truth of the judgment we have now so long maintained—the judgment that between the intellect of man and the highest psychical power of any and every brute there is an essential difference of kind, also involving, of course, a difference of origin.

This position we believe to be at one and the same time a dictate of the highest science and of the simplest common sense. We know that our infants grow into rational beings, but we have no reason to suppose that they undergo, while under our care, a profound transformation of nature. Common sense therefore concludes that they are essentially "rational" from the first. On the other hand, no race of men has anywhere been found destitute of speech or incapable of plainly showing by gestures that they have a meaning they desire to convey, and that, by their gestures, they intentionally seek to depict their ideas and to converse by signs. At the same time, no race of animals has anywhere been found possessed of speech or capable of plainly showing by gesture that they have a meaning they desire to convey, and that, by their gestures they intentionally seek to depict their ideas and to converse by signs. Common sense, therefore, concludes that man has, but that animals have not, a nature capable of rational language, expressed orally or by gesture.

No facts brought forward by Mr. Romanes contradict these dicta of common sense, nor what we believe to be the dicta of the most developed science. Nevertheless, there is a widely diffused prejudice amongst both leaders and followers of physical science, which indisposes them to assert the existence of such a fundamental difference of nature. We are persuaded that this prejudice is largely due to a merely imaginary cause. Many men feel strongly the difficulty of imagining the first advent of man upon this planet, or how either a new creature could have been suddenly formed, or a new nature infused into one which already existed. Now, we should be the last to deny the difficulty of "imagining" such things ; since we uncompromisingly assert that it is simply impossible to imagine them. For who even pretends to have witnessed the formation of a new creature, or the infusion of a new nature ? While what we have never experienced, we can never imagine. But whenever we are convinced we have really good reasons for accepting as true the occurrence of something whereof we have had no experience whatever, surely the rational thing to do is, to say that we assent to its truth, while affirming the impossibility of our imagining it.* The besetting sin of our day—the sin which leads to the degradation of art and science alike—is "sensationalism." This it is that would reduce painting and sculpture to an exclusive reproduction of what the mere eye sees, neglecting what the refined and cultivated intellect may apprehend. This it is, again, which has made possible novels like those of Zola, or poems like those of Richepin—not to refer to yet more nefarious productions. In physical science, also, we again encounter this besetting tendency to exaggerate the value of the sensuous imagination at the expense of the intellect; resulting in an avidity for mechanical explanations, because those are the explanations most welcome to our lower faculties, as we have already pointed out.†

* As to Imagination and Conception, see "On Truth," pp. 111, 112.

† See above, p. 30.

If the reader of these concluding remarks will calmly consider the dictates of his own reason, he will, we are persuaded, clearly see there is no evidence for him that a break cannot take place in nature of a kind and in a mode he is unable to imagine : while he must admit that, as regards the first introduction of life and sensitivity,* such a breach of continuity must have taken place. His reason will further tell him that he is impotent to imagine the first introduction of either life or sensitivity, or to picture to himself the mode in which a creature that did not possess the faculty of feeling, could have been endowed with that wonderful and unprecedented power. With a mind informed and strengthened by a free inquiry of this kind as to what *reason* declares, let him ask himself whether he has evidence that, in a world in which at least two breaches of continuity have certainly occurred, and two novel natures (the living and the sensitive), essentially different in kind, have somehow come to be,—let him ask himself whether, under these circumstances, a third breach of continuity and the uprising† of a third new nature—a rational nature—is a thing impossible or even improbable ? With a mind thus freed from the mists of imaginary prejudice, let the reader next consider the arguments in favour of a difference of kind between man and brute—the presence in the former and the absence in the latter of intellect, as manifested by language, and, above all, by language expressing moral

* See above, p. 10.
† As to the origin of man, see "On Truth," p. 521.

judgments and asserting merit and demerit.* We are strongly persuaded that he will then clearly see that language *is* the "rubicon of mind," and that it is so simply because it is the index of that intellectual power, the presence of which makes a true and necessary "limit to evolution," in the ascending series of organic transformations. It is our hope that in the preceding pages we have made it clear that there can be no such things as real signs without intentional meaning, and that unmeant signs are not language : also that there is no meaning without mental conception, and no perception without implicit judgment. Thus, as we have said, the impressions made by the objects of nature on sensitive organisms are different according to the nature of such organisms, each being affected according to its nature and innate powers. In the vital organization of the animal they excite those sensations and more and more complex feelings, imaginations, and emotions which correspond with our own lower mental powers. In the living organism, man, they call forth not only such feelings, but also, by and through them, truly intellectual perceptions spontaneously start forth, containing within them implicitly the very highest abstract ideas, even that of "being." That the prattle of the infant is the outcome of consciousness, and that self-perception and the predication of the copula not only may, but must be present in the rudest forms of language known to us, we have also, we trust, not urged in vain. The ideal portrait of primitive man sketched for us by the author

* See Ibid., pp. 243–254, 274, 275, 282–286.

we have criticized, hardly, as he himself admits, demands or can well receive a grave and serious examination, and our brief criticism of it is, we think, amply sufficient for the purpose of this work.

We desire, finally, to take leave of Mr. Romanes with gratitude and sympathy : gratitude for his honest labour, the pains he has taken, and his studious endeavour to be just and fair to us personally. We take leave of him with sympathy, for we cannot regard otherwise than with kindly regret the thankless, the impossible, task he has gratuitously taken upon himself, and which has wasted so many well-meant efforts. Heartily do we wish that he would consent for a time to put physical science on one side, and devote his very considerable energy and ability to the study of science properly so-called. Would he only consent so to do, we feel a strong conviction that unmixed good to himself and others would be the by no means distant result. We are persuaded that a patient study of philosophy would, in a mind so candid and open to conviction as we believe his to be, lead to a permanent reconciliation between the author of " Mental Evolution in Man" and the thesis he at present opposes, as well as to a prolific union between the declarations of objective Reason and the subjective psychological conceptions of Mr. Romanes himself. We have selected his work for careful examination because in it may be found an exposition of all the most recent hypotheses in favour of the evolution of intellect from mere sentience. In examining it, we have examined these hypotheses to the best of our ability, and now offer the results at which we have arrived to the judgment of readers interested in that problem which we deem the most important one of our time—the problem which concerns the distinctness or non-distinctness as to nature, and therefore as to origin, of human reason.

INDEX.

A

A name more than a word, 46, 53
Abbé Sicard and deaf-mutes, 143
Abnormal condition of deaf-mutes, 164
—— man may be lower than brutes, 8
Absolute distinctness of man shown by ethics, 273
—— truth and mechanical hypotheses, 30
—— truths, knowledge of, 29
Abstract concepts and deaf-mutes, 145
—— idea of danger and animals, 76
—— —— "time," expressed by gesture, 145
—— ideas, 56, 59
—— —— of ripeness, appearance, detection, direction, and surprise, 142
Abstraction, 47, 51, 54, 64, 70
——, power of, not in brutes, 42
Absurd tale about a cockatoo, 136
Accidental acts, 122, 127
——, unintentional, making of facts known, 192
Accidentally isolated children and language, 231
Accoucheur, illustration from, 281
Acquired semiotic value asserted, 283
Acquisitional signs, 123, 127
Actions instantaneous in nature, 12
——, irrational, of animals, 124
—— misread, 85
—— of parrots explained, 154, 161
——, volitions, and primitive man, 234
Acts, conventional ones, 122, 126, 127
—— formally and materially intentional, what they are, 122
——, imitational ones, 124
——, impulsional ones, 122

Acts, intellectual, not necessarily reflex, 125
—— of salutation apparently similar may differ profoundly, 219
—— reveal inner nature, 49
Adam, 33
Adjectives and substantives, 248
—— by position, 248
Adoption of the easiest imaginations, 30
Adumbration of higher natures in lower, 21, 22, 83
Adverbs and pronouns, 245
Affections, sensuous and cognitive, 59
—— (sensuous) and ideas, relations between, 94
Africa, South, and children, 232
Agglutination, 262
Agglutinative language, 231
Agriculture and primitive man, 33
All men are bipeds, meaning of, 257
Alternative, an, may express a conjunctive sentence, 144
Amalgamation of feelings not an idea, 45
Ambiguity of phrase "Arise out of," 43
—— of the term "conventional," 122
—— of the term "discriminate," 67
—— of the term "know," 154
Ambiguous expression, growth of consciousness, 247
—— use of the term "seen," 186
—— use of the word "understand," 151
Amœba, psychical principle of, 73
An avowed prejudice of Dr. Weismann, 10
Analogy between flight and thought, 172
—— indicates discontinuity in evolution, 14

X

Y

PRINTED BY WILLIAM CLOWES AND SONS, LIMITED, LONDON AND BECCLES.

www.ingramcontent.com/pod-product-compliance
Lightning Source LLC
Chambersburg PA
CBHW030924050726

47498CB00003BA/883